Sean Condon is the author of seven books in a variety of genres. He lives in Melbourne with his wife and daughter.

Splitsville

Sean Condon

First published by Momentum in 2013
This edition published in 2013 by Momentum
Pan Macmillan Australia Pty Ltd
1 Market Street, Sydney 2000

A CIP record for this book is available at the National Library of
Australia

Splitsville

EPUB format: 9781743342138
Mobi format: 9781743342121
Print on Demand format: 9781743342398

Cover design by Vincent Casey
Edited by Jo Jarrah
Proofread by Melissa Kemble

Macmillan Digital Australia: www.macmillandigital.com.au

To report a typographical error, please visit momentumbooks.com.au/
contact/

Visit www.momentumbooks.com.au to read more about all our books and
to buy books online. You will also find features, author interviews and
news of any author events.

For Sylvie, my beautiful daughter.
You changed my life.

Wizard of Oz: As for you, my galvanized friend, you want a heart. You don't know how lucky you are not to have one. Hearts will never be practical until they can be made unbreakable.

Tin Man: But I still want one.

*On any given evening in any given city –
London, Hong Kong, Sydney, you name
it – there will be a certain number of
people squirming through a first date,
a certain number sitting side by side
staring at a television screen wondering
how they ended up there and where it's
all going, and a certain number of
people – about 1250 – desperately trying to find the courage to squeeze the
last gasp of life out of a dying relationship. This is the story of some of those
beginnings, middles and ends – mostly
the ends – and it starts on a sweltering
Tuesday night in New York not long ago.*

TUESDAY

New York

Not long ago on a sweltering Tuesday night in downtown Manhattan, Chester Polglase stifled a nervous yawn and glanced at his watch; the pumpkin soup that he hoped would change everything was due to arrive at the table in precisely five minutes. The restaurant was busy and Chester wondered if the food here was any good; whether, in fact, it was real. If it was, he realized, he'd most likely be paying for it. All of it – every single appetizer, entrée, dessert and drink in the whole place. Then again maybe all the dishes were props, like those plastic models you saw in the windows of Japanese restaurants. But no, the steak that just passed by on the hotplate was visibly sizzling. Unless – could they somehow fake sizzle? He knew only too well that the people behind this whole thing were capable of almost anything. They had to be – people's lives were at stake.

Chester Polglase looked up, swallowed thickly and offered his fiancée a nervous, watery smile. He hoped that when the moment came, when it was too late to stop the whole operation and turn back and make everything the way it was, he really hoped he wouldn't cry.

*

Not far away Dwight Kitchener, an older gentleman with a silver crew cut, strode down the middle of a near-empty street on the outskirts of the Meatpacking District. His heavily lined face was tough and weathered, and it was easy to imagine his mouth turning to a bitter scowl at the slightest displeasure. A pair of highly polished black shoes cracked along the still-blistering sidewalk, looking incongruous at the bottom of the stained grey coveralls he wore. Poking at a lump of fresh scar tissue on the inside of his cheek as he took careful note of his surroundings, he removed a map from his pocket, studied it for a moment then glanced at his watch. It was thirty seconds before eight; four and half minutes until Chester Polglase would be shot.

He turned a corner and came upon a police cruiser parked by the side of the road. Inside, one of the officers was lazily smoking a cigarette. Dwight rapped his knuckles on the driver's window.

"Put that out," he growled. "You know they're not allowed to smoke in uniform."

Trying to hide the look of chagrin on his face, the man behind the wheel butted the cigarette.

Dwight continued along West 15th Street, past a block-long former slaughterhouse that was now home to a half dozen thumping clubs and bars. He paused and regarded the young and beautiful clustered in desperate, disorderly queues outside – couples locked in passionate entwination of finger, arm or tongue – and he wondered how many of them he might one day be called upon to prise apart.

He rounded a corner into a dark, narrow alley, stopped outside a dimly lit doorway, shook a Marlboro out of a pack and stuck it between his lips. He left the cigarette sitting there for a short, sweet moment before flicking it into the trash bin opposite. He took a deep breath of warm Manhattan air and then, in a single, elegant movement, unzipped the front of his coveralls and stepped out of them, turned around and pushed open the door.

The busy restaurant kitchen froze in silence as Dwight entered, wearing a perfectly pressed tuxedo, crisp white shirt and thin black bow tie. His extremely short, extremely neat hair looked as though it had been freshly cut moments before. He glanced across the wide-eyed, pale faces and singled one out. "The soup ready?" he asked.

"Yes, sir."

"Great," he said. "Stay on your toes, people. And good luck."

Dwight shot his shirt cuffs and continued through the kitchen then out onto the small, bustling restaurant floor. Immediately, his hawk-like gaze settled on the couple sitting in the middle of the place:

Chester W. Polglase, thirty-one years old, five feet nine, born Rockville, Maryland, moved to New York City to study law at NYU. Junior partner at Carlson-Kavanagh, has harbored a secret fondness for all forms of corduroy since he was twelve, and – most obnoxiously where Dwight was concerned – recently-converted Yankees fan.

Sitting opposite Polglase was his fiancée, Sara Mary Alice White, twenty-six, five-five, one hundred twenty pounds. Manhattan born and bred. Attended Brearley, Fieldston, Blackstone and Geneva where she was mercilessly mocked for her pronounced lisp before three years of exthpenthive thpeech therapy eradicated it almost entirely. It still appeared when she was especially upthet or nervouth. Account manager at PPK Publicity; "accidentally" stumbled upon her husband-to-be's fondness for corduroy three days after they moved in together, and – Dwight gnashed his teeth – diehard Yankees fan.

He narrowed his ice-blue eyes and watched as Sara tilted her head slightly, to match the slight angle of her slight smile, and bent forward, slightly.

*

"Can I ask you something, Buttons?" Sara said, smiling and reaching for her superbeloved fiancé's hand.

"C'mon, honey, not in public," Chester said, looking around to see if anybody had overheard. "I sound like a poodle when you call me that. One with a fancy haircut."

"All right, *Chester*." Sara retrieved her outstretched hand, pausing only briefly to admire the ring on her finger, and removed an overstuffed binder from the bag at her feet. "Floral arrangements, specifically tulips. Specificallier, what color?" With a cutlery-jangling thud, the huge folder fell open to the section marked "Floral Arrangements."

Chester regarded it with dread, as though she'd placed a tombstone on the table. "Sorry?" he said.

"What color tulips – red or white?"

He had no idea, no opinion on the matter. Flowers were flowers, weren't they? Did people even notice what color? Where were these tulips meant to be going?

"We also need to think about aperitifs, and I'm thinking sherry. The Basque region of España is about to be very in. I'm thinking one to one and a half five ounce glasses per guest …"

In a daze, Chester watched his fiancée's motile mouth, losing himself in the pink-lipsticked black hole that he still loved to kiss if not necessarily listen to …

… *we will have three children, eighteen months to two years apart, all girls, with names that rhyme but nothing cute, they'll attend Steering Prep then Bryn Mawr or Smith, you'll have made senior partner or vice-president or whatever because you'll be working six days, eighty to ninety hours a week to pay for the house in Rhinebeck which will be very large and constantly redecorated, costing huge sums of money that you'll work yourself to death to earn, there'll be no time for your friends or golf or fishing or whatever it is you like doing to relax and, according to all available sources, I'm the last woman you will ever sleep with …*

He felt something cold tapping the back of his hand. He looked down and saw the engagement ring sitting proudly on his fiancée's long, slender finger.

"Honey?" she said, with such a sweet smile that once again he began to consider calling the whole thing off. He figured he still had a ten-second window. "Your soup?"

Chester looked up. A waiter was standing beside him, holding a steaming tureen and a ladle. "Oh, thank God," Chester said.

"Careful, sir," the waiter said. "It's hot."

Chester nodded gravely, and said, "I know." He looked at his watch – his four minutes were up; the window was closed.

His own life was almost over, and his fiancée's was surely about to be horribly ruined. Chester Polglase looked out the front window and saw two policemen peering in. He took a deep breath and said, "Let's do it."

*

Dwight watched the waiter dip the ladle into the tureen then lean over the table, dangling it above Chester Polglase's bowl. Perfect.

Except for some reason the waiter all of a sudden froze.

Dwight quickly scanned the room and noticed two cops outside, their faces pressed against the glass at the front, staring in. He quietly swore then found what he was looking for – Eduardo de Villalobos, a few seconds late, taking an order from one of the diners.

A moment later Eduardo was off, quickly threading his way between tables to where Polglase was patiently waiting to be scalded. Right on his mark, Eduardo stumbled and bumped heavily into the other waiter, who poured boiling pumpkin soup into Polglase's lap.

Polglase leaped from the table with a semi-convincing scream of pain, his lap steaming and orange. The other customers turned, opened-mouthed and wide-eyed.

Dwight checked his watch. The soup waiter put on an appropriately mortified expression and tried to stammer out an apology.

"You complete nitwit," Dwight whispered to himself, anticipating the line he and the team had rehearsed with Polglase over and over again.

"You complete nitwit!" Polglase shouted.

The soup waiter said nervously, "We'll get you cleaned up right away, sir."

"Cleaned up!?" said Polglase. "This is a …"

The waiter raised his eyebrows expectantly. Sara looked across the table in shock.

Polglase said, "Seven …"

"Nine," Dwight whispered sharply.

"I mean nine hundred dollar suit, you …" Chester Polglase was by nature not much of a swearer and he struggled with the next word. But Mr Kitchener had warned him not to deviate from the script, so he swallowed and said, "… asshole!"

"I'm terribly sorry, sir, but it was an accident," the soup waiter said. "Please watch your language."

"Watch my language!?"

"Buttons?" Sara said, beginning to become a little alarmed at her superbeloved fiancé's behavior.

"Buttons?" Dwight said to himself.

Chester turned to Sara, and said mildly, "Please don't call me Buttons, honey. Chet would do fine as a nickname." Then he turned back to the bumbling waiter and immediately resumed fuming. "Watch my language!?"

Then something in Chet Polglase snapped and he began improvising. Maybe it was the heat that had been broiling the city all day, maybe it was the Buttons thing or maybe it was part of him wanting to call the scheme off. Whatever the reason, he suddenly put his coddled, manicured hands around the waiter's throat and began throttling him.

As Sara went to get up from the table, Dwight raised his right hand and muttered into his cuff; immediately a nearby diner stood up and headed straight for the tiny blonde.

The choking soup waiter began turning red as Polglase held fast and babbled about sherry, floral arrangements, children with rhyming names and a very large house in Rhinebeck. The scrambling diner reached Sara just in time to stop her from joining the fray, although whether she'd try and pull her fiancé off the waiter or help him strangle the guy, Dwight wasn't sure. A look of genuine concern set in Eduardo de Villalobos's face as his colleague began to turn blue. He glanced at Dwight, who gave an imperceptible nod.

De Villalobos pulled the gun from inside his jacket and aimed it at Polglase. "Let him go or I'll shoot!"

"Buttons! Stop!" Sara pleaded.

Polglase's hands stayed put as the soup waiter's eyes rolled back into his head.

De Villalobos said, "Let him go, Buttons!"

Polglase looked pleadingly at his fiancée. "Please, honey!" he shouted. "Not in public."

De Villalobos cocked the pistol and said, "Seriously, Mr Polglase, I think you're really killing him."

Buttons Polglase held fast.

De Villalobos fired. A bloom of red appeared in the middle of Chester's white shirt. He looked down at it, truly stunned. It wasn't meant to go like this; he was meant to be standing up when Eduardo shot him, not on the floor strangling whoever he was down here strangling. He clutched his shirt, his hands came away slick and red. The soup waiter took a huge gulp of air as Chester slumped to the floor. Red pooled around him.

"You've killed him!" Sara shrieked, her wail mingling with a siren outside. The two police officers rushed through the front door.

She was desperate to go to her superbeloved's side, but she was being held in her chair by a customer standing behind her.

Eduardo de Villalobos dropped his gun. One of the cops cuffed him as two paramedics rushed in to attend to Chester. A tense and complete silence fell over the restaurant as everybody inside waited for the verdict. A woman at a table near the kitchen moaned. Two others held hands and prayed. But it was only moments before one of the medics gave a sorrowful shake of his head. "He's gone."

Numbly, Sara's gaze moved from her fiancé to the folder lying open on the table. She read the words "Floral Arrangements," and immediately thought of memorial wreaths. And even as she began sobbing, she wondered what refreshments people were serving at funerals this season. Satisfyingly hot and plentiful tears blurred her vision as she watched the policemen taking the waiter away, and then the paramedics placing Chester's limp body on a stretcher, clearing a blurry path to the blurry door of the blurry restaurant.

The firm hands on her shoulders lifted and Sara suddenly felt so light – so utterly and completely out of herself – that she wondered if she might float away. And then a hand was placed over hers; it was leathery, yet warm, and there was something fatherly in the gentle touch. She blinked away her tears and found herself looking into the grizzled but friendly face of the maître d'.

"I'm so terribly sorry about what's happened," he said, with a voice that was deep and soothing, like a psychiatrist crossed with an airline pilot. "Please, come with me to my office."

He had a strong face, what they used to call lantern-jawed, with pale blue eyes and the distinguished gray hair of a classic silver fox, like that man who played the burglar in … She couldn't remember the movie. Or the actor … What the heck was she doing? Her fiancé had just been killed in front of her eyes mere weeks before their wedding and she was getting all tied up in knots trying to remember an actor's name. Grief certainly worked in mysterious ways. She released a fresh clutch of sobs then suddenly stopped – was it Lee something?

*

Half a block down the street the two cops shoved Eduardo hard against a brick wall. He could taste a little blood on the inside of his mouth. "Hey, take it easy," he said. "You've arrested me – the show's over."

One of them said, "The show ain't over until we hear from the boss."

Eduardo told the guy that the boss, Dwight, was probably pretty busy right now and they could maybe start acting with a little autonomy. "Starting with taking these cuffs off me."

The other one said, "Not 'til Dwight says. And keep your trap shut or you'll be up for resisting arrest."

Eduardo couldn't believe what he was hearing. "You're kidding, right?"

Both of them pulled their weapons – the idiots actually cocking the hammers. Eduardo shook his head, laughing. "Go ahead," he said. "Shoot."

*

Sara White sat in the tiny office behind the kitchen with a glass of '96 Krug in one hand and a non-vintage Kleenex in the other. She sipped and sobbed and dabbed. Pretending to be the restaurant's manager, Dwight Kitchener sat on the other side of the desk with his arms folded, hoping that he looked trustworthy and sympathetic. He wasn't sure if the tuxedo helped or made him look like a boxing referee.

Sara took a sip of Champagne, wishing it was just a little more chilled. "Shouldn't I be with the police giving a statement or something?" she asked.

"Oh, we'll take care of all that in due course, Miss White," Dwight said. "Right now, your wellbeing is the most important thing to worry about. You've been through something deeply traumatic." He paused as she finished her Champagne and held out the glass for a refill. "But I want to assure you that you'll get over it, and sooner than you think. Everything's going to be all right." He removed a card from a small wooden box and handed it to her. "Call this number if you need to talk with somebody," he said.

Sara took it and immediately felt better; she'd been searching all over Manhattan for exactly this for months. In between her thumb and forefinger was high quality 350gsm card stock, cream colored, with a subtle matte laminate finish. It was absolutely beautiful. And perfect for the wedding – no, wait, *funeral* – invitations!

She tried to stop herself. She tried, she tried, she tried. But then it came blurting out anyway. "Who's your printer?"

Dwight gave her a name and address in midtown which she wrote on the back of the card.

Then she went back to grieving, discomposing herself by sobbing, sniffing and wiping her nose with the Kleenex. "I can't believe that Buttons is … That my fiancé is dead." She drank half the Champagne then wiped her mouth, careful, even in her bereavement, not to smear her lipstick. (It was, after all, a limited edition Guerlain.) "We were going to be married in a few weeks."

"I know," Dwight said, tightening his mouth grimly. "It's a terrible thing. Sad and tragic and terrible. Someone so young."

"Actually, he was thirty-one." Sara took another sip. "But he had a young face." She finished off the glass. "And I'll never see it again." She began a fresh round of sobs, dabbing at her eyes with the wet Kleenex even as she held out her glass for yet another refill.

"That's right, Miss White," Dwight said, reaching for the almost empty bottle of Krug. "You'll never see him again. I know it's hard but you have to get used to the idea. That's why I think it'd be in your best interest not to attend the funeral. Or contact any of Chester's friends or family. May I offer you a lift home, Miss White?"

"Thank you," Sara said, smiling wanly. She wasn't sure this was exactly the right time – although part of her knew that, of course, there was no better time – but she really wanted to hear how it sounded, so she gave it a shot. "And please, call me Widow White."

Midtown

The weird thing was, it felt a little like a date. Even though it couldn't possibly be a date – and *wasn't* a date – it had all the qualities of a date, a real classic: a man meets a woman outside a train station, they have some dinner then catch a movie.

So here they were, Charlie and Sallie, side by side in the cool darkness of the tiny theatre, the real estate on their shared armrest successfully negotiated, popcorn almost done, drinks warm and mostly backwash by now. Only Charlie was having difficulty concentrating on the movie – *The Awful Truth*, a Columbia number from 1937 starring Cary Grant, a terrier named Asta and a lady with a terrific overbite named Irene Dunne – because of how much this thing could be mistaken for a date. Not that either of the parties involved – to whit, himself and Sallie – would be doing such mistaking but you never knew what was going on in the mind of another person, no matter how close you might be to them. And so now he was starting to wonder if he ought to hold her hand, not to be romantic, obviously, but to be reassuring.

Cary Grant said, "There can't be any doubt in marriage, the whole thing's built on faith and if you've lost that you've lost everything." So true, Charlie thought to himself. Not that he'd ever been married but he knew a thing or two about religious faith, and how it wasn't so much a foundation as quicksand. Or so he believed.

It had been almost a year since Charlie had spoken with Sallie. He'd missed her, and he was pretty sure she'd missed him right back but given her circumstances, there wasn't a whole heck of a lot they could do about it. Sallie was twenty-eight and lived in Lancaster County, down in what Charlie rather childishly insisted on calling "Pennsyltransylvania," and had no phone or Internet or anything. None of the modern communications. So they wrote one another letters, sometimes a postcard; hers about who got born lately in the community, occasional livestock updates, the "English" and her increasingly rocky relationship with Jesus and their father, Hank, and the Ordnung; Charlie's were mostly about where he was living and the hot water he kept on getting into at his various jobs. Charlie had had a lot of jobs, in a lot of different cities all across the country, the only common element being that he somehow found himself in hot water in almost every one.

His latest was his favorite so far; he was a reporter at the *New York Sentinel*, the city's third-most prestigious and authoritative newspaper. He'd been there almost a year and had loved every minute, notwithstanding the unfortunate incident with the Moonies a few months back. He was somewhat on the older side for a junior reporter but Charlie sincerely believed that he compensated for his advanced years (all thirty-plus of them) with both youthful eagerness and zesty brio, both of which may in fact have been the same thing. He also liked to believe that he brought with him a certain wisdom and life experience with which his juniors – due to their very juniorness – could not possibly compete.

Among the places and things he'd been were: a carpenter at Bennington College in Vermont; a logger in beautiful Concrete, Washington; a Las Vegas masseuse (which did not end happily); a trainer of a variety of animals in a traveling circus; an advice columnist in California's political capital; television comedy writer in California's cultural capital; orderly in a VA hospital in Abilene, Texas; driver for a storm-chasing photographer in Kansas; house-painter in the Florida Keys; short stop for the Triple-A Sacramento River Cats; fry cook throughout the northeast; door-to-door salesman for the Gibraltar Aluminum Siding Co. of Baltimore, Maryland; Latin dance instructor in Portland, Oregon; Dean Martin Gift Shoppe clerk in Steubenville, Ohio; crane operator at the Port of New Orleans; a bailiff in the Municipal Court of Fort Collins, Colorado; river guide on the Tunica Lake section of the mighty Mississippi, Arkansas division; and bowling pin resetter in the jewel of southwest Michigan, Kalamazoo. His professionally aimless and desultory existence had helped him develop strength of mind and body, sharp reflexes, a fine sense of rhythm, a greater appreciation of jurisprudence and animals, culinary skills, an eclectic vocabulary and some impressive scars and bruises, most of them literal.

Charlie valued all of these things, and wouldn't have changed a moment if it meant forsaking any of them, even the scars. Growing up the way he had, cloistered, spoon-fed and backward, as soon as he'd become smart enough to wonder about the world he knew that he didn't want to die wondering *what if?* about anything so he tried to fit in just about everything. It had been exhausting. And such a peripatetic and unsettled life had also meant that he had not been able to develop any truly substantial relationships with anyone other than his own self. The closest he'd ever come was with a colleague on the TV program back in Los Angeles and, boy, had that ever ended dismally. Or rather, boy, had Charlie ever allowed it to end dismally. More than a year later he still felt guilty – even experienced phantom flashings of pain on his cheek where she'd slapped him whenever he thought about it.

He found himself wondering whether he'd like to be a father, or whether an intelligent wire-haired terrier nicknamed Smitty would be an adequate surrogate for a child. People would look at you funny if you shouted "Smitty! Come back here, Smitty!" after a runaway baby. The thought of fathers and fatherhood made him a little woozy and he tried to refocus on the screen.

As Cary Grant chased a Frenchman through an enormous apartment it occurred to Charlie that this might very well be the first movie Sallie had ever seen and he wondered if perhaps he ought to have taken her to something more ... modern, something with some action and special effects in it. But why? Apart from the fact that most modern pictures were spectacle and noise, the ideas and themes in *The Awful Truth* were as rich and relevant right now as they'd been in 1937, as they always were and always would be.

In the movie Cary Grant and Irene Dunne are trying to break up with each other but can't because they both want custody of their dog, Mr Smith, aka Smitty. They go on various dates with ingénue showgirls and oil barons who call their mothers "Maw" and they get engaged to the wrong people and have a swell time ribbing each other and trying to kid themselves that they're not still crazy in love. It was the kind of movie where people played squash and drank eggnog with nutmeg out of a huge silver bowl; where the most unlikely person sat down at the piano and started playing something transporting and grand. There were lots of fur coats and elaborate hats, and at the end various parties got all dressed up, climbed in cars and headed for a weekend getaway place outside New York City. It was smart and sophisticated and funny and full of a rare kind of verve that you didn't encounter much anymore, in movies or in life. Charlie wished it was all real; he wished he could meet someone just as full of verve and teeth as Irene Dunne, or at least her character. Tall would be nice, too, but height was certainly a negotiable factor. Nobody was perfect and Charlie didn't exp –

A sharp shushing parted the hair on the back of his head.

*

Immediately Adelaide felt guilty, even a little embarrassed about what she'd done. What she couldn't help herself doing. Shushing the man. This muttering oaf, this blue-ribbon sap sitting right in front of her, had been murmuring and blathering away to himself for almost the entire movie. And this was dialogue-driven entertainment, not some car-chase, shoot-'em-up where it didn't matter if you missed a line or two or all of them. This was one of her favorites. This was *The Awful Truth*, one of the finest, frothiest, fluffiest confections ever concocted. Words mattered in *The Awful Truth*. Why someone would bother coming along to a Film Society presentation and then talk all through it was completely beyond her comprehension. He was probably just here for the air-conditioning. The oaf. The sap.

Still, she didn't like to be rude and spent quite some time internally debating the pros and cons of leaning forward and ever-so-quietly apologizing. It would be terribly disrupting for both of them, and she'd already lost enough *Truth* time on him. On the other hand, this was New York City and if you chose the wrong person that *shush* could be your last breath. But he was sitting with a companion, a very pretty blonde, from what Adelaide could see when she craned her neck, and did whackos even go on dates, anyway? Actually, she supposed they did, not least because she herself had been on quite a few thousand before she met Rob.

She wished Rob was with her right now. Or, more accurately, she wished he'd *want* to be. But this wasn't his sort of thing. This was about something other than Rob Dolen and he had limited time for anything not directly concerned with Rob Dolen, including his wife, Adelaide Carter.

Stop it, she told herself. Stop being so mean! You love your husband. And not despite his faults, because of them. All of them. Every single one. So that's a huge amount of love, right there.

Adelaide cleared her throat and was just about to tap the man on the shoulder when Irene Dunne arrived at the party. It was her favorite scene. The gentleman in front would have to wait. Well, either that or kill her.

Irene Dunne crashes a soiree, pretending to be her almost-ex-husband's Swiss-educated sister so she can meet his new fiancée and maybe get between them and their forthcoming nups. She's at the fiancée's parents' house and she says to the mother: "May I have a drink? I had three or four before I got here and they're beginning to wear off. And you know how that is." Adelaide absolutely loved the combination of breezy and brazen in Dunne's delivery; it knocked her out every time she heard it. And just like every other time she'd heard it – because she couldn't help it and didn't want to anyway – she threw back her head and released a great big "HA!"

And so, at the very same instant, did the blue-ribbon sap sitting directly in front of her. That was interesting.

Chelsea

Larry P washed the dishes while Larry D dried them. Larry D was older – as he never stopped reminding Larry P – so he got to choose. But only when it came to chores; everything else was up for grabs. They stood side by side in sudsy silence for a while, listening to an ornate bel canto by Rossini coming from the reel-to-reel player in a far corner of the art-strewn loft.

Larry P dropped his plastic scourer into the lukewarm water and turned, his arms folded across his chest.

Here we go again, thought Larry D. And they were off.

Larry D said, "I don't see any boxes or packing tape lying around."

Larry P said, "No, Larry, you don't."

"So I guess that means you're planning on staying?"

"Yes, I am," said Larry. "You?"

"Certainly," countered Larry. "I never had any intention of leaving."

"Nor did I."

"Screw you, Larry."

"Same to you, Larry."

Larry D threw his dishcloth onto the bench top. It made no noise, and Larry was disappointed. As an artist working in the obscure and ephemeral field of aural soundscapes he liked to employ non-verbal punctuations to quotidian remarks such as the one he'd just made, giving them extra weight and oomph. His last gesture lacked both.

"I've had enough. I'm going to bed," Larry D said.

"Me too."

"Oh, for crying out loud," Larry D said. "Can't you give me a break for just one night?"

Larry ignored Larry and stalked off toward the king-size bed on the other side of the loft. Larry followed. And as he crossed the enormous darkened room it occurred to him that if he played this Rossini piece backward at half-speed it actually might sound halfway interesting.

Back in Midtown

The movie was over. The final credit – a single card with 'The End' written over the begowned Columbia lady and her shimmering torch – had clacketed into its cannister. The small cinema was dark and silent and empty. Except for the two of them – herself and the blue-ribbon sap.

Adelaide told herself that she was just sticking around for the air-conditioning but another part of her – the one she kept quiet most of the time – knew better. The actual truth was that right after their simultaneous eruptions of joy, she'd begun to develop a curiosity about the fellow in front of her, and that mild curiosity had quickly grown into a fixated compulsion which had now metastasized into a sort of a mini-obsession which she realized was unutterably and embarrassingly schoolgirlish of her – at thirty-four, no less! – but which she absolutely had to resolve because, what the hell, you're only thirty-four once.

So here she was sitting right behind him, waiting for him to get up and leave so she could sneak a glance before he rejoined his blonde companion who was probably tapping her foot and anxiously choking down a smoke on the baking sidewalk wondering where the hell her date was.

So why wouldn't he leave?

*

Why wouldn't she leave? The lady who'd shushed Charlie and his hair was still sitting behind him even though the awful truth (that whether they liked it or not, Cary and Irene were made for each other) had been revealed and resolved minutes ago and all that was left in here was velvet curtains and stale air.

And her.

And him.

Chelsea. Bedtime

Larry D lay unsleeping on the very edge of the king-size bed with his back to the middle. In the middle of the bed was Barbara B. She rolled over and put her arms around Larry, cuddled him and kissed the back of his neck. "G'night, sweetheart," she whispered, tingling him with her breath the way she knew he liked. She rolled over the other way, to the edge of the bed where Larry P lay, silently praying to the Catholic Jesus forty-nine per-cent of him so fervently believed in. Barbara patted Larry three times on the ass – a favorite of his – and kissed his shoulder. "G'night, sweetheart," she said, then rolled back into the middle and closed her eyes.

Barbara was almost asleep when, through the sizzle and buzz of the traffic down below, she heard singing and violins coming from the other end of loft. She opened her eyes and said, "Larry, one of you has gotta go turn that music off."

The Upper West Side

While she waited for the elevator, Adelaide thought about
the list of things she didn't want to think about. Some
– like her nauseated revulsion for cats' whiskers – were
perennials, having been with her since The List began to
form when she was six years old, and which she knew
would be with her forever; some were as fleeting and tax-
ing as a summer cold; others crushed and slumped her for
years, only to one day take flight as suddenly and inexplicably as they had descended upon her. Some she knew
she deserved; some were just plain unfair. On that torrid
Tuesday night, the uppermost rungs on Adelaide's ladder
of things to shun were:

Fruit and vegetables, and why she didn't eat them more
often.

Her husband, and how very long it had been since he'd
last ravaged her.

Her marriage.

The broad-shouldered, square-jawed, blue-ribbon sap
in the cinema and what he might have looked like (she

didn't get a chance to see for herself because she'd been hustled out of there by an overeager usher). Weird, probably.

The multi-billion-dollar company she inherited, owned and ran. And how she sometimes wished it would just disappear. Or never have been invented.

The break-up of Chester Polglase and Sara White.

Her increasing enjoyment of alcohol. Or if not enjoyment exactly, then reliance on its calmative ... Oh, hell, she liked a drink or two – big deal.

Herself, generally.

Herself, turning thirty-five.

The blue-ribbon sap. Again. Sure, he had his faults but he was there, wasn't he? Whatever else, he was a fan of *The Awful Truth*. And why was she acting like a teenager all of a sudden? Again.

Her mother's presence in Dallas in 1963: the secret to end all secrets. And how long she could keep it bottled up inside her.

All forms of cancer.

The fact that she was extremely almost thirty-five and didn't have children.

The blue-ribbon sap. Again.

The fact that she didn't want children. Probably.

The word 'probably'.

The List itself and how impossible it was not to think about the things on it...

The doors slid open. Tim the elevator man winked and said, "Hot out, huh, Ms Carter?"

The casual remark made Adelaide wonder if the weather showed on her – if she was perspiring or there were dark patches in the armpits of her agnés b. blouse

– but she stopped herself from checking. "Yes," she said, entering the small elevator car. "It very certainly is." She was tired and the words came out wrong so she quickly added, "I'm not trying to be sarcastic, Tim. It really is hot."

"How would it be sarcastic, telling me something I already know?" Tim had a very distinct attitude that Adelaide was never quite sure was naivety or surliness or an especially dry sense of humor. Maybe it was an annoying, confusing combination of all three. Whatever it was it made her nervous and self-conscious. And she hated being made to feel that way. He was bearded and young; the young could be challenging.

"Sorry," Adelaide said. "I had three or four drinks before I got here and they're beginning to wear off."

Young Tim didn't laugh. "I guess booze is an occupational hazard in your line of work, huh?" He pressed the button for the top floor. "Must be tough being in PR. What was it tonight – theatre world, art world? Was it fashion? You hangin' around with the beautiful people?"

"No," she said. "Nothing like that." She looked up at the bank of lights – six more floors to go.

"Your husband's home," Tim told her. "Got back around seven after a workout at Gold's on eighty-ninth. Upper body mostly. And I don't mind telling you, he's looking pretty good. For his age."

For his age? She tried to dial back the incredulity. "He's only twenty-eight."

"I know that," Tim said. "But I'm twenty-three."

The elevator stopped and the doors slid open. "Okay," Adelaide said, stepping directly into the penthouse hallway. "Well, good night, Tim." She didn't turn around but could almost feel the twenty-three-year-old checking out her ass. She hoped it looked good – for a woman who'd be thirty-five in just a few days. Either way, she vowed, next time she was taking the stairs, all fifteen flights.

As soon as the doors closed she looked under her arms and was immensely relieved to see that there were no dark patches there. She took off her shoes and flicked through the letters piled on the high table in the hallway. The mail was, she thought, even duller than usual and she let it fall from her hands and spill across the parquet floor. If there was an early birthday card somewhere in the scatter she wasn't interested in reading it.

In the unlit living room she placed her Valextra handbag on a side table, went into the kitchen and thought about fixing herself a drink – maybe a whisky sour – before beginning the search for her husband. She opened the refrigerator and cooled off, deciding that she – and her thirty-four-year-old butt – didn't really need any more alcohalories.

Was it the fact that she was getting "old" that accounted for Rob's apparent disinterest in her? And her own indifference developing into something approaching contempt toward him? They'd been married for only two and a half years, together for three, and yet the stagnation felt as rich and aged as vintage wine. As soon as she'd poured herself that nice glass of metaphor, Adelaide wondered if her fondness for alcohol was literally boundless. Was she an alcoholic? That would be very bad. She definitely drank a lot – not as in tons of booze or like there was a keg tube permanently attached to her mouth, but a lot as in rather often. Several nights a week. If "several" meant "every." She supposed it was because she was bored. Because she was bored and because it made life with Rob a little easier, everything she couldn't share with him;

"everything" meaning "everything." Every single thing. Adelaide was tired of keeping it all hidden. She wanted to share her life with someone she could share her life with. Someone who knew her inside and out and wouldn't be stunned and horrified by it all. Someone like ... There was no-one. There was not a single person in the whole entire world in whom she could confide who would not run screaming. Okay, now she was just babbling; it's not like she was hiding the fact that she was a werewolf or something. It was the heat. The heat was making her crazy.

"Rob?" she called out, a little surprised to find herself still standing at the refrigerator staring at a crisper full of wilting green things. "Are you in the vicinity?"

After looking in the media room, her office, the library, all three bedrooms, the bathrooms, the laundry (you never knew), the dining room and once again in the living room, Adelaide opened the French doors to the terrace and stepped out into the heavy, humid night air. Through the stand of linden trees, she could see that the lights were on in Rob's bungalow office at the far end of the terrace, the corner that overlooked West 75th Street and the park. The terracotta tiles felt warm and rough on her feet. "Rob?" she shouted, as she approached the bungalow door.

"Hello?" Rob said from inside. "Who's that?"

"Adelaide Carter," she said, then added dryly, "We're married."

"Great! Come on in."

Face to face with her husband at last, Adelaide leaned in for a kiss.

He smiled and shook her hand. "Good to see you," he said, as though he'd run into an old college buddy. His hand felt clammy. "Did you eat?"

"Some fruit," she said. "In a cocktail."

He mentioned that it was late and, almost as an after-thought, asked her where she'd been.

A book launch, she lied. "For this book about things that ... people who ... " Her whole life hidden from her husband. It was absurd; she decided to tell him everything right there and then. "Listen, I – "

"Sounds great! Here's the thing, babe, I need the advice of a professional." He paused and smiled, as though this were a sales pitch. "Which one of these do you prefer?"

Covering the large drafting table her husband was seated at was an array of eight-by-ten-inch headshots of himself; Pensive, Playful, Concerned, Sympathetic, Rakish, Smoldering, Hysterical, Moody, Coy, Playful (again), Haughty, Whimsical and Imperious. She took in all the handsome Robs looking up at her, his teeth the brightest thing about every shot.

"Hmmm ... " she said, trying hard to make it sound considered. This revealing-her-entire-life-and-family-secret business would have to wait until more important matters were addressed. "They're all very nice. But isn't magazine publisher usually more of a behind-the-scenes type of role?"

Rob nodded. "I'm shaking things up a little."

"I see," Adelaide said. "Well, I still don't know about these photos." Especially the one where he wore a pair of black-framed glasses that clearly had no lenses in them. Could this really be the same person who once said to her when they were shopping in Williamsburg, "Brooklyn is the Manhattan of the other boroughs"? It was the sharpest thing he'd ever said and she treasured the memory. Clung to it, actually, allowing that one clever remark to excuse several thousand, er, less sharp ones.

"I hear ya, babe. It's really tough, isn't it?" He pointed to Moody. "In this one, I think I look a little like Kennedy – not the dad or the plane crasher. The uncle – the car crasher. What was his name?"

A dark memory made her cringe. She shook it off and focused on her husband. "You know his name, Rob," she said. "Don't you?"

"Of course. I'm just having a mental, uh, breakdown," Rob said. "C'mon – what's his name?"

She waited a moment before saying, "Groucho?"

And as Rob snapped his fingers and said, "That's the guy!" Adelaide dearly wished she'd made herself that whisky sour.

Kiko's Diner.
368 West 31st Street

Charlie looked across the scuffed and stained Formica table top at Sallie. Even under these godawful fluorescent lights, and dressed the way she was, plain and dour, her long straw-blonde hair pulled back so tight and severe under her black bonnet, his sister was really a knockout, even without a hint of make-up. He knew he shouldn't be having thoughts like that but he couldn't help it; he just wanted what was best for her.

"Leave him," he said, flipping his coffee cup upside down and resting it in the saucer.

"I can't," Sallie said. She looked disappointed with him. As though he was being obtuse.

"Why not?" said Charlie. Even to himself he sounded unsympathetic. And obtuse.

"Come on, Charlie," she said. "We've been through this so many times. You know why not – it would break Father's heart. I couldn't live with that."

"But what about your own heart, Sallie?" he said, making sure he didn't sound too pleading or whiny. Or, for that matter, too much like a Hallmark card. "When are you going to give that a chance to –"

She cut him off. "Not every situation in life demands that we put our own interests before those of others, Charlie. I think you know that."

"I do," Charlie said. "I understand that, of course I do. But life shouldn't simply be one sacrifice after another." As it most certainly had been for the first eighteen years, he did not add aloud.

"Nor do I see it that way."

He tried to stop himself, he really did, but before he knew it the words were already out. "I'm not sure you know enough about life to make an informed judgment."

"Do you mean enough to enable me to make patronizing remarks like that?" The barest hint of a smile creeping into the side of her mouth softened the comment.

"Gosh, it sure was, wasn't it?" Charlie said, shaking his head. "I apologize. I just want … " What he wanted – what he told himself he wanted, anyway – was for her to experience life the way he had. A little of it at least, see what she made of it. "Come live with me, just for a while, and see how you like it. I've changed, Sal. Not necessarily all in good ways, I admit, but the last few years I've –"

She quieted him by clasping his hand in both of hers. "I'm happy about that," she said. "And not in some vague, distant way either. I feel real happiness for you. Especially now that you're back from the west coast. I'm not sure you belonged there. How're things between you and Lainey?"

Despite – or perhaps because of – being polar opposites, Charlie's ex-girlfriend, Lainey, and Sallie had been fast friends from the moment they'd met. Just another of the many things about his little sister that surprised the hell out of him.

"Somewhat thawed," he told her. "She's coming around to forgiving me. Probably. Maybe. You know her sort of people, they're very emotional." Charlie's eyes glazed over as he remembered how things often were with Lainey – the tantrums and fights and slaps across his face. There were six-year-olds who had more control over themselves. "Gosh, that was mean," he said, snapping out of his brief reverie. "Did I say that out loud?"

"What?" Sallie asked. "That she was emotional?"

"Uh, yeah, that's right," Charlie said, relieved that the "six-year-old" remark had been contained. Especially after what had happened in the cinema earlier, being shushed and so forth. Then having to wait until the shush-er left the cinema before he could leave because he was pretty embarrassed about accidentally speaking aloud in there. "Emotional."

"You know she would have done anything for you, right? Anything you asked."

"I know," said Charlie. "I know that. But I guess I just didn't know exactly what to ask for."

"Maybe not. But you always knew what you were looking for, Charlie," said Sallie. "You always have."

"Is that right?" he said. "What am I looking for?"

"Perfection," she told him. "But you won't find it. Not in this world, anyway." She joined her hands and spoke to him over the steeple of her index fingers. "The only per-fection we can hope to know is God."

"So I'll look for a goddess," Charlie said, with a flip-pant wave of his hand. "This is New York City – they're everywhere."

When Sallie wryly cocked her head he could tell she wasn't buying his Mr Casual act. "I have to go," she said. "Are we far from the station?"

"Don't want to be late for the time machine, huh?"

"How do you mean?"

"Well, you get on the train at Penn Station but where you get off, where you end up, you're two hundred years in the past. Back in Pennsyltransylvania."

She smiled briefly and thinly but otherwise chose not to respond.

Charlie flipped the coffee cup back over and looked at the thin, finger-shaped remnants running down the inside; in some cultures you were supposed to be able to tell your fortune by looking at that stuff.

"Any clues?" Sallie asked, surprising him once again; how the heck did she know about this?

"Not one," he said, smiling. "About anything."

As they stood, Charlie helped Sallie on with her coat, slipping his fingers inside, brushing against her back, telling himself that he was just checking out the lining.

*

"That's Madison Square Garden," Charlie said, as he and Sallie walked along West 33rd. "They play basketball in there. Concerts, too."

"Madison *Square* Garden?" Sallie said. "But it's round."

"Yes, it is," her brother answered solemnly. "That's another joke, right?"

Sallie nodded, but added that Madison Square Garden was still round, which didn't make much sense to her. "Unless it was named after the president," she said. "James Madison Square."

Charlie was surprised; her sense of humor was almost as irrepressible and goofy as his own. He laughed. But a small part of him still couldn't help wondering if she really thought the fella's name was James Madison Square.

"I know his name's James Madison," she added. He laughed again, already missing her; five years younger, but she could always read him like a cheap dime novel.

As they entered Penn Station he slipped his arm inside hers and pulled her close to him, wanting her to feel protected. A busy train station late at night was no place for a woman. Especially a woman like Sal; dressed the way she was she was just asking for trouble. "Let go of me," she said, wriggling. "It's too hot." He slipped his arm back out, but stayed close to her.

They reached the platform for the train to Hartburg. As they stood by the door to her car Charlie asked his sister if she'd be all right.

She told him that she'd be fine, that she was a grown woman and that this wasn't her first time out in the world all alone. In the pause, he couldn't be sure whether she was angry with him for being so patronizing all over again and was maybe building up steam for a blast of invective that he surely knew she was capable of when she was riled about something, and just when he thought he'd burst with nervous dread, she gave him a smile that was so dazzling in its purity and warmth and grace and beauty that for a moment he wondered if maybe there really was a God and he was staring right at the proof.

He closed his eyes for a moment, dismissing the thought and the smile. He opened them again and looked up at her, framed by the carriage doorway. "You still walking from Hartburg station?" he asked, telling himself not to scold her no matter what the answer was.

"Yes," she said. "If there are no buggies. I like to walk anyway. It helps me think." She gave him a bemused look and said, "May I have my ticket?"

He put on a blank face, hamming it up a little. "Your ticket?"

"Yes," she said. "The one you removed from my coat at the restaurant."

"You knew?"

She told him he needed more practice, and as the train's whistle blew he handed her the ticket. "I'll call you," he said.

It was the best joke of the night, and both of them laughed heartily. She looked out the window and Charlie waved, tears beginning to well in his eyes as the train pulled out, taking her back to what passed for life.

Greenwich Street, between Horatio and Gansevoort (and back again)

Dwight held open the passenger door of the convertible 1955 Porsche Spyder, immaculate and gleaming under the streetlight. Sara got in, a little wobbly from Champagne and grief. As Dwight walked around the front of the car he smiled at her through the windscreen. She smiled back, more brightly than he was expecting; mourning had added a definite *joie de vivre* and luster to the Widow White. And her teeth.

Sara nodded absently and examined her nails. "There's no roof on this car," she said, as though informing him of something he might not be aware of.

Behind the wheel, Dwight hit the ignition, let the engine rumble for a moment and then took off. Miss White's apparent grace in the face of shock notwithstanding, Dwight wanted this night – this debacle – over as soon as possible. He hated playing grief-counselor, even if the person being counseled wasn't grieving a whole hell of a lot. He was, in the weary words of countless screen characters around his age, getting too old for this shit. He was tired and he wanted a drink. He wanted to sit at the end of a bar with a drink and a cigarette and a couple of people near to his own age who knew more about life than what they learned from the goddamn TV or the goddamn Internet. He wanted out of this. He wanted to sit back and take it easy. He'd earned it, and now he wanted to retire and spend every minute he had left listening and laughing and talking. With Claudette.

He put all that aside and was in the middle of explaining the twisted history of this particular roofless silver Porsche Spyder when he saw the ambulance with his paramedic in the driver's seat, waiting for a light to change. Before Miss White noticed the vehicle, which in the interest of verisimilitude should have been long gone by now, he executed a swift and smooth u-turn. "Short cut," he muttered.

As it eased into the lane heading back the way they'd come, the Spyder's headlights caught Eduardo and the two cops loitering in front of a brick wall. Just standing there, like they were waiting to be caught. Dwight made a mental note – ream them. He continued the turn, making it a full circle. The ambulance crossed the intersection and quickly disappeared down Gansevoort Street. Miss White hadn't seen a thing and before she knew it the Porsche was back at the lights.

"But what's the hurry?" Dwight said, trying to contain his fury; retirement would have to wait – he was going to have to go to work and kill a few people tomorrow morning.

88 West 75th Street

Adelaide stood in front of the bathroom mirror studying her face, looking for signs of her encroaching thirty-fiveness and trying not to be vain about it. Vanity was for kids and really good-looking people, she thought, and she was neither. There were a few small wrinkles around her light brown eyes, and two or three grays creeping into her long black hair, but she regarded these things with simple curiosity rather than any kind of dread or despair. She was not unhappy with the way she looked. Except for the distinct lack of fire and passion in her eyes. Her eyes, she thought, seemed pale and dulled by dissatisfaction. Which was disappointing.

So that was how she looked on the cusp of her mid-thirties, and all things considered it wasn't too bad. But who she was – or who she seemed to be becoming lately – was a different story. One that she hoped wasn't too late to change. Step One – be nice to Rob.

Adelaide switched the ensuite bathroom lights off and went into the bedroom. Rob was on the bed, lying there like a catalogue model, the sheet modestly covering his groin, the rest of him – all broad and tanned – on display.

"I've narrowed it down to three," he said.

"Three what?" she asked.

He swept his hand over three of the eight-by-tens scattered across the bed beside him.

"God, did I marry the vainest man in New York?" Adelaide said, looking down at Pensive, Rakish and Moody.

Smoldering looked back at her and said, "Maybe not the vainest, babe, but definitely the studliest."

Adelaide winced at the last word, scooped up the photographs and tossed them onto the floor. She put her mouth to Rob's and forced his thick lips apart with her tongue. Before he had time to tell her that he had a headache or his period or some other bullshit excuse, she'd removed her black Eres Organza de Rêve bra, straddled his groin and placed his hand on her hardening nipple. He squeezed it, dutifully at first, but with an enthusiasm that she could feel quickly growing between her legs. *And about time, too*, she thought, becoming warm and wet. Rob reached down and began rubbing the head of his dick against her. She shuddered, kissed him harder and deeper one last time before pushing herself away from him. "Gimme a second," she panted, backing toward the bathroom.

"No!" Rob said, his hand still clutching his throbbing joint. "C'mon, Addy, don't do that. Come back to bed."

"I have to, honey," she said. "Let's not get into this right now, huh?"

Rob turned on his side, away from her. "Ah, just forget it."

She said, "I don't want to forget it. I want to keep going. Come on, make it an early birthday present." But already the warm tingle she'd felt all over her body was fading, turning clammy.

He sulkily told her that there was no point.

She told him that of course there was a point. "Pleasure."

"Pleasure I can take care of myself," he said.

Adelaide's temperature leaped. "Oh yeah?" she said, pointing down to the photograph she was standing on. "Is that what these're for? Inspiration?"

"I want to make a baby, Adelaide," Rob sighed. "And for that I need you."

There were so many things wrong with what her husband had just said; the infantile expression "make a baby," like they were fourth-graders; his almost defiantly unsexy and non-intimate "need" of her, like she was merely an element in a chemical equation. "Oh well, now that you put it like that," she said, "I'll just jump right back in."

"Cool!" he said, enthusiastically. "I hate wasting a Viagra."

She couldn't believe what she was hearing. "You took a Viagra?"

"No …" Rob swallowed nervously. "Maybe." He desperately searched the bedroom for inspiration. Nothing. "I thought it was an M&M."

"You need Viagra?" Adelaide said. "You're only twenty-eight!"

"It's not me, it's you," he said. Then paused; that didn't sound right. "No, the other way around. It's you, not me. No! Jeepers, you've got me all wound up, Addy." It was true; the sheet was now coiled and twisted, snaking in and out of Rob's arms and legs like a cotton cobra. "I'm all confused. Here." He pointed to his head. "And here." He pointed to his groin.

"Well, I can't help you," Adelaide said. "At either end."

The last thing she saw before she slammed the bathroom door was Rob folding his perfectly-toned arms and pouting. Most couples' sex lives ended up on the rocks because they had kids; hers and Rob's was finished because she didn't want them, and he'd only "entertain" her in the interest of creating one. There was an irony in that, she supposed. A fucking bitter one. She switched on the light above the mirror, not at all pleased with what she saw. Except for her eyes – where at last there was a hint of passion.

A bar called "A Bar Called Heaven"

By the time he finished his fourth vodka tonic Clayton Townsend had forgotten the name of the place he was sitting in. He tried to catch the attention of a barmaid and noticed some fluffy clouds and rainbows and golden rays of sunlight and these fat-cheeked grinning things that could be cherubs or angels painted on the ceiling. The place was pretty crowded and Clayton had the weird feeling that he'd seen almost everybody in there somewhere before, as though they'd all appeared in various television shows sometime over the past couple decades.

He turned to the woman sitting on the stool next to him, Elodie Frontenac, but her attention was elsewhere. Clayton followed her green-laser gaze; in the far corner of the room a woman threw a pink drink into a man's flabbergasted face. It was like a clichéd scene from a cliché-ridden telemovie. Clayton found that that sort of thing happened often in New York City, birthplace of so many of the world's most enduring clichés.

Elodie turned around and said, "Well she doesn't need any help from us. Good for her, eh?"

"I'm about done here," Clayton said, pointing to the warm dregs in the bottom of his glass. "You want another?"

Elodie nodded.

Clayton widened his eyes and arched his brows, even planted the faintest trace of an anticipatory smile in the corner of his mouth as he tried to engage the attention of one of the many, many not-particularly-busy barmaids behind the large and not-particularly-busy bar. They looked near him and beside him and above him and behind him, just to the left of him and just to the right, and even gave brief, quizzical consideration to what might pass for the fuzzy outer edge of his aura or his soul, but not one came close to actually seeing him. There is a very specific shade of ignominy in being ignored in bars (and while, as is the case with so many other of life's highs and lows, it may seem more acute in New York City, it is not unique to that place; the ignoree is cloaked in unnotice wherever he goes) and Clayton had become so used to it that sometimes he even began to doubt his public quiddity, at least where the attention of females who wanted to overcharge him to inflate that very same sense of self was concerned.

He gave it another minute, maybe four, then gave up and turned his attention to a couple necking heavily on a crowded couch. The guy had the muscular physique of a professional refrigerator-lifter while his date was built like some sort of waterbird, all sharp bones and twitchy, long-necked movements. They were really going at it, too, with a brazenness that Clayton considered extremely European, even though he'd never been there and had no real knowledge of how the Europeans went at it.

"Probably their third date," Elodie said. "He's done

dinner twice and that's all he's willing to stump for unless she gives it up tonight. Which she will. Possibly right here in the bathroom. I give 'em six weeks."

"Six weeks?" Clayton said incredulously. "They can't keep their hands off of each other."

Elodie shook her head. "Take a closer look – the guy's eyes are wide open. He's scoping the room for backup flesh in case things don't elevate in the next ten minutes." She finished her Gin Rickey. "What a terrible, terrible person."

More terrible than me? Clayton wondered. More terrible than you?

He squinted for a moment, convinced as he was that momentary squinting gave him extra long-range vision. Sure enough he saw that the muscle man's eyes were wide open. "So who's coming to ReStart – him or her?"

"The guy," said Elodie. "The broad's a goner. Look at the way her little hand is wrapped around his fat neck. She's not letting him go anytime soon. She's almost thirty. The way she's thinking, it's this guy or bust. Things don't work out with him I may as well kill myself or get me to a nunnery."

"Right," Clayton said, awed by how sharply and quickly Elodie thought. It got him excited, even a little breathless, as he added: "Meanwhile he's looking around at all this sweet, sweet trim thinking, I gotta check out all the flavors before they take away my spoon."

"Exactly," said Elodie. "Please don't ever say 'sweet sweet trim' in front of me again."

"Is it the 'sweet' or the 'trim'?"

"It's both," Elodie told him. "And the combination. And the repetition. Just say 'women'."

"Will do," Clayton said, meaning it. In a perhaps misguided effort to win Elodie's affection and respect, he always took her advice and followed her commands. Always too quickly, always too eagerly.

"So if he came to us what would we suggest?"

She leaned over and whispered hoarsely in Clayton's ear. "Some kind of set-up like the Albanian Spinster Pillow Fight."

"Perfect," he said, forcefully stopping himself from shivering at her warm breath spilling over his neck. The Albanian Spinster Pillow Fight was one of their most effective operations – subtle, swift and emotionally merciful. But another scheme from a few months earlier offered a superb finishing touch. "Just add the banana movement from Sayonara Lunchtray, and bang – Splitsville."

Just then the young woman on the couch noticed Elodie staring at her with such unabashed interest. She flipped the bird at Elodie with her wedding finger, on which there was a modest engagement ring. She mouthed the words "He's mine" to Elodie, who finally averted her eyes.

"You keep on believing that, sister," Elodie said quietly, more to herself than the other girl. It was one of the more dastardly ironies in her life that despite what she did for a living – devising deceptions designed to disintegrate duos – Elodie strongly suspected that most people were only truly happy when they were part of a pair. (Also, she had a weakness for occasionally lapsing into attenuated alliteration that she was urgently trying to kick because it was as annoying to herself as much as to others. As was her habit of often speaking and thinking parenthetically. And sometimes *en Français*.)

The French thing she couldn't help. Elodie Frontenac was twenty-nine years old, the wise and (mostly) dutiful daughter of two United Methodist ministers from Jonquière in rural Quebec, "about which there is nothing interesting to know or likely to ever be known," she often said. She'd graduated from Concordia with a degree in sociology, which had in no way led or helped her to spend the years immediately following graduation as an ad agency producer in Montreal. She loathed her French-Canadian accent (which to her ears sounded like Celine Dion after she'd gone deaf and had a tonsillectomy and then been punched in the throat) and worked hard to get rid of it and pass for "a regular Canadian." As a producer of television commercials, Elodie had displayed a knack for cost control, organization and creativity that made her an ideal recruit for Level 102 at ReStart, where she'd been for the last three years.

The ReStart recruitment was – and this was obviously no accident – almost ecclesiastical in its pitch, and its pitch and yaw made Elodie swoon. "Do you want do something meaningful with your life?" the recruiter had said as Elodie stood in line outside Schwartz's Delicatessen on Saint-Laurent; it was freezing that day but Elodie had a susceptibility toward smoked meat that she was ashamed of but powerless over. The recruiter just came right out and said it – "You're in advertising – you want that to be your legacy?" – and Elodie had expected to be clobbered with the Book of Mormon or a brick of Jehovah's Witness pamphlets. The line inched forward. Elodie was just starting to wonder how this *bouffant* knew that she was in advertising when the woman presented Elodie the most incredible offer she'd ever heard. "You will be paid millions and your work will change people's lives," the recruiter concluded. "Literally and literally."

Elodie farewelled some of the world's finest smoked and herbed pastrami and two weeks later she was in New

York City, pulling down almost forty thousand dollars a week (literally) and (literally) changing people's lives …

Clayton tried to flag a waitress but, gosh, her cuticles were absolutely fascinating her. He watched as all ten were thoroughly examined then he gave up and asked Elodie if she wanted to go do something fun.

"Maybe," she said. "What do you mean by fun?" Elodie sometimes found herself suspicious of what other people considered fun. Fun in Jonquière often meant tipping cows or being groped on the back of a snowmobile. Fun was crude and dangerous and not worth being unbuttoned for. Up in northern Quebec, fun had gotten a pretty dubious reputation for itself. Of course, what passed for fun here in New York City for people around her age also left a lot to be desired, Elodie believed. This thought led her to wonder if she was perhaps opposed to fun in general.

"How about …" Clayton had no suspicions whatsoever surrounding fun and the having of it; unfortunately he also had no idea of what Elodie Frontenac might accept as fun at that particular moment. He was pretty clear on what he'd consider fun right at that moment but was far too solicitous to suggest it. Maybe another drink would help him get the words out. Or the thought out of his head. "How about staying right here on these stools and having another drink?"

"I like it. We're better off in here, don't you think? It's air-conditioned, there's alcohol, no cows are in danger of overbalancing and there's people of the opposite sex, meaning there's a faint glimmer of a sliver of a microscopic chance that you might get laid." She smiled at her colleague. "That'd be nice, wouldn't it?"

Even as he blushed, Clayton's heart stammered at the

smile. He wasn't quite sure what she meant by the cow remark.

When Elodie suddenly began rubbing her green eyes with the heels of her hands Clayton knew what was coming; a sentence, an invitation, a demand he'd heard hundreds of times in the three years they'd been friends and co-workers. "Tell me a secret."

He was ready. "My reaction to most contemporary music makes me feel really old. The way I hear it it just sounds like men complaining about various matters backed by minor chords and insipid rhythms." He waved his right hand in the air in a small circle, capturing the music that was drifting from the speakers above them. "Do you like this stuff?"

Elodie said that she did not, but also that she was probably the wrong person to ask since she'd heard precisely one piece of music in her entire life that had moved her in any way – a thirteen-minute lament for voice and cithara (an ancient Greek lyre-like instrument, she kindly explained) called 'Dolorum Solatium' by the twelfth-century avant-garde composer and philosopher Peter Abelard, who wrote the piece for his beloved Heloise.

"So was it the tragedy of the Heloise and Abelard story that drew you to it?" Clayton asked. "Their passionate affair undone at the devious hand of her uncle?"

"No," Elodie said. "It's an amazing piece of music. It doesn't need anything else."

"I'll just go see if it's on the jukebox," Clayton said, slipping off his stool. "Now you tell me a secret."

"I genuinely wish I was more empathetic toward young people, but it's hard. Especially with the current crop of youth being the way they are. Look at 'em – has there ever been a more undeservingly self-obsessed generation of goof-offs and yahoos?"

"I agree," Clayton said. He tried to catch the eye of a waitress, maybe order that next drink. Nothing doing. "Although it's very possible that at the same time there's never been a better-looking generation of humans. Which would go some way toward explaining why they're always taking and sending each other photographs of themselves."

"Or it's the other way around, right? Maybe the media has created the mug."

"Like natural selection – they've had to become better-looking to survive."

"I hate the young."

"We are the young." He looked at her, at the tiny contrails of red around the green planets of her irises. "Aren't we?"

"Then I hate us."

"Cheers to that," Clayton said, raising his hand where a cocktail should have been.

Splitsville

Chester Polglase lay in the back of a fake ambulance. Two fake paramedics stared down at his prostrate, unconscious body which was covered in cold orange soup and some sort of red goo; he looked like Halloween gone terribly wrong. "That's his name?" one fake paramedic said. "Seriously?"

"I kid you not," the other replied.

Both of them laughed.

"What's it mean?" one asked.

"No idea," the other said. "Maybe the dude's a clown."

"Right. Or a tailor."

They both laughed some more.

Until Chester opened his eyes and looked up at them. Clearly he had no idea where he was or what was going on. "What happened?" he said groggily. He looked down at his red-stained shirt, moaned, then closed his eyes and laid his head back on the gurney's mattress.

"You fainted after Eduardo shot you," one of the fake paramedics said. "It was a nice touch. Very authentic."

"Oh. Right," Chester said dismally, suddenly remembering everything. His fiancée was now his ex. He was a bachelor, a free man, all the women of Earth re-available to him.

He wanted to cry.

"What happens now?" he asked. "Where are you guys taking me?"

"You are now an official resident of the happiest place in the world," one of the men explained. "Splitsville, USA …"

A very real tear plopped out of Chester Polglase's eye.

"… Buttons."

Murray Hill

Holly Hohenzollern sat at her kitchen table and reviewed the letter she'd almost finished,   skipping over the dull bits and reading aloud her favorite parts to see how it would sound in the ears of its recipient. "Dear Mr Van Linden," she began. "Blah blah blah … Blah blah blah … reptile cage at the Bronx Zoo, two gallons of strawberry ice-cream … blah blah blah … sudden reappearance of his supposedly dead parents …"

She took a sip of Pink Lemonade Snapple and underlined "supposedly," to give it a bit more skeptical weight. Then she added some exclamation points where things slowed down, and continued.

"Blah blah blah …" she said to herself. "Blah blah … Later, there was a bicycle pump but I don't want to go into that right now!! Blah blah blah … blah blah … I'm telling you so that you can expose these sick, evil people for what they are. Yours …"

And here was where she was stuck, looking for just the right word with which to sign off. Something intriguing yet believable but not too crazy-sounding because she knew how easy it would be to come across as a little nutty considering what she was writing about here. And God knew she saw enough of exactly that sort of crazy every day at work.

"Sincerely?" she said. "Faithfully? Respectfully?"

None of these was right.

"Single-ly?" she wondered aloud. It sounded good, and she tried again. "Single-ly! Single-ly yours, Holly Hohenzollern." That was good. But it needed one last thing. So after her name she added a single word and underlined it. "Miss."

Miss Holly Hohenzollern folded the letter, put it into an envelope and wrote the name of the recipient on the front: CHARLIE VAN LINDEN. It looked good to her, the way she wrote his name all in capital letters. There was no way the reporter could ignore it, and there was no way he could pretend he never got it either, because she was going to hand deliver it to his office her own self personally. The hell if it was almost midnight and stinking hot outside. She grabbed her handbag and her gun and left the apartment.

Holly Hohenzollern was, not to put too fine a point on it, out for revenge and nothing was going to stop her – not the stupid heat, not the stupid lateness of the hour and certainly not the stupid, diabolical company that put her into this situation of single-ness in the first place.

Rivington Street,
Lower East Side

In the middle of the small, sparsely furnished room, Dwight Kitchener concentrated on his movements, and on the gentle burn of whisky in his throat, and attempted to have no other thoughts. Barefoot, wearing black tuxedo pants and a white t-shirt, he breathed in deeply and exhaled slowly through tightly pursed lips. He held both arms straight out in front of him, with his hands bent back sharply at the wrist, then moved them to the left. He took a step forward, placing his weight, the balance of his core, on the front leg and turned his torso to the right. He wobbled a little and tried not to think about the fact that it wasn't all that long ago that he'd have been practicing Tae Kwon Do movements, something much more rigorous, threatening and useful than this bullshit Dim Mak Tai Chi, which was for invalids and goddamn seniors. Breathing in, he quickly straightened up and swung his trailing leg around, overbalanced, and fell heavily to the floor. Goddamn seniors like himself.

He slumped onto the Murphy bed in the corner and lay there panting for a moment before reaching down and removing a pack of cigarettes, a Zippo lighter and a clean ashtray from under the bed. He lit the cigarette, allowed himself a deep drag then blew out a long stream of smoke.

"Yeah, yeah I know," he said to the framed photograph of the woman on his bedside table. "It'll kill me. And you know what, Claudette? I hope it damn well does."

But he stubbed out the cigarette anyway. And as he did, he took a long look at the open bottle of whisky up on the shelf on the other side of the room before deciding it was too far away to bother.

Outside Heaven

Elodie and Clayton lingered in the still heat that radiated from the sidewalk outside the bar. Clayton looked up above the doorway and saw that the place was called A Bar Called Heaven. Probably named after a line in that old Talking Heads song because that was the sort of thing that passed for clever these days. They'd been at – or in – Heaven since around ten pm, so they were both a little oiled by now, but not swaying or about to get mawkish or ribald or anything. Unfortunately.

"Well, thanks for the drink, Clay," Elodie said. "Despite the odds, I enjoyed it."

"Me too," he said, trying to sound casual, almost ambivalent, about it. Clayton liked drinking a lot, but he absolutely loved drinking with Elodie, and if people around them mistook them for an unlikely item – a total fox like her and a borderline dweeb like him – so much the better. "So maybe we should …" He didn't want the night to be over but it was near midnight and they both had an early start the next day.

He glanced over Elodie's shoulder as a brassy blonde with a heap of curly hair piled high on her head came marching around the corner with these big purposeful strides like she was in a parade or something. She had dimples and big brown eyes and there was a kind of blithe eagerness in her face and her bearing that made Clayton think she might suddenly burst into song at any moment, start singing the praises of Love or Spring, just like that. Maybe even accompany it with a little tap or shuffle. She appeared to be wearing one of those pointy bras from the 1950s. There was an envelope sticking out of the back pocket of her jeans, and as she loped away Clayton saw her left hand reach behind and pat it with her fingertips, as though she was making sure it was there.

"Wow," he said, nodding. "I wonder if she's single." He turned back to Elodie, eager to see if his remark had gotten a reaction from her.

She looked mildly startled. "Oh she is," Elodie said with certainty.

"How do you know?"

"We made her that way."

Clayton drew a blank, and his face showed it.

"The big lizard, the ice-cream and the parents from beyond the grave," Elodie said. "Remember?"

"That's *her*?" he said. "The girl from Night of the Living Iguana?"

Elodie nodded slowly and contemplatively.

"Gosh," said Clayton. "I wonder if she's eaten strawberry ice-cream since."

"I would guess not," said Elodie gravely.

"Man, I hate it when this happens. Seeing someone after an operation," he said. "One of our marks. I hate having to acknowledge that they're, y'know, real."

Clayton sighed, remembering where they were before old Holly Whatsername suddenly appeared and threw him off. He'd been busy not wanting things with Elodie to end. So should he suggest another drink? Maybe the Aspen – that was around here someplace. Or maybe a nightcap back at his place? He took a deep breath and got ready. "So listen, maybe we could –"

"*A demain*, Clay," Elodie said quickly.

It was almost like she'd known exactly what he was about to say, what he had in mind. And, God, how he loved it when she spoke French. "Sure," he said, as though it was nothing, no big deal, absolutely fine with him. "G'night, El." And without so much as a handshake to formally end the evening he took off.

But after just twenty paces he couldn't help himself; he turned around. There she was, her gorgeous back to him, her gorgeous red hair dipping between the shoulder blades of that gorgeous back, heading home, gorgeously. Clayton watched for as long as he dared. Then he turned around again and kept walking, just missing the green-eyed glance Elodie threw over her shoulder at him.

God, she was gorgeous.

Chicago

Morton Havisham hated the television program "Lulu & Fred." He hated and loathed and despised it with such a fierce and unyielding passion that he absolutely never missed it. Every Tuesday night at ten pm, CST, he reclined in his BarcaLounger, dressed in silk pajamas, staring clench-jawed at the brand new 58-inch plasma screen television with a vodka highball in one hand and his Colt Python in the other.

A few feet away, Morton's wife Dolores sat in her own BarcaLounger, similarly-dressed and similarly drinking, but completely unarmed.

On this particular Tuesday night they watched as a perky, playful young couple bounced around their enormous, bright sitcom living room, jumping over furniture, throwing orange lobster shells and spraying each other with water pistols.

"Tell me who lives in Manhattan in a place like that with no visible means," Morton said to his wife. "Tell me. Who?"

The same question every week. Fifty-seven years old and her husband could still act like a spoiled kid.

"Nobody, Mort," Dolores said, lustfully eyeing the box of Xanax on the marble coffee table. "Except people who aren't actually real."

"That's right," Morton said. "That's exactly right. Whatever bunch of ninnies and schlemiels produce this program hasn't set foot New York City in the last forty years if they think anybody could live there the way these two do without they're being drug lords or something. Jesus!"

"These two" were the titular Lulu, a petite, purple-haired twenty-something unemployed opera singer who was afraid of birds and nickels (and not a drug lord), and her boyfriend Fred, a dumb-but-lovable former house painter who was trying to make it big in the Manhattan art world despite having absolutely no formal training and even less natural talent (and who was also not a drug lord).

Lulu and Fred and their coterie of dippy, wacky, quirky and zany pals were the CBC network's number-one smash-hit prime-time four-quadrant must-see comedy blockbuster for the fifth year running, reliably collecting Emmys for writing, directing and acting each season. The network loved them, the media loved them, and the public loved them. Sometimes it seemed that the only person in the entire country who didn't love them was Morton "The Meat King" Havisham of Kenilworth, Illinois.

"I *hate* 'em," Morton said, crushing an ice-cube between his teeth. "Especially him. Why would somebody like her put up with a chucklehead like him?"

The same questions, every week. Dolores sighed and said nothing. She liked life here in their 12,000 square foot home in Kenilworth, the wealthiest, whitest, most exclusive enclave in the Midwest. She liked it plenty but, oh, she paid a price. Every Tuesday night shortly before ten, Dolores Havisham paid a price for life in the gilded kennel. She picked up a pair of military-grade safety glasses from the side table.

Lulu squealed and giggled as Fred fitted lobster claws over his hands. "Who knew shellfish could be such fun?" she fluttered.

Fred waited for the laughter to die down, then said. "It's the outfits."

The studio audience erupted once more.

"You know what, Fred?" Lulu said, panting with what might have been desire but was more likely exhaustion. "I think you took me to that res-tah-raunt just so you'd have an excuse to wear a bib." She paused for one and a half seconds. "You big baby!"

Fred turned, revealing that he was wearing a lobster bib! When the audience was spent, he said, "Let's go to bed. Baby needs his rest."

Fred and Lulu linked arms and made for the bedroom. Behind the closed door Lulu giggled and tittered for two point eight seconds before Fred ran back into the living room. "Whoops! Forgot something!" He hunted around the cushions on the fat blue couch, pulled out a rattle and a pacifier then ran back to the bedroom. The door slammed. Lulu squealed with delight.

The Millionaire Meat King of Chicago said, "And now they're eating futzing *lobster*?"

As the peppy theme music began and the audience began its final round of applause, the screen exploded and Lulu and Fred's impossible Manhattan living room disappeared in a cloud of smoke and pulverized television parts.

"Every week, Mort?" Dolores said.

"You know how I feel about these two, Dolly," Morton growled. "You don't like it, go do a crossword puzzle or something."

"I've tried," she said. "I get distracted by the gunfire." She removed the safety glasses and reached for a Xanax, wondering if there was enough left in her drink to help swallow a pill.

NYCNYUSA

Charlie had been a resident – or, he wondered, should that be citizen? – of the world of New York City for coming up on a year now and he'd loved every sense-battering moment of it; the ceaseless sensory stimulation (although obviously a person needed to get away from all that and rest up about every ninety minutes or so); the astonishing beauty, variety and height of the architecture (although for skyscrapers he had to admit he preferred Chicago); the depth, breadth and powerful historical punch of the city's contribution to American culture (although you had to credit an awful lot to New Orleans just for giving the world Buddy Bolden and the first blasts of jazz. And gumbo); the way the city grimly accepted extremes like the Arctic winters and the steaming, febrile summers, like Brownsville and the Upper East Side, like the *Post* and the *Times*.

In almost every way the place was the opposite of Los Angeles. Which was kind of odd in as much as Charlie had also loved living in LA. How could you love one thing that was the complete opposite of another thing you loved? Maybe it was because really, actually, honestly he loved pretty much all of America's cities (at least the ones he'd seen and, boy, he'd seen a lot of them), which in turn was because for an awful long time he hadn't really had much experience of the world outside of a tiny green plot of rural Pennsylvania. And in actual fact it wasn't until Rumspringa, when Charlie was sixteen, that he'd even gotten close to feeling the pluck and thrum of city life, the "city" in that particular case being little old Kleinhooftersville, barely more than a strip of convenience stores, auto shops, a funeral home for dead horses (or so he seemed to recall) and the Kleinhooftersville Motel and Eating House, famous for offering "a taste of Oude Holland," Kleinhooftersville being the sole place outside historical Holland that actually desired such a taste. But even little old K-town had been more than enough for Charlie to know that he wasn't made for a life on the land, a life of chopping and cutting and sweating, of sowing and hoping, much less for the bizarre and backward belief system in which he and his sister had been raised by their devout and devoted *moeder* and *vader*. So as soon as he was able Charlie cut himself loose – he fled all of it, all of them.

And there hadn't passed a day – perhaps not even so much as an hour – in all the years since that he didn't feel completely weighed down by guilt for his flight.

Nevertheless there they were, the facts of his one-and-only life, in increments annual, professional and geographical: a twelve-acre farm outside Hartburg, P.A (age 0–17); pursuing the Liberal Arts at Penn State University (17–22) and taking his sweet time about it; spending at least a week in every contiguous state in the Union (22–30) supporting himself by any kind of work he could get, from professional-level yodeling to catalogue-level modeling; writer of humorous words and situations in Burbank, Los Angeles (30–33) before deciding that he really ought to pursue a career somewhat more noble, and if nobility in a job proved too elusive then something more meaningful, and if meaning in labor was impossible to find then at least something whose success wasn't measurable by ratings and quadrants (never mind the fact that emotional problems between himself and one of his colleagues – a very important one of his colleagues, as it happened – had greatly imperiled that TV job in Burbank anyway); and somehow talking his way into his latest position at the semi-old age of thirty-something.

All right, Charlie thought as he found himself out front of his building, a converted firehouse on West 27th, so there was the annual, the professional and the geographical, but what about the emotional? Where was the measure of that?

Well actually the less said – or thought, because he wasn't actually speaking out loud (he hoped) – about all that the better. There had been women, of course, all of them terrifically attractive and interesting, one of them even foreign – a French girl who baked macaroons in Abilene, Texas of all places – but not one, sweet and lovable and Gallic as they may have been, not one had set a true and piercing path all the way from her heart to his.

Oh, he'd been *in* love plenty of times; the honest truth of falling in love and out again was that it could happen in the length of a bus ride, without your ever having spoken a word aloud to the object of your eye's desire, an overactive imagination taking the place of the history between you and she, the whole before and after and every moment in between, until the bell dinged and she got up out of her seat and left you for real and forever, nothing to remember her by but the tiny little ache of not and never knowing even so much as her name.

There'd been hundreds of those, maybe thousands. What Charlie wanted was to find the one that made him jump off that bus and run until his heart stopped – or re-started. He wanted that piercing pain, the chest-bursting jolt of true love.

He wanted that and he also wanted to feel just a little less of that other needling emotion – guilt – about abandoning his little sister. He sat down on the ledge of a window that overlooked the rectory of a Lutheran church. He had no idea that he'd even gotten home, or how long he'd been there. And he had no idea of how to lose the guilt or find the love. Oh well, he may or may not have said out loud. "Oh well."

Trinity

Larry couldn't sleep. It was partly because he was abuzz with anticipation and excitement at what was supposed to happen tomorrow night and partly because young Larry P and bounteous Barbara B were making urgent, fetid love just inches from where he lay, roiling his bed and his thoughts. But if all went to plan this was likely their *coitus finalis*. Hooray! Hoorah! Huzzah!

When he'd first heard about the... scheme? the scam? the service? Whatever it was called, Larry D had thought it was a put-on. Either a put-on or the greatest idea for and execution of conceptual art he'd ever heard of – elaborate pieces of staged performance designed to ruin relationships. Wonderful! Incredible! Scandalous! This was about a year ago, over dinner at the Waverly Inn (food: toothsome! clientele: loathsome!) with his friend Harry Ramjet, a private detective. Larry D had been complaining bitterly and lengthily about how young Larry P refused, utterly and intractably, to get the hell out of Larry D's loft and love life. And Barbara B's pants. Harry had suggested, in terms shady and initially vague, that there was "an outfit" that could "take care of" "the situation." "For a price," he added. (Most of Harry's speech was uttered in utterly unnecessary quotation marks.) Larry, of course, immediately thought that Harry was implying that young Larry P could, "for a price," be clipped or iced or whacked or "taken out." And as the Berkshire pork chop (dry! lonely! $34!) was presented before him, Larry began to give the idea deep and serious consideration.

"I don't mean having him killed, which I take by your silence and the look on your face is what you think I mean," Harry told Larry. "This isn't a movie."

In that case, Larry asked Harry, what do you mean?

Harry explained that there was a company which, if you said the right things – not like a code word or something stupid like that – but if you gave the right answers to certain questions during an interview process they kicked you up to a higher level, a kind of an inner circle, where they offered you a whole different service to take care of your "relationship issues." A completely different service than the one they advertised. It cost you a bomb but there was no blowback and, if you were lucky or immoral, no remorse.

"How do I find them?" Larry asked.

Harry hunched over his chicken potpie, looked askance theatrically and whispered, "They're everywhere."

After dinner ($585! unforgettable! unforgiveable!), as they made their way past the black phalanx of limousines arrayed in waiting on Bank Street, Harry had asked Larry what the other Larry's "fears and weaknesses" were, because a knowledge of these would come in handy if and when the company took on his case.

"He's frightened of higher judgement."

"Isn't everybody?"

"I suppose so, in one way or another. But he's not sure if God exists. Fifty-one percent of him doubts His existence. But if he finds out he's wrong he plans to renounce everything earthly and sinful."

"Like especially threesomes?"

"We're no longer a threesome," Larry said. "We may have begun that way – well, we *did* begin that way – but it's no longer sexual. We're now more aptly described as a triumvirate."

"I'm sure the Father, the Son and the Holy Spirit appreciates the difference."

And so here he was, a summer later, just one night (steamy! sleepless! sex-adjacent!) away from freedom.

"Why don't you join us, Lar?" panted Barbara. "We have a number of openings right now."

At this Larry P giggled. Of all the things that had soured Larry D on Larry P it was this giggle (sniveling! shrill!) that had most acidulated in Larry's heart and ears. (Sound was, after all, Larry D's beloved medium and he loathed and despised any offence to it.) If he was honest, though, he also hated Larry P's youth, his smooth, un-blotched skin, his unhooded eyes, his unbridled future, his relentless erections, his still-more relentless optimism. Larry P was twenty-nine. Twenty-*nine*! *Under thirty*! Under thirty and at that very moment also under Barbara B, who refused to divulge her age but who possessed the vim, vigor and verve of someone half her age, no matter what that age was. And Larry D wanted it all to himself – all that vim, all that vigor, and all that verve – not shared with some sniveling giggler, some giggling sniveller who was exactly, impossibly, unforgivably half his own age!

Hot minutes passed by. Barbara came, extravagantly. Young Larry followed, youthfully. Moments later both were snoring as Larry D lay still on the now quiescent bed (awake! awake! *awake*!).

620 9th Avenue, New York, NY 10036

Holly Hohenzollern handed the envelope to the security guard manning the reception desk but didn't let go of it. "And you'll make sure that he gets my letter, personally?" she asked. "Charlie Van Thingamacall?"

"I'll see that it's delivered," the security guard said.

"Personally?"

"I will personally place it on Mr Van Linden's desk but I will not personally wait for him to pick it up and read it, ma'am."

"It's miss," she said. "Miss Holly Hohenzollern. If you're wondering about the last name, it's actually from Prussian nobility."

"If you say so," the security guard said. "But listen, I have to ask. This isn't any kind of love letter, is it? Only Mr Van Linden gets quite a few and we're supposed to discourage them."

"It's not a love letter," Holly said, curling her lip at the thought. Love had wronged her and she was done with it! For now, anyway. "In fact, it's an un-love letter."

"Well we're not supposed to deliver hate mail either," the guard said. "Your highness."

She laughed. "It's not hate mail," she said, finally letting go of the envelope. "Tell him if he handles it right he might even win a whaddayacallit … a Pulitzer."

Miss Holly Hohenzollern thanked the guard for his help and strutted toward the exit, thinking that people needed to lighten up a little here at the *New York Sentinel*.

WEDNESDAY

It will surely come as no surprise to learn that for as long as people have been getting together they've been breaking up as well. One of the earliest and worst break-ups was between Jason and Medea. Poor old Medea the barbarian: she bore two sons for Jason, and helped him find a ram with golden fleece and he *still* wouldn't commit to her. He couldn't pass up the opportunity to marry a royal princess, but hoped to someday join the two families and keep Medea as his mistress. She wasn't so keen on the idea. To avenge herself Medea sent the princess a poisoned robe that made her burst into flames and die an agonizing death. Unfortunately – but probably not surprisingly – this didn't win Jason back and so, to completely and utterly destroy him, Medea killed the two sons she'd had with him then escaped to the heavens on a chariot pulled by dragons, satisfied at a job well – perhaps over – done.

It's this sort of fallout that ReStart can help you avoid.

290 Park Avenue, 102nd floor. 8.30am

Dwight Kitchener had woken a little bruised and in a dark, heavy mood which he hadn't been able to shake off – because he hadn't really tried – by the time he reached the office. The previous night's operation had been just the latest in a long line of close-calls, foul-ups and downright disasters. He was tired of them. And he was tired of waking up with the dank taste of stale whisky on his tongue because of them. Because of one in particular.

Once he was in his building's elevator, Dwight slid his passkey into the slot, punched in his nine-digit security code and hit the button for 102, the private top floor. As the elevator car began to ascend he bit down hard on the inside of his cheek. Biting his mouth was a technique he'd developed a long time ago when he needed to take his mind off something that was bothering him. The issue he was trying to evade – which had, in fact, already drawn blood – at that moment was the first and biggest debacle of his professional life. Sure it was fifty years ago, but goddammit, it had changed the course of American history. And not in a good way. All for the sake of fifteen lousy inches …

Tearing a large chunk of flesh out of the inside of his cheek, Dwight forced the pink, spongy memories from his mind. He stared at the bank of elevator lights; fifty-three floors to go.

The operation Dwight was fifty-three floors below was divided into two discrete but symbiotically connected departments which occupied the two top levels of 290 Park Avenue. On level 101, the lower floor, was the corporate headquarters of ReStart, the nationwide chain that ostensibly offered counseling for troubled relationships, whether that relationship was sexual, emotional, fiscal, musical or marital in nature; whether that relationship involved two, three or a dozen people; whether that relationship was three days or three decades into its inevitable decay. Conflict Resolution. Intimacy Restoration and Enhancement. Correction of Self-reinforcing Maladaptive Patterns and Negative Interaction Cycles. Outright Hostility Control. ReStart offered all these services and many, many more. "We'll Make It Right" was the company's slogan, and its promise. And it wasn't a lie, not entirely, anyway.

But the real reason for its existence was to identify relationships that were ripe for breaking up. More specifically, operatives posing as counselors offered a very special service to one of the parties mired in a relationship that had become more sedimental than sentimental – the chance to get out without having to go through a protracted, painful, and often financially crippling break-up. For a fee, Emotional Architects and Extrication Engineers on the 102nd floor of the ReStart headquarters would devise a scenario in which you would never have to wrench out the words, "It's over." ReStart was all about mitigating that most corrosive and enduring of emotions – guilt. Or at least the appearance of it. And people were willing to pay a very high price for innocence. Or at least the appearance of it.

Naturally, there was a price to pay above and beyond the financial; sometimes it was relocating to another city, state or even country; other times it was a complete physical, emotional, psychological and spiritual makeover. And on that one particularly unfortunate occasion that Dwight was tearing into his cheek over, it was the loss of America's innocence. In the previous night's scenario, the added price Chester Polglase had to pay was having to pretend to be dead for the rest of his life.

And Dwight wasn't happy about that. Not at all.

The elevator pinged, the doors whooshed open and Dwight strode into the office. Despite housing more than ninety hard-working employees, the vast space was almost silent, emanating an ambience of sinister industry that always reminded Dwight of his time with the National Security Agency. Barely the hum of air-conditioning or the dull clunk of a photocopier could be heard. All doors to all offices and meeting rooms were almost always closed. All telephones were set to vibrate. Dense wall-to-wall carpet absorbed the fall of every footstep. There was no water-cooler around which to gather and gossip; no canteen for long, loud lunching; no music spilling from iPods or Muzak wafting down from ceiling speakers; no media room broadcasting the ceaseless calamity murmur of television news. It was an ambience – a culture – which usually pleased Dwight. But not today. Today even the sound of his own breath pissed him off.

He headed straight for the last office on the left side of the floor. As well as the door, the plantation shutters on the inside of the glass walls were closed but he knew Clayton goddamn Townsend and Elodie Frontenac would be in there, hatching some idiotic goddamn plan. As their boss, it was his prerogative – no, his duty – to stop them.

Dwight stood still, took a deep breath and tried to calm down. But even as he reached for the handle he knew it probably hadn't worked. He could feel his blood pressure skyrocketing as he yanked open the door.

"Good morning, Elodie," he said, his voice a low rumble. "Clayton," he added, even lower and quieter, without looking at the subject. "I hope you both had a pleasant evening last night while I and several of your colleagues were carrying out your latest live production. On the subject of that particular operation and others forthcoming may I offer the following: No more goddamn deaths!" he shouted. "Ever!" Then he slammed the door closed with such force that it cracked a pane of adjacent glass.

In the desert of silence that was the 102nd floor this outburst was like an atomic detonation.

He turned and headed across the room to Adelaide's office. There was a slight spring in Dwight's step now; he'd scared Townsend so much that the goddamn bonehead had actually fallen off the couch he'd been lying on. That was nice. Dwight almost smiled. He removed a handkerchief from the inside of his double-breasted jacket and wiped his bloody mouth. He looked down at a crushed star, rust-colored, in the middle of crinkled white and thought of the 35th President of the United States.

10th Avenue, between 27th and 28th

It was hot and dry and cloudless and it occurred to Charlie that of the many thousands he'd seen since he left the farm his favorite movie was *Singin' In the Rain*. Either *Singin' In the Rain* or *The Texas Chainsaw Massacre*.

"Ha!" he laughed out loud, accidentally cracking himself up.

Seriously though (he may or may not have audibly added), did it make him kind of a sentimental sap, placing *Singin' in the Rain* at the number one spot in his cinema-lovin' heart? Probably. But he didn't care. It was an absolutely terrific movie – smart, funny, inventive, self-aware and charming – all the qualities he loved in an entertainment. And a human being, too, come to think of it. And when you got right down to it, what was actually wrong with a little sweetness and sentimentality? Absent our more tender emotions and feelings and we may as well be rocks.

As far as Charlie Van Linden was concerned, the world could use a whole lot more sweetness and sentimentality. Sweetness and sentimentality and men wearing human-leather masks wielding chainsaws. You had to have diversity.

Adelaide Carter's office

"How'd it go last night?" Adelaide asked as Dwight sat down on the other side of her Danish rosewood desk. The faint trail of blood seeping from the corner of his mouth gave her a clue. She knew that he was trying to hide it, which meant that he'd been thinking about the other thing, which meant –

"It was a mess," he said. "Elodie and friend have gotta work a whole lot harder and a helluva lot smarter. If I have to deal with one more grieving spouse I'm gonna retire. I feel like a goddamn funeral director, instead of a …"

Adelaide poured a generous measure of Talisker single malt into a glass and handed it to him. She deliberately made herself not look at the time; it was well before noon, though, she knew that.

Dwight took a belt, and said, "… instead of whatever the hell I am."

"I'll tell them," she said.

"I already told them."

Actually, it wasn't even nine o'clock yet. But no big deal. "So what went wrong?"

"Plenty," Dwight said, after another slug. "One: The removal team took that idiot Eduardo less than a half a block away from the scene, where the Widow White almost ran right into him while he was supposed to have been 'arrested'. Two: The disposal team arrived a pretty unlikely three seconds after the squib popped. Three: That idiot Eduardo used the client's real name in front of the mark and number four, on top of all that, Buttons went nuts and damn near throttled one of our operatives – for real."

"Buttons?" Adelaide said.

"It's what the Widow White called him when she thought no-one was listening."

"Why Buttons?"

"What makes you think I'd know?"

"I thought the widow might've opened up to you. Because of your consolatory charms." She could tell that Dwight was cooling off a little by the coloring in his face, a little less flushed and angry now that he'd finished the whisky and vented. She decided to kid around with him. "Why, I'd tell you anything you wanted to know." She vamped it up, enjoying herself. "Anything at all."

"Is that so?" Dwight said bluntly, obviously not yet in the mood for fun and frivolity. "Then how about you tell me why you're *still* married to the prince of blandness, who *still* thinks you work in PR?"

The remark wasn't exactly stinging, but it rankled. What surprised Adelaide, though, was how she'd misread Dwight, thinking he'd calmed down enough to take a joke. She wondered if her ability to gauge people was slipping, which would be a definite liability in her business. That Columbia psych degree really *was* a waste of four years of her life. "How can you feel so harshly toward someone you've never even met?" she asked.

"I don't need to've met the guy, Adelaide," said Dwight. "I see the look of emotional stupor on your face when you come in every morning." It was too much and they both knew it. Dwight didn't want to hurt Adelaide, the closest he'd ever come to having a daughter. "You can do better than him, honey," he added.

Adelaide raised the delicate points of her arrowhead-shaped eyebrows. "Things really got to you, didn't they?"

Dwight said nothing; not admitting it, but not denying it either.

"But why last night?" she asked. "We've had hiccups before. It's a tricky business what we do. You know that more than anybody."

"Tricky, and goddamn dirty besides." He tongued the bloody pulp inside his mouth, wanting to spit. But if he did, Adelaide would know he'd been thinking about it, the whole mess. So he swallowed – blood, nausea, history and all.

"Better no relationship than a bad relationship," said Adelaide.

"So she always said."

"She was right though, wasn't she?"

"She was almost always right," Dwight said quietly.

"Almost?"

Dwight looked her right in the eye. "We *all* make mistakes, Adelaide." And he hit his emphasis hard.

She looked away from his steely gaze, down to the framed picture of her mother, Claudette. "I miss her, too, Dwight," she said. "Every day and every night."

He nodded, his lips held tightly closed.

"What did my mother call you when no-one else was around?" Adelaide asked.

"She called me Dwight," he replied, leaving the office and heading straight to the men's room where he spat away the bitter taste in his mouth.

10th Avenue,
between 30th and 33rd

It was hot and getting hotter even though it hadn't cracked nine am, and as he passed the Hudson Yards development it occurred to Charlie that if it was still like this tonight he might have to see what else was playing around town, maybe some Preston Sturges or Ernie Lubitsch, just for some relief from the heat and also maybe to take his mind off the fact that if he let himself think about it for too long he'd have to admit that he was heading toward getting lonely.

Clayton and Elodie's office

It had taken him a while but Clayton was finally back on the couch, staring up at the framed portraits that lined the walls of the large, comfortable office he shared with Elodie. Rendered in pure Warholian Pop style were big, bright paintings of Woody and Mia, Tom and Nicole, Liz Taylor and Richard Burton, Brad and Jennifer. These couples, all so dramatically rent asunder, were Clayton and Elodie's inspiration – and, in at least one case, their clients.

How could they have broken up?

There were a couple of minutes to go before the debrief that was held after every operation. It was a meeting that Clayton was in no hurry to get to and he needed some time to try and relax, get his circulation flowing again after the arctic wake-up squall that Dwight the K had delivered earlier. He may have been imagining it, but Clayton could've sworn he saw blood flying from Dwight's mouth as he screamed at them. Actual, literal, O-positive blood.

"This not killing people business is going to make things a little more challenging," he said.

"Yes, it is," said Elodie. "But they pay us a lot of money, right? So it's not unreasonable that we work hard for it, don't you think?"

"Sure," Clayton said. That was another thing he enjoyed about Elodie – her equanimity. It was a quality in short supply in Manhattan, along with sanguinity, serenity and sangfroid. "Although I guess it depends on what you consider 'a lot', salary-wise." He waved a pair of apostrophical fingers over "a lot."

"I think anybody would consider an annual salary of twenty-five million 'a lot'." She waved her own fingers over "a lot" right back at him. And somehow managed to make them incorporate sarcasm, as well.

"Twenty-f – *what?*"

Elodie looked blank. "Oh …" she said, deflating it a little. "I … I just assumed that because we were partners doing the very same job with the same amount of experience we were getting the same salary." She looked away from him, down at her left Christian Louboutin. "Forgive me, Clay, I shouldn't have mentioned it." This in a tight-lipped mumble.

"You're telling me that you're pulling down twenty-five million dollars?" He was really trying to keep it together, but it wasn't easy. He'd do the math later but at this early stage in rough calculation Elodie was claiming to earn approximately eighteen times his own salary. That couldn't be right. "Bullshit. That's junior hedge fund manager coin. No way!"

"Sure," she said quietly. "That's right. Of course I don't. That's ridiculous."

She'd backed off way too quickly and easily. "Oh my God," he said, almost falling off the couch again. "You do!" He really needed to develop his own sanguinity and/ or sangfroid – whichever was easier.

She smiled. "No, I don't."

"Yes, you do."

"Don't you find this whole conversation somewhat ... *qu'est-ce que le mot juste* ... gauche?"

God, he loved it when she spoke French. When she spoke French and when she smiled, how that smile made her cheekbones pop out and the way it revealed the two sharp incisors that added a literal bite to her expression of amusement. He tried to make her smile as often as he could. Smile and speak French. So whatever else happened he'd at least achieved two goals this morning.

How could they have broken up?

She removed her tortoise shell glasses, huffed a breath on the lenses and cleaned them. It was very casual. Maybe too casual ...

He couldn't tell if she was playing him or not. She probably was; Clayton was easily played and he knew it. Especially by her. The two of them had taken a few improv classes a year ago and they'd quickly developed a fluid, easy rhythm along with a theatrical and intellectual empathy with one another. But as well as the better performer, Elodie had always been a beat or two ahead of Clayton, either able to anticipate the direction he was headed or to guide him to the place she felt they ought to be.

Elodie put her glasses back on, blinked at her partner three times and said, "I truly, honestly, sincerely and not-lyingly do not get paid anywhere near twenty-five million dollars a year for busting up unhappy couples, Clay." Elodie looked at the office door a split-second before Adelaide knocked and entered. "And fortunately neither do you."

Adelaide smiled. "You don't what, Clayton?"

"Never mind," he said quickly. "It's nothing. It's personal. It's between … nobody." As he got off the couch and left the office he began to wish he'd never brought up the whole salary issue with El. Although – wait a minute – he didn't. *She* did.

How could they have broken up?

10th Avenue,
between 36th and 37th

It was hot and there was no shade and as a man and wo-man holding hands who must've been in their eighties slowly shuffled toward him it occurred to Charlie that his parents, Hank and Dortje, had been married for almost forty years, staying together because of their children, be-cause that was how it went in their community, because they had no choice, because divorce wasn't sanctioned by the church. They may have loved each other, too, but that was beside the point because whether his folks were happy or sad together, whether or not they belonged together, whether or not they planned to grow old together, it was only his mother's death that had allowed them to be untogether.

Boy, it was really getting hot now. And kinda depress-ing. There needed to be singing; there needed to be rain.

ReStart Meeting Room A-102

Adelaide and Elodie entered the meeting room bursting with chatter, both of them talking at each other at once. Clayton slunk in behind them, hunched, hoping not to be noticed. Already seated were six other creative teams who reported to Clayton and Elodie, as well as the head of casting, Pete Valentine, several assistants and a stenographer. At the business end of the long wooden conference table was Dwight, founding partner, director of operations and all-round fun guy, scowling at everybody simultaneously, waiting for the morning babble to dissipate.

It took too long. "Quiet down, please, people," Dwight said, shooting his cuffs. "We've got a lot to get through. Pete, how's the guy from last night? The strangled soup waiter?"

"He's okay," Pete said. "I slipped him an extra thousand and told him I'll use him regularly for the next year."

Dwight nodded. "Good. I'd also like you to have a word with that id – I mean, Eduardo about some of the basic operational rules. He used a client's name last night and nearly blew his cover. And on the subject of last night's operation – there will be no more like it. Except what's already in play with that dame down in Tallahassee, there will be no more death scenarios. They're expensive, they're risky and a general goddamn pain in the ass. Especially mine. I don't care what you so-called creatives do instead, but there will be no more killings. We almost lost an operative for real last night. If it makes your job harder you have my permission to blame Frontenac and Townsend. Especially Townsend."

Clayton couldn't help himself. "Why especially me?" he said, slumping further into the leather that seemed to envelop him, as though he were a child at the adults' table.

"Because I don't like you, Clayton," said Dwight, his voice low and mean. "And I want more people to feel the same way." He paused, glared and waited for Clayton to say something else stupid; wisely, Clayton kept his mouth shut and focussed on the cufflinks Dwight was wearing, a nice silver and blue pair in a kind of Moroccan pattern. "Moving on: There are four new assignments today. Except for the last one, Elodie'll decide who gets what."

Dwight turned to the whiteboard behind him, where a list of names and locations had been neatly written in blue marker. "First up Mrs Q of Danbury, Connecticut wants a painless conclusion to her marriage of twenty-nine years; coincidentally Mr Q of Danbury has also engaged our services. He, however, has requested considerable torment and pain for his wife who, it seems, has been less than faithful throughout those twenty-nine years. We're taking both assignments and I'd like them to be handled by the same creative team. Second, Mr Larry D wants Mr Larry P eased out of a *ménage a trois* type situation in order that Mr D has sole access to Ms Barbara B. Apparently they're some kind of artists and all three, predictably, live in Chelsea."

Dwight took a deep breath; this one was so far out there he could barely bring himself to say it. "Last of all, a Mr Morton H of Kenilworth, Illinois wants … he wants Lulu McGee to divorce her husband, Fred."

The conference room erupted in laughter.

Dwight smiled a little despite himself. "I'm well aware that these last two are a television couple and therefore, in many ways, do not exist. But our client is, as well as a little deranged, extremely wealthy and he's paying well above the usual fee for his request. So we're gonna do everything we possibly can to meet it. Elodie, I want you and Townsend on that one."

Elodie couldn't help herself. "I understand your not liking Clay, Dwight, because he *can* be annoying. But why am I being punished with this assignment?"

"What can I say? You're the best we've got."

"He's right," Clayton said, straightening up in his chair as some of the confidence he'd lost earlier finally returned. "We are."

"Not you," said Dwight. "Her. One last thing before we're done. I know you've all heard this before but after last night it bears repeating: Only one thing's kept us in business for fifty-odd years, people. And that's absolute secrecy and silence."

Clayton couldn't let this one go. He cleared his throat and said, "Or, as the acronym goes, ASS."

Everybody laughed; everybody except Dwight. He decided Townsend could wait, and continued darkly. "Never talk about what you do. Never offer our services to anyone you know. For all intents and purposes, this company does not exist." Dwight went around the room and gave every person – except Clayton Townsend – a brief taste of his hardest stare. As he dismissed the group two assistants jumped up and wiped the whiteboard clean.

Clayton was almost out the door when Dwight said, "Townsend, please join me in my office."

*

A minute or two later, things were going pretty much as Clayton expected them to; Dwight in his chair behind his oversized desk, hands clasped behind his enormous block of a head, this sort of bored-yet-disgusted look on his craggy face; Clayton seated before his boss in a chair that he, Clayton, was convinced that Dwight had had the legs of shortened so that whoever sat there was just that little bit more of a tiny hunched supplicant, trying not to look too insolent and arrogant but knowing that no matter what he did with his face and his tone of voice, insolent and arrogant was, unfortunately and accidentally, the way he came across anyway, which was a problem he'd had ever since junior high (possibly even grade school but he may've been too young and dumb to know it then) and one which had dogged him all though college and then at every place he'd worked since graduating – the magazines, the ad agencies, the film production company he'd wasted a couple of years in before being fired for ardently recommending the purchase of one of his own scripts – and which continued to dog him right up to now, when he'd finally found his way into his dream job of inventing ways to disintegrate integrations. Clayton blamed his face, in particular its many shortcomings in the area of what one might call "manliness" (he could not grow even a hint of a mustache until he was twenty-eight) or "maturity" (even the mo he could grow now looked like he'd stolen it from an Asian teenager) or "character" (when he was preoccupied he looked as though he was on the verge of tears) for the ongoing misunderstanding between himself and the world. His face, and the regrettable yet unavoidable whiny nasality of his voice, which made most of what he said sound either sarcastic or carping. People tended not to like that so much. His face, his voice and his inclination to say whatever was on his mind. People seemed to especially hate that last one. So Clayton had learned to rein it in a little. All of them, actually, but especially that last one.

Dwight was doing that silent thing he did, waiting for Clayton to say something, to break like some kind of a guilty freakin' schoolboy in front of the principal. *Well not this time,* Clayton thought. *I'll sit here all day before I open my mouth to satisfy you.* He reviewed his last thought, realized how it sounded and closed his eyes, trying not to laugh. But of course it wasn't more than a few seconds before he let out an extremely insolent, arrogant, whiny and sarcastic-sounding guffaw.

Dwight didn't make a sound until Clayton stopped laughing. Then he said, "You know I wasn't kidding out there, Townsend. I really do not like you."

"I never got the impression you did," Clayton said, his mouth making all these distressed, distorted shapes he couldn't control, like he was having some sort of mini-stroke. "And I'm pretty sure no-one else did, either." Shapes that would look to Dwight like smug smirks, he knew it.

"Good," Dwight said, his jaw furiously tight, as though there was a grenade pin clenched between his teeth. "After five years here, son, you know me. You know I'm a man who prefers action over words."

"And a fine thing that is. A fine thing, ind –"

"Shut up," said Dwight, spitting the words out like two bad oysters. "On this particular occasion, however, I'm going to employ a combination of words and action. Here are the words: Nail this Lulu and Fred McGee operation or else I will fire you. That's the action part of the arrangement. And if I hear you've gone bawling to Adelaide about this I'll kill you *then* fire you. Is that clear?"

Clayton's mouth felt like electric putty. "Yes," he said. "I won't let you down."

"I almost hope you do," Dwight said, then told Clayton to wipe the idiot grin off his face. "What are you, some kind of a goddamn schoolboy?"

New York Sentinel Building

It was cool and calm and quiet in here and it occurred to Charlie, as he leaned back in his ergonomically sound but not particularly comfortable chair and placed his leather-shod feet up on the desk, that back in Los Angeles, back in the making-things-up-for-TV-business, they'd practically fire you for wearing a suit and tie and sitting at your desk with both feet on the floor. Charlie tried to tell himself that he missed being on the west coast – that year-round sunshine vibe they had going – but it didn't ring true. For better or worse, he figured, he belonged in the east. "Although maybe with somewhere like Chicago you'd get the best of both sides ..."

He looked around, wondering if he'd said the Chicago stuff out loud. It had been a habit of his since he was kid, talking aloud to keep himself company when he was baking bread before dawn or mending broken fences with a hand-tooled hammer – the usual chores of a childhood mired in the nineteenth century. And it was a habit he was never sure if he'd completely broken.

Nobody nearby was looking at him so he assumed that the words had only been spoken in his head.

He loosened his tie and took another look at the letter he'd found on his desk when he arrived. The thing certainly was busy, full of capital letters, underlinings and exclamation points, words urgently crossed out and replaced, the sure sign of someone unhinged – possibly even deranged – being responsible for it. This particular unhinged person was a woman; Holly Hohenzollern, she'd signed it, then put "Miss" in brackets after her name, as though that was something. Of course, in the particular context of what she'd written him, Charlie supposed it was actually something. Near as he could decipher, the letter was all about this company headquartered here in New York City that busted up people's relationships on the sly if one of them in it paid enough. Crazy.

He noted the address where she'd told him to meet her ("at 10 am, SHARP!!") and put the letter inside his coat pocket along with his notebook. In order to leave the newsroom he had to walk right by the boss's glass-walled office, where the daily assignment meeting was taking place at that very moment.

Hang it, Charlie thought, the lady might not be crazy – maybe she just enjoyed the visual thrill of an exclamation point after every couple of sentences. Besides, if he stuck around Art would probably put him back on that union corruption story that Charlie believed was going nowhere. He stood up, and as he passed Mr Munro's office the kind and avuncular boss smiled and waved Charlie in. Charlie returned the smile politely, waved back politely and kept walking (as politely as possible), wondering what

Miss Holly Hohenzollern would look like. A little on the Prussian side, probably. Big hat, blonde hair, curly mustache.

Manhattan, not Brooklyn

Clay was half-singing/half-humming some song from some Broadway show. It was rich and syrupy and really beginning to turn Elodie's stomach. It was also bringing back some unpleasant memories of a certain weekend in Rhode Island the previous year, the unanswered questions it raised … "You know, you're really sending out some mixed messages regarding your sexuality with this unabashed love of show tunes, Clayton," she warned. "It gives off an air of libidinal uncertainty, with a definite leaning toward the homosexual."

"I don't like show tunes, per se, Elodie. I just happen to like certain songs from certain Broadway shows," Clayton said. "That doesn't make me a gay person."

"And saying 'per se' in general conversation doesn't help your case much."

"You're very snarky, you know that."

"Don't say 'snarky', either. That might play over in Brooklyn, but when you're here in Manhattan, try to keep the standard up." She grabbed the thick job folder from her desk. "Let's get to work."

"Okay," Clayton said. "First thing, does our client in Kenilworth think that Lulu and Fred actually live here in New York?"

"No, Clayton, he's not insane," Elodie said, looking at pictures of the troublesome client, his sultanic financial statistics, somewhat shaky psychiatric profile and general life history. The Intelligence Department had really gone to town on Morton Havisham; there was stuff in the brief that even his best friend (Ames Pleuvaber, test-pilot, born four fifty-seven am July 1st, 1951 under a waning gibbous moon in Oklahoma City, Oklahoma) wouldn't have known. "He just doesn't like them as a couple and he wants it to be over between them." She closed the file and looked at her partner, on the couch as usual, popping a ping-pong ball in and out of his mouth.

"Because he wants to make a move on Lulu?" asked Clayton, between ping-pong pops. "Or Elaine whatsername – the actress who plays Lulu?"

"No. He's married. To a …" Elodie opened the file again. "To a Dolores."

"I wish I was married to a Dolores," Clayton said. "A Dolores could make me happy, I think. Or a Eudora. If the guy's so extremely rich why doesn't he just buy the network that owns the show and exercise some creative control?"

"He already tried to."

"Seriously?"

"Seriously," said Elodie. "He really is that wealthy. And that committed. So, Lulu and Fred – that is, the actors who play Lulu and Fred, Elaine Reardon and Thurston Brown – are coming to town tomorrow for a couple days' promotion and some charity ball appearance. It's timing we'd be foolish not to exploit somehow, agreed?"

Clayton popped the white ball up out of his mouth. While it was in the air he said, "Sure," then let it fall back into his open mouth.

"Moving on," Elodie said. Man, she wanted to smash that stupid ball. Clay had a bunch of different techniques he employed to come up with ideas – mind-mapping, the Salvador Dali spoon-drop and assorted other idiocies. The ping-pong ball was part of his "inspiration through play" arsenal. "Any thoughts on the threesome?" she asked, dreading the answer a little bit.

"I find it's enough of a challenge keeping just one other person in bed satisfied and entertained," Clayton said. "I honestly don't know what the pornographers are thinking with all their combos and props, raising the expectations and standards for all of us non-porn per-formers. Now everybody expects pornography-style sex, with all the self-narration and the lights blazing. A lot of it doesn't even take place on a bed. And here's another thing – you show up to sex these days without a shaved or at least heavily trimmed pubic area and people look at you like you're some kind of freak."

"When have you had sex lately?"

"I'm saying *if*."

Elodie figured that Clayton had been watching a fair amount of porn lately.

"I haven't been watching a ton of porn, if that's what you're thinking," he said.

Right. "Right."

"But I'd be lying if I said the Internet hadn't thrown some my way when I was searching for –"

"Sneezing pandas and cats who enjoy hamburgers?"

"You know me too, too well." He spat the now glistening ball up into the air again. "Our time as a nonprofessional couple has given you some real insights into the general splendidness of my character."

It was rare for Clayton to mention the fact that they'd dated but he forced himself to occasionally, just to remind her that it had actually happened. The truth was that sometimes he had trouble believing it himself. But they *had* been a couple, for a good few months, right up until the weekend in Newport, Rhode Island. The time they were together had been the happiest of his life; how and why they'd broken up was still a mystery to him. Elodie must have had her reasons, though, he knew that. Probably something to do with how annoying he could sometimes be. Like right now, with the "general splendidness" remark. "And those insights often lead you to be vexed with me. I understand that, though, I really do. I can be very vexing. Vexing, irritating, annoying, repulsively loquacious and yet – and this is the truly sad part – overwhelmingly trivial and banal."

His self-awareness was one of the things Elodie liked most about Clay. Not that she wanted him to know that, at least for now, so she regarded him without expression before saying, "Okay, shut up now. I've got an idea how we might pull off the love triangle thing, kind of a hybrid of the Czechoslovakian Handbag Shuffle meets Our Father Who Art in Cleveland."

Clayton spat the ping-pong ball out and sat up eagerly. "I like it!"

The ball bounced off the couch then rolled across the carpet toward Elodie, who flattened it with the heel of her shoe, easily the highlight of her morning so far.

Opposite the Waldorf-Astoria

Charlie van Linden lingered in the shadows on the north-west corner of 49th and Park. Lingering was one of his specialties and one of his favorite things to do, requiring little in the way of effort from himself and plenty by way of entertainment from others. Nothing gave him more pleasure than simply standing around listening to other people talk.

A sweating fat man on a cell phone: "I saw this young couple over by Tompkins Square Park, young and completely in love with each other. I wanted to kill 'em so bad."

A frizzy-haired girl in pink Lycra shorts: "Every Friday night I get drunk and go hunting for dick. Why is it always dick on my mind?"

Her friend, in between spoonfuls of shaved ice: "Because otherwise you'd be a lesbian?"

A woman with two large bottles of cold water and two very large breasts: "Men're constantly staring at my tits. Like they've never seen none before. Haven't they seen their mother's or their wife's or their girlfriend's? The other day this guy asked me if my tits were real, I said to him, 'Is your penis real?'"

A woman in her late-twenties with a sweat-wetted mop of curly blonde hair: "Hey! Mr Van Whatsyername – what's so funny?"

*

For a few minutes Holly had watched the *Sentinel* reporter, this Van Whosamit, as he stood in the mid-morning heat, laughing out loud to himself at something she didn't know what. He was tall and thin and handsome as a bastard, this guy. Like a movie star, with his tan and his suit jacket slung over his shoulder and loosened tie and beard stubble and perfect white teeth and dreamy blue eyes. It made her sick. When she marched up to him and asked him what was so funny he'd said something about fake boobs and dicks that didn't make any sense at all and she began to wonder if she'd made a mistake bringing her story to this particular guy. He didn't seem too bright. But if she backed out now, she'd seem like a crazy person. And she was *not* a crazy person.

So they went to a café, sat in a red leather banquette all by themselves and ordered coffee even though it was kind of too hot for hot drinks. But whatever.

He annoyed her right away, with his very first question. "Now, I don't mean to be rude or insulting here, Miss Hohenzollern, but I have to ask before the horse gets its fetlock caught in a spoke, what you wrote in your letter, it's all true, right?" he said, opening a green leather notebook. "Not just some fancy kinda revenge?"

"No," she replied evenly. "I have something else in mind revenge-wise. All what I wrote actually happened.

My slimeweasel of an ex-boyfriend paid a company to organize this whole bizarre trick so that he didn't have to break up with me like an ordinary normal human being."

"A company broke you two up?" Van Linden said. She could tell he was trying to go easy on the skepticism. "Using strawberry ice-cream, your boyfriend's dead parents and an iguana?"

"That's right," she said, as though it was nothing. "That's what they do. They ruin people's lives."

"Okay." He scribbled something in his notebook. "How did the bicycle pump get involved?"

"That came later," she said.

He asked what kind of work her boyfriend did.

"What does that matter?"

He told her that everything helped, and that if the guy was, say, a Green Beret, Charlie would try to avoid him. "Probably."

A Green Beret, Holly thought. Boy, that was a laugh. "He's a magazine art-director."

"Okay," Van Linden said. "They're usually pretty harmless."

"His name is Felix," she added.

"Even more so," he said, grinning this lopsided grin at her. He probably practiced it, for maximum cuteness, but she had to admit it worked. It was cute. He was cute and he was pretty funny, the bastard. She was beginning to warm to him despite the fact that he was … a man. "Okay, so how do you know the break-up was a set-up?"

"A woman knows," Holly said.

"I understand, but –"

"Also, I saw his supposedly dead parents off-Broadway a few weeks ago."

"You mean on a street near Broadway?"

She looked at the reporter coolly, not sure if he was serious with this boyish, naive look on his stupidly handsome face. She spoke extra slow in case he was a little simple. "No, I mean they were appearing in an off-Broadway play. I always suspected these people weren't his real mom and dad, and when they showed up in this play I knew I was right."

"Well, couldn't his folks be actors?"

"Yes, they *could* be," Holly said, patiently. "Except they're *dead*."

He looked aghast. "They died in the last few weeks?"

Holly sighed. "His real parents are dead." She really didn't know what to make of the guy, acting this way. "Are you kidding around with me, mister? With this country hick business?"

"I'm just trying to get the facts straight, Miss Hohenzollern," he said, pronouncing her name real well. Most people, when they said her name, it sounded like they were coughing up a furball. But this Van Lindner said it like a pro so maybe he was descended from Prussian nobility also. "D'you know where this company is located, by any chance?" he said.

Holly nodded and asked him if he'd heard of ReStart.

"The relationship counseling chain?" he said. They had a little heart in place of the "a" in their logo. It was cute. Or nauseating, depending on how you looked at things. "Sure."

She said, "Well it's just a front, a way of finding new business for the other company, the one that splits people up."

He nodded. "How do you know so much?"

She gave it to him straight. "I tortured my ex-boyfriend."

"Literally?"

"Yes, literally."

"How?"

"I pumped him for information," Holly said. "Literally." She pointed through the café window to the building across the street. "The head office of ReStart is right there, on the top floor. You can be up there in two minutes." She looked at him and twisted a curl around her finger. "Felix told me that except in very unusual circumstances they will only do their stupid, dirty work at the request of one of the parties actually *in* the relationship."

He smiled that smiley smile at her, like he was out of Hollywood or something. "So if I happened to meet you and fall in love with you but you were betrothed –"

"Which I'm not."

"Yes, I understand, but if you were I wouldn't be able to engage this company to break up you and any Felixes you might happen to be with. Is that what you're saying?"

"That's right," Holly said. "So do you have a girlfriend, Mr Van Limberg? A wife or something?"

"What's that got to do with …?" he said. Then the light went on; he had to be in a relationship to get out of one. "Oh, right."

"So do you?"

"Not particularly."

Holly told him that he'd need a pretty good cover story or the ReStart people wouldn't take him to the next level. "The sinister level," she said.

He told her not to worry, he had something in mind. "Something where that country hick business of mine'll come in real handy."

"You better hope it's convincing," Holly said.

"It's more than just convincing," he said. "It's real."

"Golly," Holly said, unimpressed. "One last thing you should know. While he was still semi-conscious, Felix kept saying, 'Dwight will kill me if he finds out.'"

"Dwight will kill me?"

"Or words to that effect," she said. "So you might want to be careful of anyone called Dwight."

Back across the street, at the entrance to 290 Park Avenue, Holly wished Charlie luck.

"Thank you," Charlie said. Then he asked her what exactly she did for a living.

"I work for the city," she told him. "Call me when you know something."

"I will."

"You better, mister."

Tallahassee, Florida.
10.54am

A heavy pall of humidity added depth to the air of grief
that hung over the gathered mourners in the small chapel
of the Fitch Brothers funeral home. There was sweat on
the forehead of the widower and sweat on the foreheads
of each of his ten bored and motherless young children.
The priest sweated in his robes as he droned on quietly;
the friends and family of the departed woman sweated as
they sat and listened to him in the dense, wet heat, some
of them near fainting in their dark suits and dresses. Inside the plumply napped casket the dead woman sweated,
too, as she turned her left hand ever so slightly and looked
at her watch. She noted with aggrieved disappointment
that so far she'd not heard so much as a mournful sniffle,
let alone the great salty waves of anguish she'd expected.
But the emotionless silence merely confirmed that she'd
made the right decision in allowing the ReStart people to
kill her. Because just as she was not sufficiently appreci-
ated in life, she was now not being sufficiently mourned
in death, and would clearly not be sufficiently missed
henceforth. She heard the priest say, "And we know in

113

our hearts that she is going to a better place." Very slowly, the woman reached into her pocket and smiled as her fingertips brushed the one-way ticket to Honolulu. Then she closed her eyes and went back to the afterlife.

290 Park Avenue, 101st floor. 10.56am

As the elevator approached the 101st floor, Charlie Van Linden looked into the mirror on the wall and tried to place a suitably troubled look on his face. It was his impression that he generally came across as looking rather troubled – by more or less everything – so he was careful not to go too far with his brow-wrinkling, eye-crinkling and lip-pursing.

The result made him look like someone who'd had too much to drink at a wedding reception trying to recall the name of a distant cousin spotted across the dance floor; someone drunk and not too sharp. He decided to go with his regular face.

The elevator doors opened and Charlie found his way to the quiet, dimly-lit reception area and prepared to dolefully address the young woman behind the desk. He figured that a certain dolefulness, in place of an overtly troubled expression, would be appropriate when dealing with a company which specialized in rescuing unmoored relationships.

"Hi there!" the receptionist bubbled.

"Hello," Charlie said, barely more than whispering. "I –"

"Welcome to ReStart!" The company's logo was emblazoned on the wall behind her. Only here, the little red heart in the "a" looked like it was actually beating. Charlie thought it was creepy and disturbing – no matter how you looked at it.

"Thank you, it's –"

"Do you have an appointment with one of our counselors?"

"No, it's my first t–"

"Great!" the receptionist said, handing him a thick wad of forms. "You'll need to fill these in."

"Sure. Do you h–"

"Here." She gave him a pen then reached under the desk. Before Charlie had time to speak she'd taken a picture of him with a Polaroid camera. "How can we assist you today?"

"Well …" As the flash dazzle faded he waited for her to interrupt him again. But she simply looked up in silence, her little mouth hanging open slightly, her eyes widened in expectation. She had short, red-brown hair pulled into two pigtails at the back, a kind of grade-school look that Charlie suspected he was supposed to find attractive, but which was yet another aspect of modern life that troubled him; she looked like an eight-year-old, and the last time he'd taken a second look at an eight-year-old he was eight years old himself. He wondered if she rode a bicycle to work, packed crustless sandwiches in a pink plastic pail.

"Well," Charlie said. "It's kind of complicated …"

Some time later he was sitting in a small office watching a male counselor with a wispy beard leaf through the forms Charlie had filled in. It had taken a while; Charlie had completed the forms with a dense – but supportable –

tangle of lies and half-truths. Fortunately, making things up about himself was something of a specialty of his, as well as a professional necessity. The counselor stroked the hairy tendrils on his chin then looked up from the papers to Charlie, who nodded in personal affirmation of the web of b.s. the guy was clawing his way through. "That's right," Charlie said. "That's me."

He was in his mid-thirties – not old, but not especially young, either – and his emotional history was tattered and bleak, all the way back to his first love at thirteen and right up to his most recent, which had soured last summer in Los Angeles. He realized with a dismal jolt that the story of Charlie Van Linden and The Women of America Plus One Lovely French Girl had been twenty years of false starts, pointless diversions, regrettable dalliances and heart-hardening near-misses. And now here he was, about to tell a complete stranger about his most enduring and most complicated relationship with a female; and not a word of what he was going to say would be untrue.

"Okay, I think I've got enough background information to go on," the counselor said. "Now, this particular predicament of yours? What are its particularities?"

"Well," Charlie said, sighing in preparation. "They're kinda complicated, but here goes …"

About twenty minutes later, while Charlie finished explaining the particular particularities of his predicament, the counselor had rubbed his beard almost clean off; he looked pale, tired and shocked. "Wow," he said. "Okay, I think I'm going to have to refer you to one of our more experienced counselors." He rolled the last remaining hair on his chin between two fingers and barely noticed when it came out. "Actually, you know what? I think this should be handled by our most experienced counselor."

Television City,
Los Angeles

Elaine Reardon took a long, slow look at the group of eggheads, knuckleheads, dickheads and department heads sitting around the conference table in the board-room headquarters of the CBC broadcasting network. On Elaine's left was her lawyer, "Cold" Herb Cohen, and a junior associate from Herb's firm, Cohen, Cohen, Cohen and Greenblatt; next to them, taking up the whole left flank of the table, were half a dozen network executives, several of whom she believed were named Steve, seated in ascending order of importance, the least important be-ing closest to Elaine. At the opposite end of the table, close to the window and the bowl of imported Italian mints, were the creators and producers of "Lulu & Fred," Fat Tom and his whippet wife, Trudy From England. Working back toward Elaine, down the other side of the table, were Tom and Trudy's assistants, some more net-work bozos – these ones mostly named Hal or Al – then Elaine's idiot co-star Thurston Brown, Thurston's three lawyers and Thurston's personal assistant, a kid named Mitzi or Ditzy or Shitzy or something, and Thurston's other personal assistant, an unctuous little twerp called Sylvian who'd tried to stick his tongue down Elaine's throat at last season's wrap party. A bigger bunch of creeps and morons would be harder to find, Elaine thought.

Creeps and morons; morons and creeps; all human life is there. She hoped Henry James wouldn't mind the misappropriation.

They'd been here for more than an hour already, trawling over this one single issue, a bizarre and obnoxious idea suggested by the network and eagerly adopted by Tom and Trudy. And, naturally, Thurston. It was a notion that Elaine was flatly refusing to go along with: that she have a baby – an actual human baby – with Thurston.

"All we're saying, Elaine, is give it some thought," one of the Steves whined. "Won't you even think about it? Why won't you just think about it?"

"I've given it all the thought it needs," Elaine said. "A full three seconds. And the answer is ..." She turned to her lawyer. "What's my exact response, Herb?"

Herb delivered the response by rote, icily, and without a trace of inflection. "No fucking way are you fucking kidding me."

"That's the short version," Elaine said.

"What's the long version?" somebody named Hal or Al asked.

"It's where I sue you for even suggesting an idea like that in the first place," said Elaine. Then added: "You fucking moron."

"Jesus," said the senior Steve, vice-president of Comedy and Light Entertainment at CBC. "It's not like we're asking you to screw him live on TV. Just announce your plans on Steve Lamont tomorrow night in New York."

"We're talking about history-making telly, Elaine," Trudy From England said. Next would be something about how it was done back in Old Blighty, since Trudy never tired of reminding everybody that she wasn't from here, as though her hideous accent, drinking tea at all hours of the day and night, and referring to TV as "telly" didn't already provide enough clues. The way she spoke made Elaine's skin crawl, and she wondered how Fat Tom could possibly even kiss his wife's prim, thin-lipped, English accent-speaking mouth, let alone slip his American dick into it. "Think July twenty-nine, 1981," Trudy continued.

Everyone at the table looked at Trudy blankly. Despite the vacant look she planted on her face, Elaine knew exactly what Trudy was referring to. But there was no way she was letting on.

"The marriage of the Prince and Princess of Wales?" Trudy said, raising her too-thin eyebrows accusingly at everyone.

Fat Tom nodded respectfully.

Nobody else had a clue what Trudy was talking about.

Two of the Steves conferred briefly but came away from one another's hot whispers none the wiser.

Elaine suppressed a smile.

Trudy huffed with exasperation. "Charles and Di?"

A smattering of *oh sures* and *of courses* rose from both sides of the room. "The dead lady in the car accident, right?" Thurston's first assistant said. "Princess Diana of Monaco?"

Elaine burst out laughing; she could have kissed little Mitzy or Ditzy for the look of pure outraged horror that her gorgeously ingenuous remark had planted on Trudy's foundation-flecked face. Fat Tom rubbed his wife's brittle spine, bringing her back from the brink of sovereign sobs.

The senior Steve respectfully asked that the meeting return to address the issue at hand.

Thurston cleared his throat. "Can I just say again that I'm completely comfortable with the idea." Thurston was in his early thirties, with the bland good looks that made him a star on the small screen but sub-second banana on the silver screen. The main problem was that he was chinless, his eyes were too close together, his brown hair follicles were too far apart and he simply could not breathe through anything other than his always-open mouth. "I would be happy to bear your child, Lulu."

"Elaine," Elaine reminded him. "And you don't bear it, Professor. I'm the woman – *I* bear it. All you have to do is throw a hump into me."

"Which I'm quite happy to do," Thurston said, as though he'd be doing her some kind of favor. "And I get to marry you. On TV. For real. In a very special episode of "Lulu & Fred" where you're pregnant with our very own special little baby daughter girl."

"Make them stop saying it, Herb," Elaine said, reaching for a glass of water. "I'm getting nauseous."

Herb spoke. "Ms Reardon would like you to cease discussion of the matter at hand as it is making her nauseous."

"I love you, Lulu," Thurston implored. "I mean, *Elaine!*"

"There you go, he loves you," said an executive. "And he wants to honor that love. What more do you want?"

"Is it money?" a mid-level Steve asked. "D'you want more money?"

"We can do more money."

"I don't want more money," Elaine said. "This isn't about that."

"We can upgrade your parking space."

"No!"

"Longer hiatus?"

"Guest spot for your boyfriend?"

Elaine said that she didn't have a boyfriend.

"Your girlfriend then."

Elaine said that she didn't have a girlfriend, either. "Although Mitzi here's kinda cute." Elaine winked at Mitzi. Mitzi looked away.

"Bigger trailer?"

"No!"

"Bigger laughs? We can do that in post, no problem. You want it, it's done."

"History-making telly, Elaine. History-making."

"She doesn't want any of that," Thurston announced. "Lulu wants to be a mommy." He reached for Elaine's hand and beamed at her. "C'mon, honey – let me impregnify you. Let's *make* that baby!"

Everybody was looking at her as though they actually seriously genuinely expected her to go ahead with this cockamamie idea, maybe even spread her legs right there on the conference table and get things going right away.

"Oh my god," she said, slumping onto the table. The whole thing was starting to seem a lot less amusing than it had five minutes ago.

290 Park Avenue,
101st floor. 11.45am

Wow.

The most experienced counselor at ReStart was a stone cold knockout. Five feet ten, easy, and dressed with an assured sense of style without being ostentatious about it, her dark hair gathered in a French twist, a silver Georg Jensen chain draped around her long elegant neck, a delicate but strong chin, and brown eyes so deep that Charlie instantly lost himself in them from the moment she shook his hand and introduced herself. "Adelaide Carter."

Wow.

"Endicott Gibbs," Charlie said, the made-up name already fitting him comfortably, like somebody else's glove. "Pleased to meet you."

"Have a seat," Adelaide said, pointing to two black Barcelona chairs on either side of a glass-topped coffee table. She had a low, smoky voice that got to Charlie as quickly as her eyes had. "So, Mr Gibbs," she continued. "There are a couple things in your file that aren't quite clear. Do you live here in New York?"

"I'm happy to say I do, Ms Carter."

"And what is it you do for a living?"

"Right now, not so much," he lied. "But I'm a writer by trade, if not by choice."

"Oh really? What kind of writing do you not choose to do?"

"Most recently it was television work out in LA."

"Is that right?"

Charlie sighed with regret – perhaps a little overdone – and nodded.

"You didn't enjoy the work?"

"No, I enjoyed the work well enough," he said. "But there were problems with myself and someone I worked with."

"I see." Adelaide scribbled something. "What sort of problems?"

"Well, you know how when you find bubbles in your milk, the cow's more'n likely been burping?" Charlie explained. "Those sort of problems."

"I see," Adelaide said, although he could see that she didn't. "And what's your marital status?"

"Un-," Charlie said. "Yours?" There was a rock the size of a golfball on her finger but he thought he'd throw the question out there anyway. Could be just a decoy.

"Irrelevant," she said, still looking at the papers in her hands. "Your situation is rather …"

"Complicated?"

"I'd describe it as unique." She looked up and smiled at him – a strictly professional move, he could tell. "We try to avoid complications."

"So do you think you can solve my problem?"

"Yours?" Adelaide said, leaning on the word. "Or Sallie's?"

"Both of ours," Charlie said, considering the complexities. "But mostly hers, I guess," he conceded.

"I gather you and your sister are still close."

"Yes, very."

"Why does she have a different last name to yours?"

"I changed mine."

"When?"

"Oh, not too long ago," Charlie said. "Will you need to see her? Because that's gonna be somewhat tricky."

"Yes, obviously." Adelaide put the papers down on the coffee table then paused a moment, looking him in the eye and sizing him up. "So what exactly is the situation here, Mr Gibbs?"

"Didn't I explain it clearly enough to the other fella? Your colleague?"

"You did," she said. "But the whole thing is pretty odd."

Charlie nodded.

"It's extremely odd."

"I agree," Charlie said. "But as we've discussed, this company is about solving problems between people, right?"

"Yes, it is." She leaned back and crossed her legs. "However the issue here is that the problem isn't between you and somebody else, it's between a third party and, well, hundreds of other people."

"Thousands, actually, and one in particular, but that's not the point. The point is somebody needs your help."

"Or so you believe."

"With all due respect, ma'am, I know it for a fact."

Adelaide took her time, looking at Charlie slowly, her right index finger tapping her chin. "Well, in any case I'm not sure exactly what you think we'd be able to do in this situation. ReStart is about keeping relationships intact not tearing them apart."

"Is that right?"

"Yes, it is," she said firmly. "Besides which, this is more of a religious matter. We don't just go around whipping up schisms out of thin air. And we're not deprogrammers, if that's what you're implying."

"You sure you couldn't …?" He waved his right hand back and forth above his outstretched left arm. "Y'know?"

"No. I really have no idea what you're getting at. Or what you're doing." She looked genuinely confused. "Are you miming someone pulling taffy?"

"No, I'm …" He didn't actually know what he was doing, and put his hands in his pockets to stop them from confusing things further. What he did know was that he truly wanted somebody to help Sallie, and if these people actually did what Miss Holly Hohenzollern had claimed then they might be perfect for the job. "Listen, Sallie could really use your help here, Ms Carter."

"Perhaps if she came to see us herself, we could –"

"That's not possible."

"Well, I really don't know what else to suggest."

Charlie looked at the woman sitting opposite him, her legs crossed neatly in her dark linen slacks, a hint of slender ankle beneath the cuffs, a nice pair of heels on her feet. He wondered exactly what it was that made her the "most experienced" counselor in the company, what special gifts she had for rescuing imperiled relationships – if that was actually what she did. Was she especially wise and empathetic? Or had she been divorced a couple dozen times and knew the warning signs? But who in his right mind would divorce someone as poised and striking as her? How would a person even get together with someone like her in the first place? The words "How about we discuss this over dinner?" clanged around in his head, loud and strong. He gulped uncertainly and said, "Did I say that out loud?"

She looked slightly miffed. "Say what out loud?"

"Never mind," Charlie said with relief. "So there's nothing you can do?"

"I really don't think so."

Reluctantly, he stood up. "I'm sorry to hear that."

Adelaide accompanied Charlie to the door where she shook his hand again. He looked down at her long fingers and cool touch, her monster of a wedding ring. "Never mind, Mr Gibbs. I'm sure things will work out."

"For the best?"

"Perhaps," she said lightly. "I'll hang on to your file just in case."

"Because you want to keep that picture of me, right?"

She took a slight step back and stared at him.

"Oh no," Charlie said, genuinely mortified. "I said *that* out loud, didn't I?"

He smiled and he could tell that it disarmed her a touch. She smiled back, this time giving him something more than curt professionalism. It was just a little but it was enough to inspire that one-word thought one more time: wow.

Back outside on Park Avenue, Charlie stood in the shade staring at 290, pretty much convinced that ReStart was on the up and up, and that Miss Holly Hohenzollern was a crackpot. Likeable and sincere – and almost a dead ringer for Judy Holliday – but a crackpot nevertheless. Which was kind of a shame, not only because a company that covertly busted up relationships might have been able to help Sallie, but also because if it existed and he could get inside, it might be the story of the year. He could almost taste the Pulitzerness of it – and he wanted a Pulitzer, bad. But it was too good to be true – way too good and way too crazy. Which was kind of a shame.

He decided to wait another moment in the shade before heading back to the *Sentinel* office, take a little time and listen to what his fellow New Yorkers had to say. Like this pair heading toward him, a gangly fellow in his late-twenties with a flaky grin accompanied by a short, pretty girl around the same age, but more intelligent-looking, maybe because of the tortoiseshell glasses she wore and this wide, happy smile she was obviously trying to hide from the guy.

She said, "Oh, I forgot to ask. How'd it go after the debrief?"

The fellow took a sip of his takeout coffee then said, "The usual barrage of threats and intimidation. I've pretty much got old Dwight the K right where I want him."

When he heard the name, Charlie decided to follow the pair. Sure, it was probably just a coincidence – Dwight was an unusual name, but not in the same league as, say, Rumpelstiltskin or Plaxico – but it couldn't hurt to see how the next few moments played out. Just in case. He tailed them into the lobby.

"Oh yeah?" the girl said, pressing the elevator button. "Where's that, Clayton? In your nightmares? I think you'd better make it 'Mr Kitchener' for a while. Or 'your majesty'."

"I'd never go beyond 'sir'." The two of them stepped into the empty elevator car and just before the doors closed Charlie heard the guy say, "You know he threatened to kill me? Literally threatened to actually kill me."

Charlie watched the elevator indicator light going up higher and higher. It didn't stop until the 102nd floor.

Okay, well that probably isn't a coincidence, he said, the words traveling straight from his mind to his tongue then bouncing off the black marble walls of the empty lobby. There was a Pulitzery taste in his mouth.

Later

Clayton sat at his desk, removed the lid of his coffee cup and tried to stop himself from licking the foam beneath the plastic top. He knew it wasn't the most mature thing to do, and he'd decided that if he wanted people to take him more seriously – and he did want that; he wanted it very much – then he would have to act less like an adolescent and more like a – God, he hated even thinking the word – more like a man. And if in the Man's world only people under, say, twenty-five got to lick foam off of coffee lids, then so be it; it would be worth the respect he'd now command from people like Dwight the K. And hopefully Elodie. The hardest thing, though, wouldn't be forswearing foam-licking, it would be to quit making stupid jokes like his ASS remark this morning, the direct consequence of which was one of the reasons for his new plan. He liked cracking jokes, though, getting away with it and making people laugh, especially his partner. Women were always saying how a good sense of humor was more important to them than looks or physique, and while

Clayton knew that that particular claim was almost total bullshit, he was also aware that in his particular case – lacking not only good looks but also, it seemed, a single visible muscle – he had no choice but to find his way into a woman's heart via the circuitous route of her funny bone. It was a drag. It was such a drag – and a risk – that he'd almost joined a gym a few weeks back, just to see how the women of New York City liked someone who was both cut *and* funny, but then the heat wave started and there was no way he was going to begin some fitness regime while the temperature was hovering around ninety degrees day and night. It'd kill him. It'd kill anyone, probably, but especially him. He dropped the lid into the waste bin under his desk and looked at the delicious chocolate-dusted white froth slowly dripping onto the wadded-up paper on the bottom. He really loved takeout coffee foam. And, God, he missed being twenty-four, all the stuff you could get away with at that age.

*

While she waited for her coffee to cool Elodie tapped Larry D's face with the end of a pen and tried to get the song out of her head, this damn thing Clay had been singing to himself in the elevator, some crazy nonsense about magic wands and the game of love and flames going out and the taste of bitter tears upon his tongue ... Then he would pause and sing quietly, in some kind of half-assed French accent "Yesterday, when I was young."

The cheap sentiment and even cheaper melody had driven her crazy in the elevator and it was still driving her crazy now as she leafed through the job folder trying to understand why on earth this Barbara B dame wanted to have a relationship with not one but two men. At the same time. In the same place. With the same name!

Elodie allowed that, yes, the sex would be interesting – for a while, anyway, once all outlets and inlets and combinations had been explored and exhausted – but incorporating a third human into the natural volatility generated between just two people was sheer madness. As their client Larry D had apparently discovered – or decided. Yep, the sex must have been amazing, Elodie thought. The kind where ... Well, actually she couldn't remember the last time she'd been part of any kind of sex – with even one other person, forget about two – let alone anything amazing. She had a pretty nice dildo – who could survive without one these days? – but to describe it as amazing would be a stretch. Preposterously long, inhumanly ribbed and predictably adequate was about it.

This wasn't good, not at all, appraising her damn dildo when she had all this work to do. She turned back to Larry P's meek, maudlin milquetoast of a face, wondering if he believed in Barbara more than he believed in God, whether he'd sacrifice faith for flesh or vice versa. An image popped into her head. She let it sit for a few moments then picked up her phone, called the Intel Department and asked them to get the blueprints of Larry's loft. She'd also need a 200-pound winch, some steel cable, a harness, and one very brave operative.

She turned around and asked Clayton the name of the incredibly annoying song he'd been singing in the elevator.

"'Yesterday When I Was Young' by Charles Aznavour," he told her.

"Sing it again," Elodie said, getting to work on the plan.

*

Adelaide was relieved to be back in her office on 102 – the operations office, as opposed to her consulting suite on 101 – because the lower floor always gave her the creeps. It was so quiet and gloomy down there, like a sprawling confessional chamber, people talking in whispers and muffled sobs, a lot of them holding back tears as they raked over failing marriages, looming divorces, relationships going to hell. She remembered the awful time eight years ago, midway through her seemingly interminable stint as a junior counselor – insisted upon by her mother – when this woman she'd been counseling for about a month came in for her regular session one afternoon. The whole time she'd sat there, this woman, she kept reaching into her handbag for tissues as well as what Adelaide had thought were some kind of hard candies, popping one every five minutes or so as she sniffed and choked her way through another relentlessly bitter dissection of her decomposing marriage. Adelaide had been hungover that afternoon, bored and distracted as this woman detailed her misery for the umpteenth time, and it wasn't until she suddenly slumped and her forehead smacked into the edge of Adelaide's desk that she realized those small, colored things weren't candy.

The woman survived the overdose attempt, and while the incident had left Adelaide shaken, it was clear evidence of just how damaging and dangerous a noxious relationship could be and it strengthened her resolve to remain in the business her mother had founded back in 1963. It had also inspired Adelaide to organize for the vomit-stained piece of carpet where the almost-suicide had collapsed to be torn up, framed under glass and hung on her office wall as a permanent reminder of why she did what she did. It was unpleasant and dirty, and if you looked at it too closely it began to stink. So it was perfect.

She opened the Endicott Gibbs folder, wanting to take another quick look at his details (and, she had to admit, his photograph) before discussing the situation with Elodie and Clayton. Just hear what they thought about it before junking the file and the handsome weirdo behind it.

New York Sentinel Building, 14th floor

It was like he'd been sitting and waiting all day. Mr Munro behind his desk, doing nought but stroking the furry lengths of his silver mustache, staring through the glass wall of his office out at the editorial floor, waiting for Charlie to return. For as long as Charlie had been at the *Sentinel* he'd never seen Mr Munro do nothing; it was as though he had that condition that sharks do where they have to keep moving or they die.

The boss's first words were loud but warm. "Where the devil have you been all day, Charlie?" Mr Munro couldn't help liking Charlie despite his many professional derelictions and shortcomings. "I've been worried almost to the point of nausea."

"Chasing a few leads," Charlie said. "Sorry to have almost nauseated you."

"That's all right," Mr Munro said, leaning back in his chair. "The truth is I feel that way pretty often. I think I might be allergic to something. Plus I'm getting old."

"You don't look old, sir," said Charlie as reassuringly as he could to someone Mr Munro's age. "Or allergic."

"Thank you. So did you come up with anything?"

"Not much. I think it was a bad tip."

"Well please check with me next time you plan to spend so long on something."

"I certainly will," Charlie said. "Probably." He hoped he'd managed to keep the last word contained; Charlie really loved his job at the paper and wanted to stay there for at least the next twenty to thirty years.

"I certainly hope so," Mr Munro said, his left hand tugging at the walrus-like droop of his mustache. "And it would be nice if you could come up with a decent story, something big. Soon, Charlie, otherwise I'll probably have to fire you. And I truly dislike letting people go. I even cried once while doing it, which was both unseemly and unprofessional. So I'd hate for you to put me in that position."

Charlie knew what was required of him in this moment in order to keep his beloved job. He sighed regretfully, nodded respectfully, and bowed sheepishly as he backed out of his boss's office. You had to hand it him, Charlie thought, for an older fellow Mr Munro certainly had spunk. He had to be sixty-eight at least. Most people he knew that age were dead.

Back at his own desk in his cubicle, Charlie removed Holly Hohenzollern's letter from his coat pocket, took a last look at it then screwed it up and threw it into the trash can. As the paper bounced on the rim of the trash bin and then hit the floor, the telephone rang.

A telephone booth on Fort Tyron Place

Officer Hohenzollern, wearing her patrol uniform, which she hated because it made her stupid fat ass look fat, was standing in a phone booth opposite the Cloisters in upper Manhattan, watching some stupid moron in the car park pull a knife on a stupid tourist couple who'd just stepped off a bus less than ten seconds ago and were already getting mugged, for God's sake, so she was a little distracted as she dialed, wanting to get the conversation over with pretty quickly.

"So how'd it go?" she asked that Van Lindberg from the newspaper.

"Well, I talked with them and they seemed pretty harmless."

"What!?"

"I'm not saying you're mistaken about what they do there, Miss Hohenzollern," he said, slowly easing into a country-style pause. That stupid hick drawl of his was really getting on her nerves, the way it made everything sound as if was being filtered through a piece of straw poking from his lips. "But I think you are."

The male Caucasian tourist approximately fifty-five years of age was handing over his wallet. "And I'm telling you I'm not mistaken," Holly said. "As a police officer, I'm *ordering* you that I'm not!"

"Ordering me?" Van Linson said.

"Whatever."

"You're a policeman?"

"Woman," said Holly, taking another look at the 10–20 in progress. "Yes, I am. And I'm telling you that that company is no good. This is a big story, mister, and if you're not interested then I'll find somebody who is!"

"I'm interested," he said. "I really am. I just need, y'know, proof."

"So go out and get it," Holly said. "What's the matter with you?"

"I'm having a small crisis of faith," he said. "Not just in you, specifically, more or less in everything."

"Okay, well here's something to get you motivated in me, specifically. If you don't get back on it, I will personally issue you a parking violation every day for a year. Maybe two."

"I don't own a car."

"That will not be a problem." The stupid mugger was now waving his stupid knife all over the place and forcing the male and female to get down on their knees, so God only knew what he was planning to do next. "I have to go," Holly said, dropping the receiver and pulling her gun as she struggled to get out of the phone booth, the stupid folding door catching on her stupid fat can.

New York Sentinel Building, 14th floor

Golly, she sure is a bossy one, Charlie thought, still wondering if Miss Hohenzollern wasn't actually a nutjob. He was about to put down the phone when he heard her shouting at someone to put down a knife, goddammit! Then some pistol shots.

Charlie hung up, convinced that whether she was screwy or not she definitely owned a gun, so he'd better keep investigating. He picked her letter up off the floor, straightened it out and put it in his drawer amongst the tangled and highly illegal mess of bugs, microphones, listening devices, recording devices, lock picking tools, counterfeit shields for various city departments and a small gold medal that convinced nine out of ten people that he was a Nobel laureate. He considered the situation for a moment and selected a few items, wondering if he oughtn't to add a Kevlar vest to the collection. At least for this particular assignment.

Across town, around the same time. In a nicer office

Adelaide sat on the couch, facing Clayton and Elodie. On her lap was the Gibbs file, which the senior creative team had just finished reading. In a nutshell, the job was to separate a young Amish woman from her community. It was a doozy of a nutshell.

"So what do you think?" Adelaide asked, looking from Elodie to Clayton.

"I think we should take it," Elodie said. "Have you run it by Dwight?"

"I don't want to bother him with something like this right now," Adelaide said. "He's kind of …"

"Enraged?" Clayton offered.

"Preoccupied," Adelaide said.

"Leave it with me and Clay for a couple hours and maybe we'll do a follow-up." Elodie pushed her glasses back up her nose. "In the meantime why don't you introduce this Gibbs to Mr Handy's polygraph and see if he's on the level?"

Adelaide nodded. Part of her was relieved, she had to admit. It was a strange case, a dog, really, but she wasn't sure she never wanted to see Endicott Gibbs again. It would be interesting to see how he reacted to the next phase, as well as to see how he performed during it.

"Oh great! Pennsylvania here we come," said Clayton. "Should I go rent 'Witness' and look for clues?"

"If you think it'll help, Clayton." Adelaide stood up, and was almost out the door and when she turned around. "Oh, I almost forgot – what about the artist thing in Chelsea?"

"It's tonight," Elodie said. "It's kind of a Handbag-Toledo combination, with a little touch of flair we've lifted from 'The Exorcist'."

"It's pretty scary," Clayton said sincerely.

"And as per Dwight's request, nobody dies," Elodie added.

"Although there may be a withering of souls."

"Who's handling it?" Adelaide asked.

Elodie told her that it was a three-man job, being taken care of by Pete V, Matt and Eduardo. "Matt's already in position on the roof of the building, along with a very persuasive outfit."

Adelaide didn't ask what kind of outfit, but she wanted to know what the plan was called.

Clayton said, "Threeways to Sunday Mass Hysteria."

"It's convoluted but I like it," Adelaide said, smiling. "Good luck."

Outside. 92°

"Wasn't you lingering here this morning?"

Charlie turned to the hot dog cart vendor. "Who, me?"

"Yeah, you," the vendor said. He was a little guy, swarthy and sweaty, with a very wide face and lively eyes. "Who else wearing a black suit on a ninety degree day am I gonna see twice?"

"An undertaker, maybe," Charlie said.

"You waiting for your girl?"

"Maybe," Charlie said. He took a couple of steps forward, putting the hot dog cart between himself and the entrance to the ReStart building, about fifty feet away. He didn't know why – or what difference it made to anything – but he suddenly wondered if the guy was Armenian.

"Matter of fact I am an Armenian. By birth," the hot dog vendor said. "Why do you ask me that?"

"Actually, I didn't know I had," Charlie said. Obviously the question had popped out, though.

"Well you did," the Armenian hot dog vendor said. "Why?"

"I really don't care if you're Armenian or not. It just popped out."

"I'll pop you out, buster, you give me any more lip about Armenia." The fella thrust his hard stump of a chin up at Charlie. "Using my cart as cover, you really should oughta buy something. Call it an espionage tax."

"Okay," Charlie said. "How much is a hot dog?"

The vendor told him two dollars.

Charlie asked how many condiments that price included.

"Condiments is complimentary," the little Armenian chin-thruster said. "We build them into the price structure of the wiener and bun."

Charlie laughed and handed over a couple of dollars. "I'll take one, please. With mustard."

"What're you?" the vendor asked, as he reached into the steaming tin tub and removed a pretty decent-looking dog.

"What am I what?" said Charlie, looking at his watch; it was a little before seven pm, golden light falling slowly.

"By birth," the Armenian explained. "What are you by birth?"

"Oh. I used to be Amish," Charlie said. "But I gave it up."

"You can't do that," the Armenian said, sounding a little indignant about it. "You can't just quit who you are."

"Maybe not," said Charlie. "But you can at least give it a shot, can't you?"

As the mustard was being squirted onto the wiener, Charlie saw Clayton and the woman who'd been with him that morning leaving the lobby of 290 Park. There was a third person with them, a muscular Hispanic guy carrying a small leather valise. The three of them walked diagonally away from the hot dog cart, uptown, maybe heading for the subway station over on 51st. Charlie hoped so; if they got into a cab and he had to follow them in another, he couldn't be sure what kind of craziness would come out of his mouth. What the heck was he wondering if anybody was Armenian for?

As Charlie grabbed his hot dog and ran off the vendor called out, "You're still gonna be American, though, right?"

Charlie tailed the trio for a few blocks and watched with a mixture of surprise and eagerness as they entered a long-term parking garage. It had been a while since Charlie had boosted a car – a skill that arose almost from necessity growing up as both an American boy who yearned to drive and an Amish boy who was expected to get around in a horse and buggy for his entire life – but he still maintained a few scruples about what he was and wasn't willing to borrow. He always tried to find a thick coating of dust on the hood and roof of a vehicle, evidence that it hadn't been used in a while. That was requirement number one – not inconveniencing anyone. Much. Number two was that he could get in and start it without any major damage, which pretty much cut out anything manufactured after the mid-nineties, when electronic anti-theft systems became standard manufacturing practice.

A dozen parking bays away he saw Clayton and his two associates get into a car. He had to make a decision fast. This orange Ford Pinto? No way on God's green earth. That gooey-looking Dodge something? Nope. An AMC Pacer? He could barely even fit into a tiny little two-door hunchback thing like that. Having auto-theft scruples could really limit a fella's choices.

Although he wasn't unhappy with the cherry red '77 Chevy Nova he left the garage with. Not too unhappy at all.

355 West 29th Street

Clayton and Elodie sat enveloped in heat and silence in Clayton's car, a 1989 Cadillac Fleetwood Brougham d'Elegance. (The optional d'Elegance element consisted of pillow-style velour seating trim and plush carpeting, neither of which was any longer in evidence in this particular Cadillac Fleetwood Brougham.) Even though it was parked in a dark pool of shadow between two streetlights it was still easy to see that it was a strikingly ugly vehicle – big, boxy, and chocolate brown to boot. He could easily afford to upgrade but the Caddy was Clayton's first car, and he loved it deeply and unreasonably. Besides, living in Manhattan nobody really needed a car, so it made even less sense to own a nice, expensive, reliable, clean, comfortable one. Didn't it?

The pair stared up through the windshield at a six-story Italian Renaissance Revival style building on the opposite side of the street, the top floor of which was lit. Up on the roof were two operatives, Pete Valentine manning a suspension rig and winch, brave Matt Kane squeezed into red latex. It was a little after eight o'clock and, now that Clayton had picked the lock of the building's entrance to let "Father" Eduardo in so he could begin the brutal catechesis that would hopefully cast Larry P out of his sin-tainted heaven, nothing much was happening. Nothing much had been happening for a while.

Clayton thought about that weekend in Newport, how he'd woken up to find all the ashtrays in their room were full of Froot Loops. It still confounded him that things between him and El had ended that way, with help from one of the most delicious yet most stupid of cereals.

As it happened, Elodie, too, was thinking about that weekend at the Chanler Hotel in Newport, about the messages written in lipstick on the bathroom mirrors. How could it have ended like that? So abruptly? So mysteriously? It was the weirdest thing, but even though they shared an office (and now a car) and spent nine or ten hours together almost every day of the week, she somehow missed Clayton. How could that be? She wound down her window, letting in a blast of hot night air. She took a deep breath, gagged a little on the humidity, then put the window up again.

"Air-conditioning's busted," Clayton said. "So's the radio."

"Sweet ride."

He looked over at her but she was studying the roof of the building. "This is really not that bad of a car, you know. Sure, it's a little busted-looking and easy to heap scorn on but it's solid, it's reliable. It'll get you from where you are to where you want to be every time. And if you're willing to look beneath the surface, you'll find plenty to like, if not fall in love with. And you know why? Because it has character. Beneath all that faded d'elegance it has real charm."

Elodie squirmed a little uncomfortably on the un-sprung, worn velour seat. "Is that meant to be a metaphor?"

"Yeah, sort of," Clayton said. "I'm the car."

"I figured."

Both of them looked up through the windscreen as Satan, red and tight and shiny as a hot dog wiener, floated gently down from the roof of the building and hovered outside one of the loft's enormous windows. He dangled up there horizontally, clutching his trusty three-pronged pitchfork as his unblinking coal black eyes stared into the living-room, his bleak gaze trained on Larry P, slowly slowly curdling Larry's very soul.

"We should have reinforced his tail," Clayton said, pointing up at the flaccid appendage hanging between Abbadon's legs, the tail's arrow pointed forlornly at the ground. "It doesn't look menacing enough. It should be angry, maybe even accusatory."

Elodie could see that Matt Mephistopheles was hot as hell up there; he looked almost boiled. "What's that suit made of?" she asked.

"Latex," Clayton told her. "But it's reinforced with carbon fiber so it can handle the wires."

As the Archfiend rose and disappeared over the para-pet, an arterial spray of lightning spattered the sky, quickly followed by the low moan of thunder.

"Wow," Clayton said. "That wasn't us, was it?"

A few minutes later both of them watched Eduardo leave the gargoyle-guarded front entrance of the building and walk down the stairs to the street. Without looking over at the lovable 1989 Cadillac Fleetwood Brougham d'Elegance parked opposite, he gave a subtle thumbs-up in its direction and headed down the street.

Not long afterward, a young man Elodie recognized as Larry P came down the stairs carrying a heavy suitcase. With a drawn and doleful look on his face, he crossed the street, heading straight toward Clayton's car and stopping just a couple of inches from the bumper. He put the suitcase down, turned back and took a final look up the brightly-lit loft then walked slowly south, headed, Elodie was almost certain, for a confessional booth at St Columba down on 25th.

Clayton hit the Caddy's ignition, praying that it would start. If not, his metaphor – and everything riding on it – was shot.

Fifty feet south of
355 West 29th Street

As he watched the big brown boxy boat pull away from the curb, Charlie wondered why the muscular Hispanic fellow had left the building dressed as a Catholic priest. Was he *actually* a priest? And what was in that valise he had with him? And who was the gentleman with the suitcase stuffed to Sunday who came out not a minute after the little priest?

Charlie waited until the Cadillac reached the corner before he hit the gas. Why was everybody carrying luggage, he wondered.

And, oh yeah, what was Satan Himself doing here in Chelsea?

88 West 75th Street

As she walked in the front door, Adelaide called out her husband's name a few times before reaching the kitchen, opening the refrigerator door and sticking as much of herself inside as she could. She could hardly believe how hot she'd gotten on the short walk from the 72nd Street station to her building; sure it was eighty degrees outside, but the perspiration matting her hair and darkening her armpits seemed unreasonable. Maybe they were hot flashes. Could it be menopause? Jesus, *already*?

She added Possible Menopause to The List.

The blinking red light of the answering machine caught her eye. She had a pretty good idea of what was coming, and the effect it would have on her, thermally-speaking. So Adelaide slipped out of her shoes and cooled the soles of her feet on the marble floor before she hit the Play button.

"Hi, Adelaide. It's Rob Dolen here. How are you, babe?"

There was a long pause. She thought about switching

on the air-conditioning; a twenty degree plunge could be just what she needed right now. Cool things down and take a good look at the situation, in general and in particular, notwithstanding the list of –

"Babe?"

Another pause. But, depending on how this message played out – if Rob ever got to the point – she might not be around long enough for the temperature in there to matter. This pause was really stretching; he was still waiting for her to respond.

"Oh right, I'm talking to the machine." He guffawed brutally. Her clammy skin crawled. She felt ashamed of how ashamed she felt of her own husband. "Listen, I'm calling because …"

"Let me guess," she told the kitchen. "You're working late and won't be home 'til you don't know when."

"… and I don't think I'll be back 'til I don't know when. Probably late, though. Things are pretty crazy here, so, y'know, I gotta keep it all under control everywhere, like such as, so we will be able to build up our future for us. Oh, great news! I finally decided which headshot to go with. The Groucho Kennedy. You think I should grow a little mustache like his? I think it might look –"

Adelaide jabbed Erase before he could utter another word. "Everywhere like such as?" She could feel the skin on her neck growing hot and her blood pressure rising. But this was no hot flash; this heat was the direct result of being married to Rob Dolen. For the thousandth time she wondered how she could have let herself stay with him for so long, and for the thousandth time she came up dry. Although there was that very witty and astute remark he made about Brooklyn that time …

Adelaide picked up the phone and dialed Elodie's cell. When she left a few minutes later she was about ten degrees hotter than when she'd arrived. The air-conditioning wouldn't have stood a chance.

The Room

The Hispanic fellow, still wearing his priestly duds, was in between the other two – gangly Clayton with the flaky smile and the small girl with russet hair. The three of them were coming straight toward Charlie, heading east on Vandam.

They'd been easy to tail; that monster of a Cadillac was hard to lose, and once they'd parked it and got out they didn't exactly hurry to wherever they were going. It couldn't have been simpler.

Charlie lowered his head, eyes to the sidewalk, as the trio drew up to him. And just as they were about to pass by, he bumped heavily into Clayton, almost knocking him over. Charlie muffled his voice as he muttered apologies and reassuringly patted Clayton on the shoulders and chest, as though preventing him from further potential harm, all the while keeping his face angled away from view. Then he hunched into himself and continued on his way. The whole thing had lasted less than five seconds.

As soon as he turned the corner on Varick and put in his earpiece, Charlie knew it had worked. "Better check for your wallet, Clay," he heard, clear as a hoof striking bitumen on a windless summer's day. "That looked like a classic snatch to these highly-trained eyes."

Charlie poked his head around the corner and saw Clayton slip his hand inside his jacket. He removed a thick lump of wallet and waved it in the priest's face. "Maybe your highly-trained eyes need glasses, Eduardo," Clayton said, a little cockily. "This fatboy is still right here and still bursting with cash."

"A thousand bucks in singles, Clay?" the girl said, mockingly. "I didn't realize we were hitting a strip club."

"Look closely, El," said Clayton, laughing. "And you'll see a couple of ten-spots."

What he hadn't noticed was the tiny radio microphone Charlie had slipped behind the lapel of his jacket. It was all going perfectly. The only thing that might be trouble was if they went into a noisy, crowded bar.

Charlie took a few paces back along Vandam and watched as Eduardo opened the door to a noisy, crowded bar called De Kamer. "Well that's not ideal," Charlie said out loud. And he didn't care who heard it.

*

Thirty seconds later, as he was headed back to pick up the Nova, Charlie's phone rang. He didn't recognize the number, a situation he hated, and it made him answer uncertainly in case it was a relative who'd tracked him down or a telemarketer telling him he'd won something really nice.

"Mr Gibbs?" said Adelaide Carter.

Wow. It was her.

"Hello," Charlie said. There was a lot of background noise on her end – jackhammers, traffic, shouting;

wherever she was it was somewhere pretty loud. Which narrowed it down to almost any neighborhood in any of the five boroughs. "Hi."

"It's Adelaide Carter," she said. "I've given your situation some further consideration and I was wondering if we could see you at our office tomorrow morning. Would that be possible?"

"Sure." He couldn't help smiling, and not just because there was now a better chance of they're taking on his – that is, Sallie's – case (if they really did what Holly Hohenzollern said they did), and therefore a better chance of his breaking the story (if they really did what Holly Hohenzollern said they did), but also because, actually, it'd be pretty nice to see Adelaide Carter again (no matter what Holly Hohenzollern had to say about it). "That'd be fine."

"We'd like you to take a lie detector test."

Okay … "Okay." Up ahead he saw a blue truck and a bunch of fellas in blue hardhats: a Con Ed crew tearing a hole in the side of the road. The heat had literally sapped the energy from this part of the city. "Great."

"You're comfortable with that?" she asked, sounding a little surprised. "I'm pleased to hear it."

He passed the Con Ed van and there she was – Adelaide Carter, clacking along the sidewalk on the other side of the street. She was wearing a navy linen shift and flat shoes, a pretty fancy-looking handbag swinging from the valley of her elbow.

Nice dress, Charlie thought.

"What did you say?" she said, suddenly pulling the cellphone from her ear and looking around.

Before her eyes hit his, Charlie dived between two parked cars, striking both his elbows on bumpers front and rear. It hurt like crazy but somehow he managed to keep his own phone in place and even in the spatter of confusion that leaped from his side of the street to hers he thought he could hear her breath quicken in surprise. He was pretty sure she hadn't seen him – she may have seen someone hitting the ground – a phantom, a blur – but there was no way she could've known that someone was him.

"High stress, I said," Charlie told her. "The lie detector thing, it's a high stress situation but that's fine with me. If it'll help Sallie then I'll take it twice." He lay panting on the hot asphalt, watching Adelaide from beneath a Ford Territory as she crossed to his side of the street and continued along Vandam. He wondered if Bob Woodward or Neil Sheehan had ever injured themselves in pursuit of a story, stubbed their toes, barked their shins, lost their wives. Excavating a deeply buried truth was difficult, dangerous work. But what was Charlie doing comparing himself to Woodward and Sheehan? Those two legendary reporters had broken stories that changed the country, that brought down a president; the possibly-true thing Charlie was chasing was big but not *that* big. Worth a chipped elbow, say, but not electrocuted testicles. A Pulitzer, maybe, but not a Nobel. The fact that there was no such thing as a Nobel Prize for journalism notwithstanding. And the whole thing probably wasn't true, anyway. People lied about everything all the time and crazy Holly Hohenzollern was probably just another one, steamed and miffed that her boyfriend had busted up with her and out for some crazy, convoluted revenge.

Still tracking Adelaide, Charlie decided to try a little lie detector test of his own. "Listen, it's none of my business, but what are you doing right now?"

"I'm about to go into a meeting. Goodnight," she said, ending the call and walking straight into the Dutch bar.

Okay, so she wasn't a liar. Well, not exactly.

De Kamertje. 9.20pm

De Kamer was the locus of über-hip Manhattan's current taste for all things Dutch. New Amsterdam had reached across the Atlantic for a six-month kick from something that had been a way of life for centuries in Old Amsterdam. It was a find it, feed it, and forget it approach to culture. The food they served at De Kamer was typical Dutch bar fare, and it was disgusting – hard lumps of sharp cheese; fat, greasy coins of cold pink meat; deep-fried balls of God-only-knew-what called *bitterballen* – but the old world atmosphere in the small bar was perfect. There was no music, no television, no hostile hostess, and the uneven wooden floor was covered in sawdust. What especially appealed to Adelaide and her colleagues was De Kamertje, a small, dim room off to the side comprised of little more than half a dozen creaky old chairs set around a well-worn provincial farmhouse table. And a sign on the public side of the door that read "Privaat."

On the exclusive side of that door, Adelaide and her employees, Elodie, Clayton and Eduardo, sat around a sparkling, forty-two-proof rainbow of one-ounce tulip glasses filled with flavored *jenevers* imported from a tiny Dutch distillery called Wynand Fockink. There was lemon, boysenberry and plum, spicy *Bruidstranen* (The Bride's Tears) and sweet *Boswandeling* (A Walk in the Woods). Just one glass of this gin-like stuff was enough to ease open the doors of recklessness; lined up in the middle of the French oak table were ten full bottles. Seemed like somebody was planning to kick those doors down.

Eduardo requested a moment's silence then bowed his head in prayer. "Oh Heavenly Father," he intoned solemnly. "We ask you to bless these various jenevers as we give thanks to the blessed fruits of the earth which make such delicious spirits possible. Amen."

"Amen," Adelaide said, taking a healthy slug of lemon *jenever*. "That was pretty convincing, Father."

"I was taught by Jesuits, Ms Carter," Eduardo said with a grin. "So I'm well versed in both scripture and booze."

Elodie knocked back some plum and told Adelaide that Eduardo had really nailed it, that Larry Number Two was out of there like a shot. "There" being both the loft and the relationship. "Cheers," she said. "To a successful – and bloodless – operation."

Clayton downed a glass of *oude jenever*. "May the traumas of interpersonal relationships continue to deliver us an endless stream of bitter, unhappy and wealthy clients." Then another. "May we continue to thrive on human misery and moral weakness."

Adelaide turned. "Gosh, Clayton, even for you that's cynical." She wondered if it was the booze making him talk like that. "You're beginning to sound like Dwight."

Elodie and Eduardo laughed. Clayton looked offended. "Oh, gimme a break."

"It's true," Adelaide continued. "Although his conscience seems to have ambushed him lately."

"Seriously?" Elodie asked.

"I was under the impression he'd had it surgically removed in Vietnam," Clayton said.

"What did you say?" Adelaide's tone was sharp; the look on her face matched her voice.

"I thought his conscience was a victim of his years in Vietnam," said Clayton. "Along with his sense of humor."

Adelaide stared. Clayton squirmed. Elodie and Eduardo waited. Adelaide let it stretch for another moment then said, "What do you know about Dwight's time in the war?"

"Well, nothing," Clayton said.

"That's right," Adelaide snapped. "So you'd be smart not to bring it up again."

"If I drink too much more of this stuff, I may not be able to help it." Clayton mimed throwing up.

"I'm serious, Clayton."

"Jeez Louise, all right."

Eduardo broke the strained silence that Adelaide had brought down on the room. "Well, Dwight reamed my ass pretty good this morning," he said. "I thought it was just because of what happened last night with Buttons and Sara."

"Last night's part of it," Adelaide said, tilting a bottle of blackberry *jenever*. "But I think his years in the business are finally beginning to catch up with him."

"We're all going to hell for what we do, Adelaide," Clayton said. He turned to Eduardo. "Aren't we, Father?"

"Almost certainly."

"If you don't like it, quit," Elodie said to Clayton, not giving it too much because she felt he'd already gotten enough. He was a goofball but he always meant well. And he was a very good kisser – not that that had anything to do with anything. What was she even thinking about that for, anyway? She blamed it on the booze.

"Well that's the problem, El," he countered. "I love what I do. And I'm not being facetious. I really do."

"And so you should," Adelaide said. "What we do is if not 'good', then at the very least necessary. My mom was right – better no relationship than a bad relationship." Which didn't apply to Adelaide herself, of course. But that was a matter for The List.

"That's another part of what's bothering Dwight, isn't it?" asked Elodie. "He misses your mother, doesn't he?"

Adelaide nodded. "There's a lot of guilt there."

"Guilt?" Elodie said, unable to contain her surprise. "They were a great couple. I've never seen two people so right for each other in my life."

"Oh, I know they were. But it's ..." Adelaide wondered if another shot – which would be what, her third? Her seventh? – would help get the words out. "It's complicated."

"Few things where Dwight is concerned aren't."

Elodie and Adelaide both shot Clayton quick looks of schoolmarmish disapproval.

"Oh come on," he protested. "I'm allowed to say that, aren't I?"

Eduardo stood up and grabbed Clayton by the elbow. "C'mon, let's go grab a breath of fresh Manhattan steam."

"Just a second." Clayton removed his jacket and hung it over the back of his chair. There was a snatch of barroom buzz as the door opened and closed, leaving Adelaide and Elodie alone in the privacy of De Kamertje.

"What's up?" asked Elodie. "Is it Rob?"

"No ..." Adelaide lied. "Yes ..." she confessed. "Sort of ..." she qualified.

"You still haven't told him what you do, have you?" Elodie had to physically stop herself from shaking her head in disbelief at her boss's staggering and attenuated deception; even by their extraordinarily high standards of duplicity and deceit this was a doozy. Then again, some people suddenly embraced homosexuality after decades of suppressing it, after being married and raising a family. Wasn't that the same thing? Kind of? "He still thinks you work in PR?"

"He wouldn't understand the truth." Adelaide sighed. "Who would? Do you ever ... Do you really believe that what we do is right?"

"If I didn't, I wouldn't do it," Elodie replied firmly. "People come to us, Adelaide, we don't approach them. They come to us because there's nowhere else for them to go. And nine times out of ten, when we're finished with them they're a lot happier and a lot better off than before."

"But we only ever see half the story," Adelaide said. "What about the other half – the dumped?"

"Screw 'em," Elodie said. "Most of them deserve what they get."

"You know who was the first one?" The words shot out of Adelaide's mouth almost before she knew it. She blamed it on the booze. "The first one who got what he deserved?"

"No idea."

"It was my father," Adelaide said.

"Do I even need to say that I don't understand what you're talking about?"

"As I mentioned, it's complicated."

*

Charlie slumped lower in the bucket seat of the Nova, now parked directly opposite De Kamer, as Clayton and the possible priest named Eduardo exited the bar. He absently watched them share a cigarette while listening with increasing amazement to the conversation between the two women still inside.

"Complicated how?" he heard Elodie say.

"So complicated it …" Adelaide paused yet again. "God, I can't believe I'm finally telling somebody this. But here goes nothing: it's so complicated that it involves killing a president."

"One of ours?"

"Of course!" Adelaide scoffed. "Whose else matters?"

"So you mean …"

"Yeah, President –"

A loud noise obscured the name of the dead president.

"Who?" Charlie said, knowing already who it was, who it had to be.

At the same time, Elodie blurted out *"Maudite marde!"* so loudly that Charlie's earpiece almost popped out. "So Dwight is directly responsible for the death of –"

"That's right," Adelaide interrupted.

"Who!?" Charlie said. He needed to hear her say it. A sharp knock on his window almost gave him a heart-attack. White-faced and open-mouthed, he turned and saw a beat cop's ugly mug looming down at him.

"Gonna have to move along, fella," the old copper said. "This is a no parking zone."

"Oh no," Charlie said, still trying to listen to the voices in his ear. "No, no, no. That's impossible."

"Impossible?" The cop raised his bushy gray eyebrows. "Like I'm gonna have to write you up, impossible? Or place you under arrest, impossible?"

"Just a second," said Charlie, patting his pockets, rummaging through his bag, tossing out the contents of the Nova's glove compartment and feeling around on the floor. In no time at all the interior was strewn with papers, wallets, plastic cards, and a pair of sunglasses with a tiny video camera hidden in the bridge. There were even a couple of fake mustaches on the dashboard. He finally found what he was looking for jammed in between the two front seats and handed it to the cop.

The grizzled veteran studied the heavy gold shield for a moment before returning it, deeply impressed. "Beg your pardon, Detective," he said deferentially. "Can I ask you one question about the French Conn–"

Charlie shook his head, quickly wound up the window and refocused his attention on the conversation he'd been listening to – and recording. Adelaide was in the middle of something.

*

"... back when Dwight and my dad were in Vietnam together. Back when my father was screwing half the population of Saigon, local and imported. So after they completed their tours, Dwight worked for the NSA and my father stayed with the Air Force. But a couple of years later they formed a private air charter business doing black work for the government. Flying dictators into and out of trouble. Hauling drugs and weapons, too, I'm pretty sure. That sort of honorable stuff. Soon after they became business partners it wasn't long before Dwight fell for my mom, hard. They'd known each other since about 1960 or '61 and I'm certain that Dwight had always tried to suppress his feelings, avoid seeing her and whatever, but now he found himself in love, badly. And he figured this was his one shot at true happiness and that if the guy she was married to didn't honor her or respect her – didn't seem to actually love her – then he didn't deserve her. So he laid it all out to my father, basically said that if he didn't step aside, he'd tell my mom exactly what kind of husband he'd been. And so one night in 1979 my father flew down to Honduras and never came back. Swallowed up by the jungle, by lies and by his own faithlessness ..." The story hung suspended on another trademark Adelaide Carter pause. "Did that come across a little histrionic?"

"Given the context, not a bit," Elodie said, her mind reeling. Naturally, she'd known that Dwight and Adelaide's mom, Claudette, had been together a long time but the circumstances that had brought them together was news. Pretty big news, actually. "Did you ever see your father again?"

"No ..." Adelaide said. "Dwight's a good man, despite what he did."

"What he *had* to do. The heart wants what it wants." Elodie gave a moment's thought to her own heart and what it wanted. The jolt of sorrow and confusion she felt surprised her; she blamed it on the booze. "Did your mother know?"

"I never asked," said Adelaide. "And I truly didn't want to know."

"But you figured she did, right?"

"Sure. She and Dwight started this company – she had to have had suspicions of her own."

"But didn't want them confirmed?" Elodie said wryly. "Just like you."

"What can I say? I am my mother's daughter."

"And a good thing, too." Elodie smiled. "So now that you've told me all this, are you gonna have to kill me?"

"No, but you're fired."

Both women laughed. Adelaide poured two glasses full of something dark and drunk-making. "Seriously, though," she said. "If you ever mention any of this to anyone I will have to throw you out of an airplane or something."

There was laughter from both again, but this time Elodie's was a little uncertain.

The door to the private room opened. Eduardo and Clayton came in, both carrying trays laden with crusty balls of deep-fried horror. "Enough gossiping, girls, let's talk shop," Clayton said. "What the hell're Elodie and I gonna do about busting up Lulu and Fred McGee? I swear to god, that case is gonna kill me. Or fire me then kill me."

The remark prompted confused looks all around the table. Everybody blamed it on the booze.

*

Charlie sat upright in his seat, completely stunned at what he'd been listening to. "Lulu and Fred?" he said, a little shell-shocked by the queasy mix of memories unleashed by this latest bombshell. Lulu and Fred? *The* Lulu? "What the heck is going on here?" he said aloud; this thing was starting to get as crazy as Rumspringa. Charlie figured he could really use a drink right about now.

Chester Polglase's safe house. Location unknown. 11.57pm

Chester "Buttons" Polglase tried not to cry but it wasn't easy; his ex-fiancée Sara was literally everywhere he looked. There she was as a little girl on the Central Park merry-go-round, outside Brearley on her first day there, outside Blackstone on her first day there, another two outside Fieldston and Geneva on her first days at those institutions. On holiday in Bermuda with her first boyfriend, Chad. Skiing at Stowe with Algernon, boyfriend number five. Shaking hands with various mayors. Cocktails and kisses with celebrities too numerous and numinous to mention.

And there they were on their first date, Chet and Sara themselves, just fourteen months ago.

Chester picked up a pair of scissors and carefully cut Sara's head off, leaving Algernon alone on a slope. He held his sweet, beautiful, smiling ex-fiancée's head between finger and thumb and stared. She was spectacularly lovely and desirable – even without that fantastic body below. They'd been so happy for so long. But then, like the Grim Reaper of Relationship Death, came the endless and painfully detailed planning for their wedding, for their future. Everything had quickly soured and before he knew what was happening he'd gotten involved with that strange ReStart company and they'd set up this whole thing where he had to pretend to be dead for the rest of his life and never see Sara again.

Chester smeared glue on the back of Sara's head then reached across the table for his copy of *American Bride Magazine*. After a quick kiss, he placed Sara's head over the face of the cover bride. His own photograph sat in place of the groom's face.

As Chester stared at the happy couple his bottom lip began a pre-lachrymosal quivering. He didn't like it here in Splitsville. He didn't like it one bit. And consequently very soon the bride's gown was alive and sparkling with his tears.

Holly Hohenzollern's apartment. 11.57pm

Glistening and freshly showered, Ho-Ho Hohenzollern stepped out of her ensuite bathroom wearing only a fluffy pink towel. She stood in the doorway for a moment and then let the towel drop, a fluffy pink puddle at her pink-toenailed feet. She smiled as she bent down and picked up her police utility belt, strapping it around her naked waist before she leapt onto the handsome man lying on her bed.

Clayton Townsend's apartment. 11.57pm

In his small, extremely neat living room, with the air-conditioning on high, Clayton sat in his Eames Lounge chair, his de-panted legs splayed out in front of him on the matching Eames Ottoman, watching an episode of "Lulu & Fred," keenly taking notes, trying to figure out a way to split up the two leads. His still-bugged coat hung on a nearby rack, also by Eames. All the *jenever* he'd consumed over the preceding few hours was still swirling around inside him so it wasn't long before, as was his occasional inclination when he was drunk, he began to talk to the television.

"Lulu, how'd you get together with Fred? Was it love or was it demographically-dictated casting?"

He watched as Fred scrambled beneath a gigantic sofa in his and Lulu's gigantic apartment. The faces he was pulling were somehow making Clayton feel drunker. "Fred, one for you," Clayton slurred. "Which is bigger – your dick or your ego? And is the one responsible for the other?"

When he then found himself wondering if sitcom

characters actually had dicks and egos, Clayton knew it was time to tune out. He fell asleep wishing that Charles and Ray Eames had designed a bed.

The street outside Clayton Townsend's apartment. 11.57pm

Charlie lay in the backseat of the Nova, the calves of his long legs resting on the windowsill. His dangling feet were bare because even though it was almost midnight it was still too hot for shoes. The earpiece was in but Charlie was no longer surprised at anything he heard through it; after tonight's revelations, some fella talking to a TV sitcom couple he was apparently going to disunify didn't seem particularly remarkable. It was odd, no question about that, but in a way it was like seeing your third two-headed calf – somehow you got used to it, and faster than you thought you would.

He wondered how old Lainey would feel about this whole thing, though. That was a whole different kettle of jelly.

Adelaide Carter's apartment. 11.57pm

Okay, it was really pretty late now and he would probably've almost definitely have turned the air-conditioning on when he got in, which would have to have been a couple of hours ago, so the apartment would have had a chance to cool down by now. Right along with his libido. *Ha!* Obviously, she wished she'd switched the air-conditioning on before she'd left for De Kamer, but that would have been environmentally unconscionable, obviously, and no matter how insanely hot it might still be at midnight o'clock in the morning she still had a few principles that hadn't melted away. A few principles and a few desires, both of them heightened by alcohol. How long had she been in the elevator? And where was Tim, by the way? He was also the garage attendant so maybe he was down there. Sleeping prob'ly. It felt like it was taking forever to –

God, that elevator ping was loud when you weren't expecting it.

Okay, the apartment entrance hall was like a desert. Even with the way-too-slippery marble. A little wobbly now so maybe she should remove her heels except bending down seemed like really a lot of effort in her current state and in this current heat so why don't we just press on? The living room felt like a sauna and the kitchen was even worse; two saunas, maybe. So probably old whatsisface, Groucho Kennedy, wasn't actually home, even though it was practically almost three in the morning. Walking carefully along the slippery, shiny wooden beams of the hallway she could see there was no light spilling from under the bedroom door. But why would he have the light on, anyway? Because he was lying in bed reading a book? *Ha*!

Door open; light on; bed empty.

Okay, so the new plan was threefold: grab the air-conditioner remote from her bedside table, getundressedandgetsomesleep ... A few steps into part one she slipped on something and found herself on her butt on the floor, pretty sure something other than booze had helped her get there. It was Rob; there he was at her feet, kind of.

One of his headshots was stuck to the bottom of her shoe, the eyes peering over the top, all black and white and "moody." She yanked her cell phone from her purse and hit his number. She got to her feet, picking up the photograph along with herself.

Heard, "Hi, you've reached Rob Dolen, publisher of 'Primo Magazine' ..." Headed straight into the bathroom. "I can't get to the old phoneroony right now, but –"

Dropped her cell into the toilet bowl. And the photograph of her husband. Flushed them both away. Ha.

Elodie Frontenac's apartment. 11.57pm

No matter what she'd been doing earlier in any given evening, whether she'd had one drink or ten, whether she was alone or with company, Elodie unfailingly followed a prescribed routine in preparation for bed.

She brushed her bright white teeth, then she brushed her red red hair.

She turned off the bathroom light then slipped into bed.

She read ten pages of whatever book she happened to be reading at the time.

She slipped a bookmark into the pages and put the book on her night table.

She lay between the sheets for a moment, staring at the ceiling, thinking about the events of the day.

She turned off the bedside light.

She took three deep breaths and then, a blank moment after the last long exhale slipped from her lungs, she began sobbing.

Charlie Van Linden's apartment. Later

"God, I can't believe I'm finally telling somebody this," Charlie heard Adelaide saying again, as he replayed the recording. "… so complicated that it involves killing a president."

It was the fifth or sixth time he'd run through the entire conversation. He told himself that it was because he was listening for clues, and while there was some truth in that, he had to confess that he enjoyed hearing that husky voice of hers no matter what it was saying.

"Yeah, President –"

That confounded noise again, wiping out the name of the dead president. The president that Dwight Whoeverhewas might have had something to do with killing. Unless Adelaide had a very dark sense of humor and this presidential assassination business was all just her idea of a joke. Which might be the case because people's senses of humor were all very different. Why, back home Abel Lindstrom thought it was terrific fun to break his own nose by running his face smack into the side of a barn every other St Michael's Day. Good times.

Charlie shut off the recorder and hid it under a spatula in a drawer in his kitchen. (Domestic security hadn't been much of an issue where Charlie had grown up and he'd never really got the hang of it.) It was a quarter after four in the morning – dawn in Lancaster County, Pennsylvania; Abel Lindstrom had about another fifteen minutes' sleep left – and time Charlie hit the hay. After he'd stripped down to his boxers, he knelt by his bed, closed his eyes and bowed his head.

"Dear Lord, I pray that you do not exist and that I am therefore doing the right thing where Sallie is concerned. Yours sincerely, Charlie." He paused then added, "Van Linden." Just in case.

He was about to pull back the covers when a thought hit him. He tried to ignore it but already he knew that it'd gnaw at him and keep him from sleep unless he acted on it so he dialed a number in Los Angeles, giving himself pretty good odds that she'd be awake, for whatever reason. "Lainey!" he said when she answered, tickled to hear her croaky late-night voice again. "How you doing, darlin'?"

Dwight Kitchener's apartment. Dawn

Dwight sat on the edge of the uncomfortable Murphy bed staring at the array of photographs spread out on the floor at his slippered feet. There was Jackie's suit and matching pillbox hat, pink and pristine in one shot; blood-spattered in all the rest. There was Texas Governor John Connally sucking in air as he's hit. And there was Jack Kennedy with his fists clenched, raising his arms spastically to his neck as the bullet comes out of his throat. Dwight tongued the scarred lump inside his cheek, sighed mournfully then covered his face with his hands. He'd liked Kennedy the two times they'd met, despite what the President had asked – demanded, really – Dwight do for him. "Christ," he said as a crack of light from the already-warm sun slipped into the gloom. "What a mess."

THURSDAY

Charlie Van Linden's bathroom

At seven o'clock the temperature was already in the high seventies. As he shaved, Charlie decided not to wear a tie; old habits were hard to break, though, so the suit jacket wasn't optional. It was black, but at least it was linen. And lightweight. And Italian. Compared with the heavy, boxcut numbers he'd had to wear growing up it was like putting on the finest bespoke garment ever made. It had been years since he'd worn traditional Amish clothing but he would never forget the burdensome feeling the *mutze* frock coat carried on the shoulders, the unpleasant scratch of rough wool against his skin. Pocketless, collarless, buttonless, colorless. As though the Amish weren't sufficiently removed from the world, and modest enough already. They really didn't need any extra help from fashion.

He left his apartment wondering why he was so preoccupied with all that. Maybe the heat was messing him up. Maybe it was seeing Sallie a few days earlier, and talking with Ms Carter about Sallie's predicament – well, what he saw as a predicament, anyway. As he made his way to the subway station he gradually became aware of what in New York was an unusual sight: simply that people were moving slowly, dazed and depleted as they were by the fifth successive day of oppressive heat. The smell was probably slowing them down a little as well, for there were some extremely noxious reeks rising from manholes, grates and garbage bins. They could really knock you around if you weren't careful, the physical smells of New York City.

Charlie hovered by a coffee cart outside the entrance to 290 Park Avenue. The cart was large and decorated in "ye olde" style, with a red-and-white striped canvas awning sitting atop four ornately-turned wooden poles, two small white wagon wheels at the front, red accents everywhere. Someone's idea of how coffee got around back in 1890. Having been raised with one foot firmly rooted in the past, Charlie could have offered the coffee cart designers of America a few tips about what the carts might *actually* have looked like, if anybody cared. But nobody did; the past was dead, and only the future lived, only the future mattered.

He heard a plane fly overhead, looked up and wondered if Lainey was on it, whether she'd boarded under her phony name. He smiled at the thought and jotted some notes in his green leather notebook.

"Y'know, mister, hanging around my cart here, conducting your business and whatever, you really should oughta buy something. Consider it office rental."

"All right," Charlie agreed. "How much for a coffee?"

"Two-fifty."

"Cream and sugar?"

"Included in the lease agreement."

Charlie laughed and handed over the rent, wondering if the guy was by any chance Armenian.

"No," he said, a little indignantly. "Why would I be? And what if I was?"

Charlie hadn't meant for the words to come out. But there they were staining the air like breaths of fog. Actually, fog was a poor simile given the temperature. So there the words were, staining the air like ...

"What're you talking about, mister, with your stains of fog?" the non-Armenian coffee seller said. "I think you should oughta move along now."

Charlie was about to apologize for ... everything when he saw Clayton approaching 290. He ditched the coffee and quickly sidled over. "Clayton, we need to talk."

"Do I know you?" Clayton asked.

"Not yet. But in about two minutes I think we're gonna be good friends." Charlie took the other man by the elbow and steered him away from the building. "Trust me," he said. "I think we can help each other."

Charlie was due to be lie-detected in about fifteen minutes – he needed to be fast.

Adelaide's office

Elodie stared at the vomit-stained carpet square hanging on the wall by Adelaide's desk. Last night's session had left her feeling a little piqued, and close proximity to the demento memento mori wasn't helping. "I know it's an unusual one," Elodie said, careful to keep the sharp note of desperation out of her voice as she brought up the Endicott Gibbs case. "Extremely unusual, but I think I've hit it, I really do."

Adelaide maintained her silence, still considering the proposition. She appeared to be giving it deep contemplation, but of course that could partly have been due to the hangover Elodie was pretty sure her boss would be suffering right now. Adelaide wasn't exactly bombed when they'd left De Kamer last night, but she wasn't exactly sober, either. And as for that confession … Jesus.

"C'mon, let's give it a shot," Elodie said, careful not to sound too jaunty.

"I don't know. Even for us this is morally perilous. We're not talking about splitting up two people. This a woman and her faith. Who are we to –"

Elodie stopped her. "It comes down to the same thing we always do, and that's giving someone a sort of freedom. We –"

Adelaide pushed back. "But *she* didn't come to us. He did, and that's the difference." Her shoulders rose and fell as she let out a long, despairing breath. "I mean, it's not as if she's involved with Scientologists or Raelians. She's Amish, for God's sake. Except for the beards, they're harmless. What he's asking us to do seems especially evil."

"Well like Clay said, we're all going to hell anyway," said Elodie. "So why not do somebody some good while we have the chance?"

"If good is what we're doing." Adelaide rubbed her forehead with the heel of her hand. "You got a name for the op?"

"Witness Relocation."

When Adelaide laughed at the pun Elodie knew she was getting close.

"I'll get back to you with a final decision after I've poly'ed Gibbs. In the meantime you can begin prelims. But the moment you feel even the slightest qualm about this, I want you to put the operation in turnaround. Instantly. Got it?"

"You know I won't."

"Obey me?"

"Suffer any kind of moral crisis," explained Elodie. "Look, Clayton says he loves what we do, and I do too. But it's more than that for me. I believe in it. It's my faith."

"As the daughter of not one but two ministers, I'm sure you see the irony in that," said Adelaide.

"Irony?" Elodie blinked idiotically. "What irony?"

"That you're –"

"Yes, Adelaide, I see the irony," said Elodie patiently. "I was kidding."

Adelaide looked mildly chagrined. "Right. Sorry. Didn't get much sleep."

"Me either," Elodie said, getting up. "Must be the heat." She took a final glance at the framed piece of carpet and wondered if it still smelled even after all these years under glass.

JFK

As the throng she was in the center of contracted, Elaine Reardon's right buttock tingled. It felt like something between an accidental brush and a deliberate fondle – a deliberadental brondle, maybe. She turned to look at her sitcom co-star, Thurston Brown, and when she saw that he was trying his best to appear composed, that his eyes contained none of the "mischief" he liked to throw about when he was in public – which they very much were at that moment, as they tried to make their way out of the airport and into their ride out front – she knew that it was him delibradentally brondling her. He was that bad of an actor, even off camera.

"Try that again and I'll pop you, Brown," she whispered hoarsely, just keeping it out of earshot of the gaggle of paparazzi that surrounded them.

They'd been in New York – here for some promotional appearances on behalf of the network, the show, their futures – for all of twenty minutes and already she wanted to jump on the next plane out. Something about the place always got to her, maybe the fact that as the self-anointed "greatest city on earth" she was practically obliged to like the hell out of it. What was it James had said about the city? New York is appalling, fantastically charmless and elaborately dire. James was always right on the money. She loved that about him.

"I do not know what it is that you are talking about, Elaine," Thurston said, suppressing a smirk. The dickless wonder.

"Seriously, Thurston, I will deck you right here in front of New York City," she said, louder now. She showed him her little balled fist. "So help me, I will."

The sea of photographers reluctantly parted as Lainey finally reached the sidewalk and the waiting black Escalade. She jumped in and quickly yanked the door closed after her. Thurston's knuckles dragged on the window. She buzzed it down a couple of inches and waved goodbye.

Then got back to chapter thirty of Washington Square: It was almost the last outbreak of passion of her life; at least, she never indulged in another that the world knew about. But this one was long and terrible; she flung herself on the sofa and gave herself up to her grief.

Elixir

Clayton allowed himself another moment of appraisal of the man sitting opposite him. He didn't *look* completely psychotic. Or crazy. Or even mildly discombobulated. In fact, he looked pretty combobulated, all things considered. "All things" being that two minutes earlier this Van Linden guy had physically forced Clayton into the juice bar they were sitting in then laid out this crazy proposal: that Clayton would locate and steal a file of Dwight's and in return Van Linden would lay the groundwork for a bust-up between Lulu and Fred McGee. It certainly *sounded* pretty crazy. Of course, he'd heard crazier things in his life; hell, he'd *devised* crazier things himself in the past twenty-four hours. What was scary, though, was that this guy even *knew* about the Fred and Lulu thing. And Dwight. And the company.

"So do we have a deal?" Van Linden asked. "I save your career, you save mine?"

Clayton pondered this for a moment. "Well, I don't really have much choice, do I?"

"Sure you do. You can lose your job and your chance to change television history. It's up to you."

He was very casual about everything, this Van Linden. Like some sleepy-eyed gunslinger playing cards in a saloon, feet up on the table, hands hanging oh-so-casually by his holsters, ready to draw ...

"How do I know you'll come through?" Clayton asked.

"I will."

Clayton said nothing. He just stared and hoped it looked intimidating. Or at least formidable.

"I promise," Van Linden said.

"How do you know that this file you're after even exists?"

"To be completely honest, I don't," Van Linden said, still keeping it casual and dude-like. "In fact, if you wanted, you could just pretend to look for it then tell me it doesn't exist. But I trust you, Clayton. I like your face. And I have a pretty good hunch that Dwight *does* keep some sort of a file."

"All right," he said. "But I really hope you're on the level with this or else ..." Clayton struggled to come up with a suitable threat. Physicality wasn't really his thing; he preferred to wield the power of words. Although he had to admit he wasn't doing real well with those at this particular moment. "Or else ..."

"Or else what?" Van Linden asked.

Unbelievable. He even made *that* sound all matter-of-fact, like he was just curious to know what Clayton had in mind, rather than trying to throw back some intimidation of his own. "You don't wanna know."

"All right," Van Linden said mildly. "So we're clear?"

"Yep," Clayton said. But he wasn't exactly sure what the plan was. Or if he'd agreed to it. At the very least he'd take a look around for this "secret file" of Dwight's. It might actually give Clayton some leverage over his boss. He was beginning to keenly hope that things really were as Van Linden said they were. They probably were. The guy was too well-dressed to be a whackjob; that suit looked expensive. And Italian.

290 Park Avenue, 101st floor. 11.56am

She was standing at the elevator bank on the 101st floor, her arms folded, this set look on her face, as though she was working security here in this empty waiting area.

Charlie was glad to see her.

Beside her was an enormous, granite-looking fellow, standing with his arms folded, this set look on his face, as though he was working security here in this empty waiting area.

Charlie was less glad to see him.

Adelaide shook his hand. Her skin was warm but – he hated to notice it – a little bit clammy. "Please come with me." She took off down the carpeted hallway, all business, in the opposite direction to where ReStart reception was located.

They came to a small room containing a table with two uncomfortable-looking wooden chairs on either side of it. On top of the table was a machine about the size of a briefcase with a bunch of lights and buttons and dials on it as well as three long, thin metal needles hanging over graph paper wrapped around a barrel. This, Charlie knew, was a psychogalvanic skin response measuring unit; it looked distinctly analog, as though it might've been sold to ReStart by Kruschev himself. He brushed his fingers along the back of his left hand, wondering if his own skin was maybe a little clammy, too, and whether it might affect the galvanic responses. For things to go the way he wanted, Charlie needed to carefully control those responses.

He sat down in one of the bony chairs; Adelaide stood close by, looming over him. The other man blocked the doorway with his arms braced across his chest, as though preparing to fend off an attack from absolutely everything all at once.

"This is just routine," Adelaide told Charlie as she folded back his shirtsleeve. "We're considering taking your case to another level of engagement." Her fingers lingered, just barely, on his cotton shirt.

Finally, she introduced her rock-like colleague. "This is Mr Handy, our head of security. He'll hook you up to the apparatus but I'll administer the test myself," she said. "Would you like something to drink? A soda or a water?"

"No, thank you," Charlie said. He actually would have loved a root beer but didn't want to seem like he was twelve. Ask for a root beer in most big cities and people often took you for a kid or a rube. You had to be careful, especially in a place like New York. In fact, even mentioning the word 'rube' sometimes made a person come across a little rubey, too.

"Are you sure?" Adelaide asked.

Charlie nodded.

"Do you understand everything I've told you so far?"

What? Of course he had. But now that she'd asked him about it he wasn't completely sure. Maybe he'd missed something buried under all that obviousness. Maybe he *should* have asked for a root beer. Maybe if you requested a soda they asked you a whole different set of questions. He nodded again, not too certainly this time.

Mr Handy slipped a rubber cuff around Charlie's upper arm. Up close, his square head looked like it had been carved from pure stone and overlaid with gristle. Another cuff was placed across Charlie's diaphragm and three Velcro bands around three fingers on his left hand.

As he left the small room, Mr Handy told Adelaide that he'd be just outside if she needed him.

Why would she need him, Charlie wondered. What did they think was going to happen in here? Charlie began to feel just the littlest bit perturbed.

Adelaide cleared her throat and looked him in the eye. "Have you ever been instructed in techniques of deceiving or evading lie detectors or similar apparatus?"

Charlie could hardly believe what he was hearing – she sounded like a CIA operative. And the weird thing about that was that it thrilled him a little. He shook his head.

"You need to give your responses aloud, please, Mr Gibbs."

The irony, he thought. "No, I have not been taught such evasive or deceptive techniques."

"Thank you."

"Are you wearing a white cotton shirt?"

He was. It was a Paul Stuart Sussex Pinpoint he'd found in a thrift store in his first week in town; he liked nice clothes and had been really thrilled to find a shirt as fine as this, which he'd never be able to afford new. Then he wondered if he'd said any of all that out loud ...

"Mr Gibbs, are you wearing a white shirt?"

"Yes," Charlie said deliberately. "I. Am. Wearing. A. White. Shirt. Do you need to know what brand?"

"No." In the pause she looked closely at the shirt. "Yes."

"Calvin Klein," Charlie said, glancing at the wavering metal needles, the tiny seismic record of his tiny lie. He looked at Adelaide; she was looking down at the device, chewing her bottom lip while making notes on the paper attached to her clipboard. He felt very ... assessed.

"Do you have a sister living in Pennsylvania?"

"I do."

"Is she Amish?"

"She is."

"Are you Amish?"

"No, I am not."

"Were you raised in the Amish faith?"

"I was, yes."

"How old were you when you renounced it?"

"I suppose my apostasy began when I was sixteen or seventeen, but I'm not sure I'll ever completely shake it. I still find myself touched by grains of faith every now and then."

"On what sort of occasions?"

He said nothing. He wanted to say something like "When I meet someone like you" but he wasn't sure if he could bring it off. If it would sound sincere or corny or like an outright lie. The fact that it was the truth didn't really matter one way or the other.

She repeated the question.

Charlie sighed. "Now and then," he said.

"Is there an ocelot in this room?"

"Is that a trick question?" He wasn't sure if maybe these people were capable of exactly that sort of thing, putting ocelots in rooms and so forth.

"Just answer it, please, Mr Gibbs."

"I'm trying to," he said, genuinely trying to sound genuine. "Is it a trick question?"

"It's a control question," she said, looking at him over the dark horizon of the clipboard. "Of course there's not an ocelot in the room."

"If you say so," he said. Then, with a gasp and a flashing of his eyes he suddenly jumped up on the chair.

Instinctively Adelaide spun around. But of course, there was no ocelot in the room.

It was one of Charlie's skills to make people sometimes believe things that weren't entirely true, however this was the first time it had ever involved any kind of wildcat. He tried not to use it for cheap or nefarious purposes but on occasion just couldn't help himself. (He'd never used his powers to get somebody unworthy elected to public office, so he could live with himself.)

When Adelaide faced him again Charlie was seated and he thought he saw just a touch of embarrassment heating her cheeks. Maybe the hint of an abashed but amused smile, too. "What's your opinion on root beer?"

She waited a moment before saying, "I'm not sure I have one."

"Well, do you like it?"

"It's *soda*." She said it incredulously, as though how could anyone even *think* about such a thing. *Soda!* But the plain fact was that Charlie had grown up without ready access to carbonated drinks, and their existence, while considered almost sinful in some quarters, was important to him. It was probably something to do with freedom of choice and what have you, if you felt inclined to analyze it.

"I know what it is," he said. "I'm asking if you like it."

"If I found myself at a child's birthday party I suppose it'd be my drink of choice."

"Well, your facetiousness aside, it's a very underr–"

"All right, Mr Gibbs," she said, ending it. "Let's continue, please."

He waited, trying to determine if the ambience in the small room had changed, maybe become a little more airless.

"Is your father a dangerous person?"

He gave the question some thought. "Well, I guess that depends on what you mean by dangerous."

"Is he violent?"

"No."

"Is he unstable?"

"No, he's Amish. We're –" Charlie corrected himself. "They're very stable, peaceful people."

"Then why are you –?"

Charlie didn't want to get into all that now and said that he thought this whole thing was to find out if he was being straight-up rather than re-examine the reasons why he had come to ReStart.

"I'm trying to determine if one accords with the other," she said. "So why did you come to us with your problem?" The twin needles scraped and wavered as the machine's black barrel rolled, scratching out the psychogalvanic facts. Charlie's chest felt a little constricted; it was getting harder to breathe.

"Because I want my sister to be happy," he said truthfully. "Do you have any siblings?"

"No," she said sharply. "I'll ask the questions."

"Would you have preferred a brother or a sister?" Charlie said.

"Brother. Have you ever lied to get out of trouble?"

"Does now count?"

"Yes it does," she answered. "Have you ever lied to get out of trouble?"

"No," he said. "Older or younger?"

"Younger. On what occasions do you lie?"

"To prevent someone from getting hurt," he said. "And to get into R-rated movies."

He thought he detected her suppressing an involuntary hiccup of laughter. "Are the lights on in this room?"

"Yes."

"Can you yodel?"

"Yes, I can," Charlie replied.

"*Seriously?*" The word leaped out with such girlish eagerness and delight that the frosty CIA mask was gone for good.

"Yep," he said with a grin. "But please don't ask me to prove it."

By the time she'd stopped laughing, wiping great hot tears from her eyes with the backs of her hands, he'd begun to feel extremely dizzy and ill, two sure signs that he was falling for her, fast and deep, and his only hope was that she'd turn out to be an idiot or a bigot or a world-class transvestite or very happily married or preferably all of those things otherwise he was pretty sure he was finished.

"Last question," Adelaide said, still a little breathless from laughing so hard. Another thing, that laugh of hers sounded familiar. Somehow it reminded him of Irene Dunne. "Do you enjoy telling lies?"

"No," Charlie lied.

Dwight's office

"Why aren't I allowed to change my mind?"

"Because you're dead, Mr Polglase. Dead people can't change their minds. We killed you the other night at the restaurant and now you're dead. In fact, you're not even supposed to be on this coast. Besides, aren't you better off?"

"Actually no. I miss Sara like crazy. I love her. I understand that it's a little inconvenient, but you guys break couples up all the time. Surely it's not too much trouble to put two people back together, especially two people as deeply in love as we are. Or were."

"It's not what we do, and it is a lot of trouble. Especially when one of the parties has apparently died in front of the other."

"I'll tell her I got better. It's not like I was shot in the head."

"You'll tell her nothing, Mr Polglase. Because you will not contact your former fiancée, understand? You will not see her or speak to her again, ever."

"But without her I really *would* rather be dead. I love her. You can't stop me from –"

"I can and I will. I've done worse than this, believe me."

"What am I gonna do without her?"

"Find somebody else or get used to being alone!"

Polglase's chin dimpled. His bottom lip quivered. His brown eyeballs began to drown.

Dwight knew that it was only a matter of seconds before the waterworks began in earnest, and he was in no mood for watching a grown man cry. No mood for it at all. "Mr Handy will show you out," he said, pointing to the enormous man-shape eclipsing the doorway.

Dwight gave some thought to having Mr Handy tail Polglase in order to make sure that he didn't do anything stupid but quickly dismissed the idea, confident that he'd sufficiently cowed the former client. Besides, how much trouble could you expect from anyone nicknamed "Buttons"?

He watched as Mr Handy and Mr Polglase made their way to the elevator at the other end of the floor. When the car began to descend Dwight headed to Adelaide's office. The door was open but she was in the middle of a call.

"A costume party? I'm not turning twelve, Rob," she told her husband. "You want me to dress as a *what?* Yeah, I don't think so. Anyway, will I see you at this Hope for Kids charity thing tonight? It's at the Museum of Natural History," she reminded him. "In New York."

Dwight heard a sharp, exasperated breath shooting out of Adelaide's nostrils. He could picture her mouth, tightly closed as she listened to that sub-moronic husband of hers. Her mother would never have put up with someone as dunderheaded as this Rob Dolen guy. Of course, Claudette Carter had put up with her own goddamn louse of a husband for many years, until Dwight had forced –

"No, I don't think you're having an affair, Rob," Adelaide said, intruding on Dwight's reverie. "Because if you were, you'd already have that damn baby you're always moaning about!"

Adelaide hung up. Dwight stormed in right away. They stared at each other.

Dwight went first. "I'm about one screwed-up job or messed-up client away from quitting this goddamn company," he growled. "Just so you know."

Adelaide's turn. "Fine," she hissed. "And just so you know, my idiot husband is not having an affair with anyone. Including me!"

"So leave him," Dwight said. It sounded almost like an order. "Jesus Christ, it's in your blood, Adelaide."

The words hung in the air like a shot of DDT. For a moment neither spoke. But Dwight knew it was up to him. "I'm sorry," he said. "I didn't mean that."

"Sure you did," Adelaide said, with a dismissive wave of her hand. "Anyway, it's not as if it isn't true. Or a bad thing."

"Yeah, well I shouldn't have said it. I don't know what's the matter with me lately."

"You've always been like this, Dwight."

"Well I'm getting tired of me." He sat down in the chair opposite the love of his life's daughter. It was odd, he thought, that despite the fact that he'd known Adelaide her entire life she'd never felt remotely like a step-daughter to him. But he loved her as deeply and unquestioningly as though she were his own. "Something's gotta give or I don't know what the hell."

"For you and me both. Anything else?"

"Yeah." Dwight's mouth curled into what passed for a smile. "Happy birthday for tomorrow."

"Damn! You remembered." She was genuinely surprised, he could see it in her face. And genuinely disappointed. "Anything over thirty-five is not a happy birthday, Dwight. It's … unspecial."

"I see. Anything unspecial planned?"

"There's a party at the Sag Harbor house tomorrow night. You're invited. Everyone's invited." There was no enthusiasm in her voice at all. After what he'd just overheard, Dwight wasn't surprised. A goddamn costume party – at her age! At his!

He got out of the chair, doing his best to hide his tiredness, his slowness, his ache. He was almost at her door when she said his name. He turned around.

Adelaide stared at him for a long while. "Never mind."

*

When Clayton became fully aware of what he was doing – trying to open locked desk drawers and filing cabinets in Dwight Kitchener's office – he asked himself a simple question: *Am I out of my freakin' mind!?*

Then he ran.

*

Adelaide removed the Endicott Gibbs file from her desk drawer. She picked up her phone, looking at his photograph as she dialed.

"Mr Gibbs? Adelaide Carter …"

He sounded like he was talking from inside a cathedral.

"Yes," she answered, when he asked if she still had his photograph. "I'm looking at it right now." She told herself not to say it, not to make this little joke, then went right ahead and did it: "As a matter of fact, I plan to sleep with it under my pillow."

Adelaide felt as though she was taking one step closer to the edge of a cliff; it felt reckless and dangerous. It felt good. "I've got some news for you."

Elodie and Clayton's office

With considerable effort, Elodie grabbed the wooden bull's head by its horns and shoved it into the suitcase, which she then tried to close. Nothing doing. The case was full to bursting with the items she and Clayton needed for the "Witness Relocation" operation: a skipping rope, a bag of dried octopus tentacles, a box of Lincoln Logs, a flare gun, several photographs of Harrison Ford circa 1985, a selection of fake beards and mustaches, a fox mask, a jar of buttons and zippers, a tube of this dark, bitter stuff from Australia called Vegemite, traditional Amish outfits for herself and Clay, and the Endicott Gibbs file, complete with his Polaroid picture stapled to the front. Elodie stood on the case but the clasp was still a good inch or two away from making the connection. She looked over at Clayton, just a couple of feet away, to see if he was interested in helping out.

Apparently not; he lay on the couch, not moving and clearly not faking the look of fearful preoccupation on his face. He looked as though he was going to start crying or singing, maybe one of those show tunes he inexplicably loved. She removed a dictionary and a thesaurus from her bookshelf and added them to the weight on top of the case. Something was definitely up with him lately, Elodie thought; he'd lost some of that wearying, glib, verbose, buffoonish, puppyish quality. Weird thing was, she kinda missed it a little bit. *Maudite marde!* She snuck another look, just to make sure he was still breathing. He blinked and she returned her attention to the squashing of the suitcase. The heavy books did the job and she locked it up.

"Let's go," she said.

Her partner remained, still, staring at nothing. Suddenly he got up off the couch. "Ah, screw him!" he said, with unusual vehemence. "I'm not risking my neck for a total stranger."

"You're not coming to Pennsylvania for the op?" Elodie didn't understand. "What're you talking about?"

"Sure I am," he said with a confused look on his face. "What're *you* talking about?"

Four Seasons Hotel.
57 East 57th Street

His lies had evidently gone undetected. Good. That would make things much easier. And much more complicated.

Charlie snapped his cell phone shut and took a moment to admire the soaring marble pillars in the hotel lobby. Lainey stayed in Four Seasons hotels wherever she went and this one was a doozy. The truly awesome magnificence of architectural New York never failed to astound and astonish Charlie. He knew that his craned neck and unshut mouth made him look like a tourist yokel, and he didn't care – what good was living in the greatest city in the world if you didn't look around and savor its greatness once in a while? Besides, city folk did almost the exact same thing when they visited the parts he was raised in. The rubes.

"Hello," Charlie said to the young woman at the reception desk.

She had frizzy hair, dyed the color of dark cherries. "Charlie Van Linden to see Agatha Ogglepopple."

The receptionist looked doubtful as she tapped out the name on a keyboard.

"It's a pseudonym," Charlie explained. "Hers, I mean. Not mine. Mine is real."

To her unconcealed surprise, the name appeared on the receptionist's computer screen. She picked up a telephone. "Hello, Ms, uh, Ogglepopple? This is reception. I have a Mr Van Real down here to see you."

Charlie knocked and a moment later, hands on hips in the double doorway to her suite, was Elaine Reardon. She looked completely attractive in all the ways a woman could. He smiled warmly.

A heartbeat or two later she slapped him across the face. It was quick and sharp and it hurt a little but Charlie didn't let the smile slip from his face.

Lainey liked a good slap; in fact, she'd slapped him at the end of their very first date. Slapped him right across the face then said, "See you tomorrow, Charles." It was the stinging start to eighteen months of bitter tears (mostly hers), a remarkable amount of non-bitter sex, an almost equal amount of bitter fights over matters both trivial and titanic, frequent misunderstandings, misapprehensions and misgivings, an engagement that was on and off more times than a set of Christmas lights, and hundreds of slaps across the face, each one with its own perfectly justified reason for being, at least in Lainey's estimation. It was also a lot of fun, their relationship.

When they first met Charlie was new to Hollywood, having gotten onto the writing staff of "Lulu & Fred" by submitting a spec script in which Fred becomes a Mennonite for the Labor Day weekend. Hilarious. It was not the first time Charlie had exploited his cloistered religious upbringing for the purposes of self-advancement. ("Well it ought to be of some use to somebody," he'd say by way of justification.) Trudy From England loved the script and thought Charlie just about the most fascinating and pitiable person she'd ever met, treating him much as her ancestors would have an African tribesman on exhibit in Victorian London.

Lainey lived in a modern marvel in Venice Beach because she could afford to. Charlie lived in an apartment in Burbank because he didn't know any better. They worked together in Television City, almost halfway in between, and kept their relationship a secret from their colleagues. It had begun oddly; one night two or three months after Charlie came on staff they were walking on the studio lot and suddenly found themselves kissing. They weren't sure why, or who'd started it, and decided to go out on a date that very evening to see if they could get some answers. They went to Musso & Frank for cocktails, the Pacific Dining Car for a steak dinner, and finally Chez Jay, a not-quite-dive bar on Ocean Avenue, for a nightcap. And when the date was over Lainey slapped Charlie across the face for kissing her *before* their date started instead of at the end of it, like a normal person.

His cheek sizzled. Her smile dazzled. Outside her suite here at the Four Seasons in Manhattan, Charlie's cheek still sizzling, they looked at each other a while longer before Lainey suddenly leaped forward and threw her arms around him.

He deposited her on the rounded nose of a white leather chaise longue in the suite's living room and sat opposite in an overstuffed chair. Hard sunlight beat down on the glass-topped table between them. The air-conditioning worked overtime. It was a very large room. There was a black baby grand tucked away in the corner; unobtrusive, but not the kind of thing you missed.

Lainey asked if he wanted something to drink from the mini-bar or room service. Charlie shook his head and told his ex-girlfriend that she looked good.

"Uh huh," she said. "Are you saying that because you feel obliged to? Or because I look good?"

"Both. But you do look good." He decided to tell her the truth: "Actually, honestly, you look great."

"Uh huh. What would you say if I looked terrible?" she asked drolly.

"I'd say you looked terrific. But you'd be able to tell I didn't mean it and we'd probably get in a fight, me insisting you look beautiful while you're standing there all pale and spotty, screaming at me what a filthy goddamn liar I am. My blood pressure'd creep up, then I'd probably start getting all loose and ragged and sniffly and, well, you remember how it used to go. So it's a good thing you really do look the way you do."

"Yeah, for both of us."

As they laughed, Charlie saw her glance slyly at her watch, the Hermès Cape Cod he'd bought her for her thirtieth birthday. "Where and when?" he asked. Less than two minutes and it was all coming back to him, why they'd broken up. Two people in the same industry – on the same *show!* – whose lifestyles simply couldn't connect. An actress and a writer; it was always doomed.

Just a touch sheepishly, she told him that she had to be in a limo out back in fifteen minutes. "I'm sorry." She did her shrinking, chagrined mouth. "I have to do a live bit on Steve Lamont and then go straight to the Hope for Kids ball."

"Price of fame, I guess."

"Not fame, Charlie, business," she insisted. "It's part of my job."

"You only wanted a clear-gloss nail polish but they pierced your listening wings and put in some diamond earrings, right?"

Not for the first time during a conversation with Charlie Van Linden, Lainey looked baffled. "Could be," she said, her fingers drifting up toward her earlobes. "I never really understood those little sayings of yours."

"Nobody does. I fashion 'em up on the spot. They make me seem a little different from most fellas."

"You *are* different, Charles." She swallowed and looked away from him. "That's why I still love you. Somewhat."

"Are you saying that because you feel obliged or –"

"Skip it," she interrupted. "I'm saying it because it's true. Somewhat."

"No, it's not." Charlie squirmed in the plumply uncomfortable seat. "You love someone else. You love Fred."

"I fucking hate Fred!" Lainey said, throwing herself backward onto the chaise. "*And* Thurston," she told the ceiling.

"Really?" Charlie asked, easing her into the territory of his idea.

"Very. I'm tired of the whole stupid show. You wouldn't believe what Tom and Trudy From England want me to do next season. I've had it with those idiots." She rolled off the chaise longue and flopped face down on the floor, giving herself up to her grief.

It was cute as hell, but not something Charlie hadn't seen a few times before. He smiled anyway. "I think I can help you, Agatha."

"Really?" Her voice was muffled by the carpet.

"Yes," he said quietly, then began telling her his plan, and what it might cost her.

A short while later, Lainey had agreed to give Charlie's scheme a try; all she wanted in return was for him to be her date at the Hope for Kids ball in a few hours. "I'll supply the tux," she said.

He was getting off easy, and he knew it.

Somewhere in Lancaster County, Pennsylvania. 2.15pm

Elodie looked at the swelling green hills, the red roofs of the barns that seemed to glow as though a scintillating, searing sun was setting inside them, the endless rows of yellow corn, the black and white cows, the white and black sheep, the horses-and-buggies driven by the "Plain People" of Pennsylvania. According to the brochure in her lap, the two most conservative groups drove white-topped buggies, another group preferred yellow tops, and two others used entirely black buggies. Here in Lancaster County, the Old Order Amish drove gray buggies and the Old Order Mennonites drove black buggies. Fascinating ...

Or not.

"How can people make entire weekends out of this activity?" she moaned. "Are they hoping to catch a barn-raising, maybe see someone shunned right before their very eyes?" She felt like a tourist, some pathetic rubber-necker come down from the big smoke to stare at the freaks. It wasn't right.

Clayton said nothing.

The trip from Manhattan to wherever the hell they were right now had taken two and a half hours. Two and a half hours of Elodie's life which would not be refunded. Two and a half hours spent in Clayton Townsend's 1989 Cadillac Fleetwood Brougham d'Elegance. Which was brown and had no air-conditioning. And because Clayton had shrouded himself in near total silence as he sat behind the wheel, the two-and-a-half-hour trip to wherever the hell they were had felt even longer and even more tedious. Wherever the hell they were was green. Wherever the hell they were was pretty. Wherever the hell they were was dull. She needed to shake things up.

"What's wrong?" she said. "You haven't sung a torch song or said anything regrettable in fifty miles."

Clayton said nothing at all and she wondered if their shared tendency toward mock-hostile sparring was maybe getting a little old, along with Clayton and Elodie themselves. Maybe that sort of thing tended to play better with young people in their twenties who preferred revealing themselves through their clothes and tattoos rather than through their emotions. And maybe their badinage was less mock-hostile than *actually* hostile; after all, there was nothing ersatz about last year's lipstick message on the bathroom mirror in the hotel in Newport. And she *did* still hate him for it a little bit.

"Seriously," she said, growing increasingly uneasy in the silence. "What's the matter?"

Clayton opened his mouth, but all that emerged was a yawn. That could be boredom, exhaustion or a show of contempt. The first two she could understand, but if he even dared harbor any ill feeling toward her after what he did that weekend in Rhode Island … But that wouldn't be like him – that wouldn't be the Clayton Townsend she was once so beguiled and besotted by. But neither was this new silent bastard.

Elodie looked out the window at a horse dragging a plow through a field and she wondered again what drew people here as visitors, especially when all the locals wanted was to be left alone. Her own excuse was business; she was here to excommunicate a woman from her life, her history and her God. Which was a far more noble reason.

Maudite marde! The way she could douse any faint spark of moral inquiry with sarcasm stunned even her. Stunned and, if she was being truthful, sometimes repulsed her.

"Clayton," she said firmly. "I want to ask you something and I need an honest answer."

He turned and looked at her; she knew that he knew she wasn't kidding around.

She took three deep breaths and let it out. "Do you hate me?"

Danbury, Connecticut.
2.34pm

The cheap briefcase in Quigley's hand was heavy. There was absolutely nothing in it – not so much as a paperclip – but it weighed a ton. He'd been carrying it from home to work and back again for nigh on thirty years now and he was tired of being dragged down by it, tired of being handcuffed to it and being defined by it, if only in his own mind. He passed the white clapboard church he always passed twice a day, once in the morning on the way to the station and once again in the evening on the way home. Zion's Hill United Methodist Church, a lovely small building in the Greek Revival style, with covered lamps on either side of the ten-step staircase that led to the entrance ... Quigley had spent thirty years at Northeast Mutual, the average year containing 260 business days, minus some vacation time, a handful of sick days and sundry other subtractions meant that that church (which Quigley had never set foot in because he was a Baptist) was almost as much a part of his life as was his own home, his job or his wife. Quigley was a claims adjuster at Northeast. Quigley had a head for figures and he calculated all too quickly that he'd passed Zion's Hill United Methodist Church about seven and a half thousand times. Which in turn meant that Quigley had trepidatiously arrived home to approximately three thousand seven hundred and fifty icy greetings from Mrs Quigley.

Mrs Quigley: loving mother, devoted homemaker, cheating whore.

Quigley passed a milk truck. He passed a mailbox. He passed a stone bridge on which sat two staring squirrels. He passed beneath clouds, power lines, and the heavy, gnarled branches of oak trees. And as he stepped from shadow into sunlight, Quigley thought about his wife, how long she'd been having the affair with their neighbor, Ben Hood, what had precipitated it (boredom, he guessed, along with frustration, anger, curiosity and probably some lust), where they did it, how often and whether she enjoyed the sexual act or, as it seemed when she was with him, merely tolerated it. He had no answers to any of his ponderings.

All he knew for sure was that if they split she'd be into him for exactly half of everything he'd worked for his entire adult life. Half the house, half the car, half the savings. Fifty percent of everything she'd contributed one hundred percent of nothing toward. It wasn't right; as he'd told the man named Dwight when they'd met the previous week, *she* wasn't the one dragging a heavy case to a hollow job day in day out.

He turned into his street, Carlyle Street, and passed a very large moving van parked diagonally opposite the path that bisected his front yard. He took the path up to his porch, and the porch steps up to his front door. He lived in a cream-colored double Cape Cod that he loved every square inch of, from the shingled roof to the basement linoleum.

Still holding his briefcase, Quigley opened the apple-red front door and stepped inside. He placed the briefcase where he always placed it – on the hall table where he'd placed it almost four thousand times before – and was surprised when it fell straight to the floor. He looked down: the hall runner that covered the floorboards was half gone, neatly cut lengthwise. The hall table was only half there, too, split precisely down the middle. Half the hooks on the coat rack were missing. The picture hanging next to the coat rack now only contained half a sea and half a sailboat.

And so it was throughout Quigley's house: in the living room half a couch faced half a television; half a bed lay in the bedroom. Every last item in the kitchen was divided down the middle. Every book and magazine and record album was halved, cut right down the middle. The floors were half-covered in carpet, linoleum, rugs. Quigley was quite stunned but far from unhappy. So this is how it was going to end; this is what the people in New York had come up with. It felt entirely appropriate and Quigley was pleased. On his face was a half-smile.

Half a block away. 2.48pm

A short distance down the street, in front of Ben Hood's two-story Victorian, Eduardo de Villalobos put the truck into gear and eased away from the Quigley house. Behind him, in the truck's large trailer, was one half of every item from the house. And a chainsaw.

Abel Lindstrom's rear pasture. Lancaster County, PA. 3.15pm

Elodie and Clayton lay flat on their backs, side by side, on a gently sloping field staring up at a cloudless sky-colored sky. The Cadillac was by the side of the rutted road, steam or smoke or some kind of cloudy gas spuming from under the hood. A Triple-A repair van was on its way but the operator had warned them that, because the only location they could offer was "somewhere in Pennsylvania," it would probably be a while. There was a cool breeze and there was silence, two things that Elodie observed were in unfortunately limited supply in New York City. She thought about where they were, and the reasons that had brought them there. She thought about the contents of the suitcase in the backseat of the car, and what she and Clayton planned to do with all those things: sever somebody from her family and her faith. To remove love from her life and replace it with doubt, and perhaps hate. Elodie thought about that weekend in Newport with Clayton a year ago, splitting up on the Sunday morning because of ...

"D'you really think we're going to hell because of our jobs?" she asked quietly.

"If there's a hell, we're definitely on the invitation list," Clayton answered. "I mean, if not us, who?"

"True enough," she agreed, although without much enthusiasm. Something had happened to her; something to do with what she remembered was her conscience. She didn't know why it had suddenly crept up on her, and she didn't much like it. "We've earned our place among the damned. Who are they to deny us our due?"

"Don't they know what we've done?" said Clayton.

"What we've worked at so hard and for so long?" Elodie's voice croaked a little. "What we've *achieved?*"

"Doubters."

"Deniers."

"They're haters."

"And liars!"

"They're dirty, lousy…" Clayton paused. "I can't think of the mot juste."

"Bastards."

"Hmmm, not quite."

He struggled to come up with something. She couldn't wait and released the torrent that had built up inside her night after night after night: "Wife-betrayers, husband-ruiners, vow-betrayers, homewreckers, lawyer-feeders, child-destroyers, family-killers, faith-demolishers, *juste de la chnoutte* motherfucking girlfriend-dumpers!"

The outburst – appearing all the more sudden, loud and vicious in the bucolic calm that surrounded them – worried Clayton a lot. This was a new level of bitterness (and volume) for Elodie, and he knew that at least some of those epithets were directed right at him. Probably the French-Canadian one toward the end. The rest of them applied to, well, just about everyone Elodie had ever met, including herself. He moved his left arm slowly toward her shoulder, wanting to comfort her, tell her that they wouldn't be going to hell – probably – if there was one – which there probably wasn't, anyway – and that things would be okay and that he was still hopelessly, idiotically, transcendently in love with her. But his outstretched fingers stopped short, and a moment later retreated without touching her.

She took three deep breaths and waited for him to do something, say something. But he did nothing. There was a cool breeze, and there was silence.

CBC Studios. 542 West 57th Street. 5.30pm

Lainey sat on the leather couch waiting waiting waiting for Steve Lamont to drop by for a pre-show chat. She hated to complain about her life – even in the privacy of her own thoughts she shuddered at the specter of ingratitude – but for all the wealth, privilege and glamor that accompanied stardom (even television stardom) there was a hell of a lot of attendant sitting around waiting, as well. On set, on call, on tarmacs, in hundreds of limousines, hotel rooms and green rooms like this one. Fortunately, Lainey liked to read, and always traveled with a book, but even as *Washington Square* sat open on her lap and her eyes ran across thin black smears of words, she couldn't concentrate; Charlie's audacious proposal kept blocking out everything else, even Trudy From Fucking England's "history-making telly" idea, the one she was supposed to hint about on Steve Lamont's show, live in front of an estimated viewing audience of 6.5 million. Followed by the YouTube audience of every last geek and troll on earth for all eternity, or until somebody switched off the Internet, whichever came first.

She tried to think about something else. How many celebrities, she wondered, had farted right where she was sitting?

There was a perfunctory knock on the door, followed by Steve Lamont's head. Steve Lamont was thirty-nine. Steve Lamont had been thirty-nine for several years now, Lainey seemed to recall. And he looked almost exactly the same as he had when Lainey used to watch him on "The Late Steve Lamont" when she was a kid; wavy blonde hair that made him look like a pretty-boy TV cop from the 1970s. Teeth. Rings. Tan. His shirt unbuttoned one button too far. Steve Lamont had been promoted to "Steve Live" a few years back, when he was thirty-nine.

"Steve Lamont says 'hi'," Steve Lamont said.

Lainey's forehead crinkled in bewilderment. "Okay ..."

Steve Lamont grabbed a handful of peanuts from the snack table and sat himself down on the couch, way, way, way too close to Lainey. "Great to finally meet you, Elaine. In the flesh-wise." Steve winked. Then smiled. Then winked again, probably in case the first one hadn't worked, Lainey guessed.

"Thanks," she said. "You too ... wise."

"Whatcha reading?" Steve asked, pointing to the mysterious thing on her lap. "A book?" He picked it up, copping a leisurely backfinger feel of thigh while he was at it. Lainey looked at the offending hand, then the offending face, but said nothing.

Steve Lamont winked – again. "So, I heard a rumor that there are some biiiiiig surprises for the end of the season – T or F?"

T or F? Lainey looked confused. *Tits? Fanny?* Was he seriously expecting some nudity on America's number-one sitcom?

"It means 'true or false'," Steve explained, throwing a peanut into his gaping maw.

"Oh," said Lainey. "I H Y B U W W D T S."

Steve looked mystified.

"It means, 'I hope you'll be using whole words during the show'," Lainey clarified.

"Riiiiight." Steve smirked. Steve nodded. Steve tongued peanut skin from his front teeth. "You're feisty."

If there was one thing guaranteed to make Lainey want to punch someone in the brain it was being called "feisty;" next would be how he liked that in a –

"I like that in a woman," said Steve. "You got a little hot Latina blood in you?" He poked her; he *actually* poked her in the breast. "Gosh, pretty small," he said.

That was it. "Okay, is this some kind of a goof?" Lainey asked, because she really wasn't sure, and she really had to know. "A character you're developing? If it is, it needs work. If it *isn't*, you need help."

Steve unstuck himself from the couch and headed for the door. "Wizzywig, Elaine. What you see is what you get. Steve Lamont is the real deal."

"Well, Elaine Reardon's real sorry to hear that."

Steve Lamont held up a warning finger. "Don't do that. Talking about yourself in the third person is Steve Lamont's thing."

Twenty minutes later Lainey was on another couch, this one made of blue velour, watching Lulu McGee present a roast turkey to her telehusband, Fred, who, not for the first time in the five series of "Lulu & Fred," was wearing an oversized bib. Thurston believed that bibs were inherently funny, and the bigger they were the funnier they were. He may have been right: the audience members here at "Steve Live" were laughing their moron heads off. The TV turkey deflated like a sinking soufflé. The audience whooped. Sitting behind his glass tonight-show-host desk, Steve Lamont clapped and wiped away imaginary tears of imaginary laughter.

He composed himself sufficiently to take care of some network housekeeping; the whole reason Lainey had flown 2400 miles. "Little preview of the season finale of 'Lulu and Fred', ladies and gentlemen, next Tuesday night at nine on CBC."

Steve Lamont primped his hair and grinned his oh-gosh-oh-golly grin as he turned to Elaine. "Lulu's a fun gal, isn't she, Elaine? How much of yourself do you bring to her?"

"Well, I'm a pretty fun gal myself, Steve. Kind of a non-stop laff riot, as you can see. So I guess without me Lulu may as well be more or less, y'know, dead."

Steve laughed nervously. "Dead? Gosh, I hope not."

"Yeah, me too," Lainey said. Then she winked at Steve and added, "I guess."

"Dead?" Steve repeated, actually sounding worried.

"She's not real, Steve."

"Right. Of course. Nevertheless, I think I speak for millions of Americans when I say that I hope Lulu remains in good health."

"What about me?" Lainey asked. "What about my health?"

"America and I wish you well, too, Elaine."

"Thank you, Steve." Lainey turned to Camera Three. "Thanks, America."

"You're welcome. So, I've heard rumors that there are some big surprises in store for Lulu and Fred fans. What can you tell me?"

"What I can tell you – but let's keep it just between us – is that Fred and Lulu's dream of having little Freds and Lulus runs into some obstacles."

"What kind of obstacles? Not 'death' I hope." Steve waggled his fingers over the troubling word.

"No, Steve, not 'death'." Lainey's own finger-waggling was both bitter and facetious. "I guess the biggest problem they have is when they discover that Fred is completely and utterly dickless." She made a shocked "O" of her mouth, framing it with palms flattened against her cheeks. "He has literally no penis to speak of."

Steve's laughter was nervous and thin. "I can see how that would be a problem."

"Oh, I'll bet you can, Steve." She leaped off the couch, scooted over to the transparent desk and reached between Steve Lamont's legs and felt around. The audience went crazy with whoops, cheers and foot-stomping. Lainey loved it, and hated herself a little for just how much she loved it, how shameless she could be when she felt the urge. "Yep, just as I thought – nothing!"

Steve turned a rattled shade of red. But he still grinned that golly-gosh grin.

"It's like a Ken doll down there!" Lainey squealed.

"Oh yeah?" he said standing up and unzipping. "Say hello to ten-point-five inches of Steve Lamont!"

The audience fell silent.

Lainey looked down and said, "Hello."

Dwight's office

Dwight was about ready to kill this ditzy dame on the other end of the line; the best he could do was strangle the telephone cord. "Are you listening?" he said. "Tell him – in big letters so he can't miss it – that I, Dwight Kitchener, called and that he, that is me, Dwight Kitchener, wants to get drunk with him, that is your boss, Arthur Munro. Got it!?"

He listened as Art Munro's PA read the message back. With each clause his veins tightened and his blood pressure rose a few diastolic notches. By the time she was finished, Dwight was ready to scream. "No, I'm not calling on behalf of Dwight Kitchener, you imbecile!" he screamed. "I *am* him!"

Arthur's office

Ten blocks south, four blocks west and eighty-eight floors below where Dwight was screaming at Arthur Munro's PA, Arthur Munro leaned waaaay back in his chair and leveled his gray eyes at Charlie Van Linden. "I sincerely hope you had a more productive day than yesterday, Charlie."

"I did," Charlie said. "And I think I'm onto something pretty big. Maybe huge. And I think you're gonna like it." Charlie's heart was beating fit to burst out of his chest he was so excited. He was on the verge of telling his boss the whole ReStart story – nothing redacted – and the capper was solving the Kennedy assassination. Not bad for a couple days' work. "I can almost guarantee us a Pulitzer."

"This is the Sentinel, Charlie. We have plenty." He waved his arm around as though Pulitzers were everywhere for all to see. And in fact, from where he was sitting Charlie *could* actually see two or three of the large gold medals right behind Mr Munro. But still.

"Well, I don't. I don't have any," said Charlie. "And I really want one. Ever since I –"

"Please stop dancing around it like a ballerina," Mr Munro said. "What do you have?"

Charlie reached into his jacket for his notebook. "Okay, this is pretty darn amazing. But it looks like one of our presidents –"

Arthur Munro's gaze shifted from Charlie over to the doorway as his personal assistant popped her head into the office. "Excuse me Mr, uh, Munro," she stammered. "I have an urgent message from a Dwight Kitchener. He – Mr Kitchener – wants you to call him, that is Mr Kitchener, asap, that is, as soon as possible."

"Thank you." Mr Munro blinked and slipped his gray eyes back to Charlie. "You were saying something presidential?"

Actually Charlie didn't know what he was saying anymore. The message from Dwight Kitchener to Mr Munro changed everything. He took a long, deep, stalling breath. He enjoyed lying and considered it one of his best skills, especially when it was used for good, like on this occasion. Or like this occasion would have been if he could come up with a good lie.

"One of our presidents, what?" pleaded Munro.

Anything.

"Well, okay, right." Charlie flipped through the pages of his green notebook. "Okay, so what I have, sir, Art – Arthur – is … approximately … this." Charlie swallowed; there was a very real chance that Mr Munro might get very upset and do something they'd both regret if he didn't deliver. And he was about to extremely not deliver. "One of our presidents seems to've passed a law about hot dog espionage tax and coffee-cart office rentals."

There was a long silence from Charlie's boss and protector. As Art Munro tilted his head far to one side a vertebra in his neck popped loudly. "You know I like you, Charlie."

"Yes, sir, I do," said Charlie. "I just don't know why."

"Well I'm sure I have my reasons," Mr Munro allowed. "Although I cannot, at this moment, recall even one." He closed his eyes for a moment. "No," he said, opening them again. "Nothing. Suppose I've only got myself to blame. I mean, you've been here, how long? Less than a year, right? And the trouble began almost immediately as I recall. I'm sure you know what I'm referring to."

A mass of silent, white-clad Unified Koreans danced in his head as Charlie nodded. Good times.

"Of course you do." Mr Munro got out of his comfortable chair and began pacing the floor. "Even someone as frequently soft-headed as you isn't about to forget a forty-five million dollar lawsuit in a hurry. A lawsuit based on your so-called 'exposé'. Streets out front jammed with all those protesting loonies."

"Moonies," Charlie corrected. "And they dropped the suit."

"Please don't interrupt me when I'm firing you."

"You're firing me?" This seemed excessive. This was the third-best job in New York journalism and Charlie really didn't want to lose it. Probably.

"Well, Charlie, I importuned you yesterday to come up with something solid," Mr Munro said, his voice cracking a little. "And all I'm hearing from you is humorous remarks about fast food and presidents. It's not fair." Mr Munro sniffed.

Charlie hoped his boss wasn't about to start crying. "Are you allowed to fire me?"

"Unfortunately, I am." Munro was standing directly

behind Charlie. "If I wasn't I wouldn't be doing it. Although somebody else certainly would."

Charlie covered his notebook with his hands, hoping Mr Munro hadn't had time or clear enough vision to notice Dwight K's name among the scribble. "I was only kidding around, Arthur. Having a little fun. I really am onto something big. Probably. Just give me another twenty-four hours and I give you my word I will never kid around or have any fun in your presence again." Arthur returned to his desk but didn't sit down. "I was raised Amish, sir – we're physically incapable of telling lies."

"No." Mr Munro folded his arms. "I don't see any way around this, Charlie. Please clear your desk." Arthur removed a hankie from his coat pocket.

"I'm not gonna beg," Charlie said. And immediately wondered if the words had actually come out.

"It wouldn't make any difference."

They had. He decided to run with it: "Don't make me beg."

"I won't."

"Cause it'll humiliate the both of us."

"I know."

"Good, because I'm really probably not going to."

"That's fine."

"There's no need to."

"That's true."

"Great," said Charlie with a big smile. "So we're agreed then?"

"About what?"

"That if I don't have something for you by five-fifteen tomorrow I'll quit. And I'll kick my own ass while I'm doing it."

Arthur Munro shook his head, and smiled despite himself. "Twenty-four hours. Not a second longer."

Charlie backed toward the door. "That's a wise decision, Mr Munro. You're very wise."

"I don't feel wise, Charlie. I feel manipulated." He wiped his eyes with the corner of his handkerchief. "I'm not crying, by the way, it's some sort of an allergy."

"Sure, Art, I know that," Charlie said. But he knew what was really going on.

"There is nothing 'really' going on," Munro insisted. "It's *allergies*."

Charlie needed to learn how to keep his mouth shut. His mouth and his brain.

Munro sniffled and said, "What was that about your brain?"

Good lord – was there no end to it?

Right out front of the *New York Sentinel* Building.
7.15pm

The limousine was precisely where she said it would be; right out front of the vast steel-and-glass entrance to the *Sentinel*, where there was Strictly No Parking Anytime – No Exceptions. But you could park anywhere if you were a media somebody, anywhere you liked. Charlie climbed in back and saw a neatly-pressed tuxedo laid out on one of the long bench seats. Lainey looked up from her book and smiled at him; there were a few thousand watts missing and Charlie wondered if she was having second thoughts about the whole thing. He unbuttoned his shirt and asked her how it went with Steve Lamont.

"This time tomorrow my television career will be officially over," Lainey said, closing the book over her index finger. She looked him up and down. It made Charlie a little bashful, his naked chest all on display like that. Not that he wasn't decently sculpted – years of yard work and dirt work had seen to that – but the last woman he'd been bare skinned with was a long time ago; the fact that Lainey herself *was* that last woman was immaterial.

"Mine too, if this Clayton Townsend fellow doesn't come through." *Or if I'm flat-out wrong about this whole thing,* he thought.

Lainey reached into a string-bound paper bag and handed him a crisp white dress shirt.

He slipped it over his brown torso. "How do you feel about giving up TV stardom? You won't be able to just park everywhere all willy-nilly once you become one of the rest of us, you know."

"I'm aware of the drawbacks, Charles. Nevertheless I feel quite liberated," she said. "And quite terrified. How do you feel?"

"Oh, not too bad." Before he knew it he'd held out a flapping white cuff for Lainey to fasten. It was sheer force of habit; Lainey had always done his cufflinks whenever they went somewhere fancy. "It'd be better if I wasn't broke, but you can't have it all, or else ..."

She cocked her head in one direction and raised her eyebrows in the other, a classic Lulu move. "Or else what?"

"Or else ... then what would you want?" He took off his shoes and pants, and, without too much indignity and slipping, managed to put on the top and bottom of the tuxedo. Outside, he saw the words carved into the stone above the great arched entrance to the Museum of Natural History: TRUTH KNOWLEDGE VISION. "How do I look?"

"Extremely fuckable," Lainey answered, then slapped him across the face. He knew what it was for; it was for splitting up with her and moving back east. "See you in there, Charles." Lainey wanted him to be her date for the night but the charity board wanted her entrance to be made with her TV-husband Thurston Brown by her side.

Such was the price of fame, and another reason why she and Charlie hadn't made it as a couple.

Charlie's cheek turned a hot shade of red as the limo came to a stop and the door beside him opened. He looked up as a gormless face peered down and in. "Hello, Thursty."

"You!" Thurston said, non-specifically.

Thurston slapped Charlie across the face and climbed in back of the limousine.

Charlie wasn't quite sure why Thurston slapped him across the face. Had to be something, though.

Pennsylvania. Night

By the time the Triple-A guy had fixed whatever was wrong with the Caddy it was dark. And not the Manhattan type dark Clay and Elodie were used to; this was rural dark – black and silent and still. This was the overwhelming, forsaken darkness of the past, of her former home, of Jonquière, QC, Canada.

Elodie needed sound so she cracked a window; outside smelled of warm earth and manure. The sloped two-lane road was straight and potholed. Every so often the car's wan headlights picked up the murky blur of a horse pulling an enamel-black buggy, but instead of looking cute and "old-timey" as it might have in daylight each one looked utterly alien and sinister. Light came from a yellow quarter-moon and distant bonfires that threw shadows against the walls of red barns. There were hitch-hikers that Elodie ordered Clayton not to stop for, not even to slow down for. Every few miles, she caught glimpses of hatchet-bearded men holding the hands of blank-eyed children standing as still death in dusty road-side ruts.

"Jesus," Clayton gasped, as they drove by a pair of goats tethered to a fencepost. "Is this still America?"

"Maybe we've arrived in hell early."

"It's too late to start the op now," said Clayton, his eyes glued to the thin, unspooling road ahead of them. "How about we find a motel?"

The words were music to Elodie's ears but she kept it low key. "*Très bien.*"

Clayton cleared his throat as he swerved gently to avoid a hole in the road. "Same room?"

That was somewhat unexpected and quite a pleasant proposition but again she played it cool. "Also fine."

"I don't mean for sex purposes."

He had to blow it sometime. "I know you don't," she said, reaching behind her and pulling the fox mask out of the suitcase. "It's because you're frightened."

"That's right," Clayton confirmed nonchalantly. "I didn't want you to get the wrong idea, is all."

There was no chance of getting the wrong idea, Elodie thought. She had Clayton Meldrick Townsend all figured out. Which was kind of a shame. She slipped the mask over her face, turned to him and said, "Boo."

Hall of North American Mammals. 7.40pm

The dimly lit hall was crowded. There were four black-headed bison plodding across the Wyoming plain, big-horn sheep standing high and proud on a snow-capped mountain peak, a pair of moose locked in combat, a family of grizzly bears, and two tense jaguars in the purple light of a Southwestern desert dusk. There were wolves leaping through the Minnesota snow on a blue full moon December midnight, a curtain of Northern Lights blazing upward from the horizon behind them. Charlie stood on the other side of the glass, alone, calmly sipping a beer, with mere seconds to live before the wolves tore him apart. He turned round and took in the room at large.

There were one hundred and fifty of New York's most wealthy and sophisticated humans milling about, creating an alcohol-fueled conversational clamor, a subdued din that had no equivalent in the animal kingdom. It was an unpleasant sound and Charlie wondered what effect it might have had upon any of the nearby creatures had any of them been unfortunate enough to be living there at that moment. At least they wouldn't have understood any of the snippets and excerpts Charlie was overhearing:

"It's so difficult for my daughter to find boys at her school. Half of them are gay and if they're not gay, they're Jewish!"

"I have another charity event after this one, for some kind of dystrophy."

"She raised three children without a nanny or a house-keeper! Can you imagine?"

Suddenly, like birds taking flight, their attention flocked toward the front of the hall as Elaine Reardon and Thurston Brown entered, arm in arm, dazzling even these polished East Coast Corinthians with their brash and dusty Hollywood glamor. The rush to be closer to the television stars created a small pocket of disinterest, in the middle of which Charlie was thrilled to see Adelaide Carter.

Wow.

She was wearing a long black dress, with a full glass of Champagne in each hand, that silver pendant dipping into the darkness of her cleavage. The way she stood there, one hip thrust to the side, her chin angled slightly upward and her long black hair tumbling in tresses onto her bare shoulders, she looked like she'd walked right off one of those vintage French alcohol posters. She was facing his direction – staring directly at him, as a matter of fact – and seemed unsurprised to see him standing there.

Charlie indicated the two glasses. "Waiting for some-body?"

"Nope. I had three or four drinks before I got here and they're beginning to wear off." She drank the glass of Champagne in her left hand and placed it on a passing waiter's tray. "So I'm catching up."

Charlie laughed loudly. Adelaide smiled and there was clear, almost rhapsodical delight in it. The line sounded familiar to him, as though he'd dreamed it or dreamed of a woman saying something like it. There was an uncontained enthusiasm for life – or at least for drinking – in what she'd said that Charlie found irresistibly, tumultuously winning.

A cloud of cheers and applause rose from the other end of the room as Lainey and Thurston took the stage. Charlie said, "Nice couple, huh?"

"I suppose," she said. "If you like that sort of thing."

"A lot of people think they're a match made in heaven."

"If heaven is a network boardroom." Adelaide looked over her shoulder for a moment then turned back to Charlie. "What brings you to an event like this, Mr Gibbs?"

"The catering," he said. "I love finger sandwiches but I don't know how to make them myself."

"You just remove the crust."

"What about the stuff in between?"

"Use anything you have that's pink or green," Adelaide said. "But stay away from the medicine cabinet."

Charlie laughed, enjoying himself. "But all my favorite materials are in there."

"Is that so? If you ever throw a party, have someone else do the food. So why are you here?"

"I'm Elaine Reardon's date."

"Really?" The look on Adelaide's face – skeptical and amused – told Charlie she wasn't buying.

"Yep. But she's kinda busy. And what brings you here?"

"I was hoping to meet my husband." She turned around again.

"Well there're plenty of suitors to choose from," Charlie said, his arm sweeping the room, presenting the men to her. "Got your eye on anyone in particular?"

Adelaide's glance whipped around the black-and-white sea. "Frankly, I don't see much difference between them, do you?"

"No, but I ain't looking."

"'Ain't'?"

"Makes me sound folksy."

"*Are* you folksy?"

"No," said Charlie. "I'm actually pretty urbane and debonair but today's lady seems to prefer folksy."

She raised her eyebrows. "'Today's lady'?"

"It's another folksification."

"Well it's not doing much for me," Adelaide said bluntly. "You sound like a simpleton."

Okay, Charlie thought, *she's got a little bite.* "What made you change your mind about my case?"

Adelaide held up a long, elegant index finger, placing it just a pucker from Charlie's lips. "Not here, Mr Gibbs. It's a cliché, but I don't like to mix business with pleasure."

He released the two tickling breaths of "uh" and "huh" onto her fingertip. "Are you experiencing any pleasure right now?"

She took her finger away. "No, but I don't want to set a precedent in case things take a turn for the better."

"Would that involve finding a husband?"

"Not a husband, *my* husband," she clarified. "I already have one."

"Oh …" Charlie said, trying to hide his disappointment. "Really?"

"Apparently."

"Is he here?" Charlie suddenly ducked and hid behind a standing plant. "Can he see us?"

"We're not doing anything."

"I know, but we ought to be careful anyway," he said. "In case things take a turn for the better."

The Old Town Bar.
45 East 18th Street

Dwight wanted a cigarette, bad. But there were about a hundred things stopping him from having one; his promise to Claudette was number one; New York City's sobsister by-laws preventing smoking anywhere a person went were the next goddamn ninety-nine. Ever since Giuliani sold Times Square to Disneyland the entire city had been prettifying and pussifying itself into unrecognizability. Wasn't too long ago that the tiled floor of the Old Town Bar woulda been covered in butts and ash and matches, the joint choking in a cloud of smoke and booze-heated chatter, the music would be different – better – and the TV would be showing a Mets game instead of another goddamn Yankee slugfest. And Claudette would be by Dwight's side, saying something wise and funny and making him love her so much he'd wonder how he'd ever gotten by without her. The place still had plenty of character – a beautiful old wooden bar, pitted and stained with decades of drinking, and a menu that was guaranteed to take a few months off your life expectancy with every choice – that wasn't the problem.

What it didn't have was the sort of atmosphere Dwight craved, where men still wore hats and a knife fight might break out at any moment.

Still, it had booze.

Dwight dropped the whisky shot into his beer and thought about what Art had just told him. "Holly Hohen-zollern?" he said to his old friend. "The name's familiar."

"It was written on Charlie Van Linden's notepad, right beside yours. Along with some pretty strange stuff about ice-cream and some sort of lizard. So I figured –"

"Yeah, I remember it now." They'd called it "Night of the Living Iguana," Dwight recalled. Some goddamn literary joke for their own amusement. Townsend was probably the one behind it. "Can you reassign him?"

"I already gave him another day," Arthur said. "Of course that was before I knew he was looking at your … business."

Holly Hohenzollern was NYPD. This was not good. At the end of a bad day in a shitty week, this was extremely not good.

"I won't run whatever he comes up with."

"Yeah, and I appreciate it," Dwight said. "But if he *does* come up with anything solid there's nothing stopping him from taking it somewhere else. Is he that kind of a guy?" He swallowed the Boilermaker in two swift gulps then burped loudly. A couple of Brooklyn types gave him a sidelong look; they reminded him of Fron-tenac and Townsend, especially Townsend. Dwight stared back, cracked his knuckles loudly and the pair looked away.

"He's persistent. And pushy. And somewhat vexing. And several people around the office want to kill him." Art narrowed his eyes. "You're not gonna kill him, are you?"

"Not if I don't have to."

Dwight shook a Marlboro from the pack, put it between his lips and looked around the crowded bar, daring anyone to say a goddamn word about it. He had no intention of lighting it – because of his respect for Claudette, not Rudy – but he dearly wanted somebody to make something of it anyway.

Kleinhooftersville Motel & Eating House. Happy Horse Road, Kleinhooftersville, PA. 7.25pm

There was "Liver & Onions & Liver" and "Haddock Served in Aspic" and "Thrice-Baked Rabbit" and something called "Estimation of Quail." The menu of "Traditional Nord-Hollandse" cuisine was discouraging enough but the smell coming from the kitchen really put the lid on dinner – somebody out there was boiling dark nappies in milk, Elodie was sure of it.

She wondered how well this obscenely authentic aspect of Dutch culture would fare in New York alongside De Kamer.

Clayton had stopped at the first motel in the first town – although "town" was stretching it; this place was more like a settlement – so here they were, surrounded by knotty pine furniture, pink and white lace doilies, old wooden farming implements hung on the wall and blinking Christmas lights strung up in the cobwebby corners. Their fellow diners were large, pale family groups out for a night of deathless conversation and bottomless soda.

Clayton asked Elodie what she was going to have.

"Nothing," she answered. "I need Mylanta just looking at this menu. Why would you bake a rabbit three times?"

"When once is already too much." He looked at the list again, even turned it upside down hoping to see something even faintly edible on it that he might have missed. "This is like European prison food. I'm just gonna ask for a lettuce. They'll have lettuce, won't they?"

"Yeah, for the rabbit," Elodie said, swallowing drily. "Before its first trip to the oven."

Clayton's stomach turned. "You know I couldn't eat for practically a whole month after we broke up."

"Well you've made up for it since."

"No I haven't!" He took a quick glance down at his gut. "Have I?"

"God, you're so vain. I'm only kidding. You look fine. You look good."

Clayton was all too visibly relieved. "So why'd you break up with me?"

"First of all, I didn't date you for your looks, Clayton. I'm sure that was why you were so eager to go out with me, but I'm not quite that superficial. I dated you because … Well, I don't remember now. Maybe I was bored one day and you said something halfway interesting. Second, *you* broke up with *me*. Remember the Lost Weekend in Newport?"

"Certainly. Do you remember the ashtray full of Froot Loops?"

"I do. And I think neither of us has forgotten the lipstick messages on the bathroom mirror, right?"

"With the endless Broadway melody medley? Of course not."

"So why'd you break up with me over it?"

"*You* broke up with *me*," Clayton insisted. "I never wanted to break up but the combination of the message in the bathroom, the Froot Loops and the endless melody, what could I do?"

"You mean what could *I* do?" she corrected, beginning to get upset. "And I had no choice."

"What're you talking about? It was your decision. You said to me the Sunday morning after the melody medley that we couldn't go on like this."

"That's right. Because it was pretty obvious that you were not interested."

"Not *interested?*" Clayton's voice broke with anguished disbelief. "I'm ... I was completely and utterly in love with you, El. I was gonna ask you to marry me." He looked away from her.

Elodie was quietly stunned by the revelation. "Then the message in the mirror ...?"

"Yeah, that really hit me," said Clayton, picturing the awful, brutal words. He still felt physically ill every time he encountered a woman wearing L'Absolu Rouge by Lancôme. "I'll never know why you wrote that."

"I didn't write it, Clay. I assumed you did, because you were ..."

He looked at Elodie again – her green eyes were shimmering – and he knew she was telling the truth. Clayton shook his head.

"Well, who the hell ...?"

As they stared at each other it hit them simultaneously; the one person who had such intense dislike for Clayton that his fondness for Elodie would be neutralized. And who could conceive of and execute a plan bizarre, fiendish and ingenious enough to end their relationship with each blaming it on the other. Goddammit!

"Dwight!" they blurted at once.

"*Maudite marde*! That bastard!" said Elodie. "I don't believe it."

"We have to get back to the city, now."

"No," she said, standing and grabbing her partner's wrist. "First things first." As he tumbled up out of his chair, the abominable menu fell onto the linoleum.

The dining room was silent; every face turned in their direction. "My apologies, people of Kleinhooftersville," Clayton said to the room. "We did not mean to interrupt your dinner with our love. Please return to your meals."

Dwight's goddamn office

Dwight's hands shook a little as he flicked through a box of files in his office. A belt from the bottle of Talisker in his desk drawer would fix that. Ease the shakes and tamp down the head of steam that had been building since he found out that there was a New York goddamn *Sentinel* reporter looking at the company. But considering what he had planned for the next hour it would be best to keep a clear head – well, as clear as it remained after that quick but intense Boilermaker session with Art.

He found the file he was after and scanned it. There was Holly Hohenzollern's picture, her address in Murray Hill, her squad number, her interests … He found the information he was after and looked at his watch – perfect. If he left right away she'd more than likely still be there.

Dwight creakily got down on his hands and knees then pulled up a square of carpet. Beneath it was the face of a floor safe. He punched in his code – 112263 – and removed his revolver, a five-shot Smith & Wesson Model 36. With a flick of his wrist the cylinder popped open; it was fully-loaded. It'd been a long while since Dwight had fired a weapon – in either pleasure or anger – and he rue-fully admitted to himself that he wasn't entirely sure how good his aim would be. His aim, and his commitment.

Maybe a belt would help with both of those things.

AMNH

Up on the stage, flanked by Thurston Brown and a couple of charity dignitaries, Lainey Reardon wound up her speech. "And so it gives me great pleasure to present this donation from all of us at the 'Lulu & Fred' show to Hope for Kids."

Charlie joined the large crowd in enthusiastic clappification. He may even have whooped. He hoped not; whooping was a folksification too far, he believed. Lainey and Thurston slowly worked their way through the room, past the jackrabbits and brown bears, shaking hands with sharks, chatting with foxes.

"Do you hope for children, Endicott?" asked Adelaide.

"I prefer to let 'em hope for themselves," Charlie replied.

"That's not what I meant."

"I know what you meant. And no, I don't. Not right now, anyway." Although maybe it'd actually be pretty nice to be a father to a little girl. Or boy. "How about you?"

Adelaide canted her head to one side and shrugged. "Eh ..."

"Now that's the kind of commitment I like," Charlie said. "So, shall we?"

"Shall we what?"

"Shall we leave? Shall we go have dinner or play a little squash or drink some eggnog or something?"

The eggnog and squash business sounded vaguely familiar, she thought. But not particularly appealing. "What about my husband?"

"Oh, he won't mind." Charlie waved away the suggestion. "We're not doing anything."

Lainey and Fred drew nearer. Lainey waved at Charlie. He ignored her; if she caught up to him and blew his cover he was finished.

"Charlie!" Lainey cried, waving more urgently, perhaps even a little theatrically.

"And your alleged 'date'?" Adelaide asked. "How will she feel about it?"

"I think she's cheating on me."

Lainey made herself even more flamboyant. "CHARLIE!" And loud.

"With someone named Charlie, apparently," said Adelaide.

"The lucky bastard." Charlie took Adelaide's hand and pulled her toward the exit. "Quick! There's an ocelot after us!"

She didn't resist – not even a little bit.

Phew.

*

Half-hidden behind a stone pillar, Holly watched Charlie Van Handsome and the pretty lady from the evil company hightail it out of the museum like they were being chased or something. As though the great big bisons in the glass case behind her had suddenly come to life and were marauding all over the place. Holly kind of wished that was true. Charlie and Mrs Whatsername looked good as a couple, like stupid movie stars, and they were even holding hands and even though this was pretty much they way she figured things would pan out it still made her a little angry and a little sad. A bit of bison marauding might take the edge off.

She patted the bulge of the Beretta in her handbag, almost like it was a little tiny baby or something. Just to know it was there, not to pull it out and shoot anybody who might deserve it for ruining people's lives!

The gun reminded her that she had to hurry out of there herself because she was late for her Thursday night appointment. Which was pretty lucky, actually, because she'd built up a lot of tension that needed releasing. "Bye bye, bisons," she said then ran out to grab a cab.

A bad part of the city. Dark

Dwight stood opposite a large unadorned brick building. He was a little tight, loose but alert, and prepared to do whatever was necessary to protect the company. This area, a dark industrial wasteland of factories and parking lots under the Manhattan Bridge not far from Pike Slip, was perfect for discovering or dumping bodies. He slipped the revolver behind his belt and headed toward a doorway in the side of the three-story building. A warm stench rolled in from the East River, or maybe from the fish market a few blocks south. The smell, the seediness, the lurking danger: this was Old New York, and Dwight felt right at home. He loved it; the only thing that could have made it better was if someone stepped out of a shadow and tried to mug him. As he opened the door he heard the distinct crack of gunfire coming from above. Beautiful. He checked his 36 one more time.

He made his way up the creaky, underlit stairway, feeling one of the stairs bend and crack a little under his weight, making a mental note to be careful on the way back down. He pushed open another door and saw her at the other end of the large room, unloading her Beretta into a human-shaped target at the end of the gallery. He was impressed; the groupings were tight and controlled, her technique confident and unhurried. *The NYPD could use more like her*, thought Dwight. It was as though she could hear his observations. She took off her ear protection and shooting glasses and slowly turned around, almost like she expected to see him standing there.

Holly Hohenzollern and Dwight Kitchener regarded one another without expression, their fingers twitching on the triggers of their weapons.

"Are you Dwight?" she asked.

He nodded. "Holster your weapon. I know the clip's empty," he said calmly. "You're coming with me."

She thought about it for a moment then did as he asked. He waved her over toward him with the barrel of his gun. "You first," he said, pushing open the stairway door with his foot. She walked into the shadowy gloom. This was going all right: Dwight was relieved not to have had to test his resolve. He was getting way too old for shooting people, especially women with nice big cans.

In fact, he didn't take his eyes off Holly's nice big can until it was too late.

Somewhere else.
Sometime later

Adelaide looked around and took stock of the situation; where she was, who she was with, what she was doing. There had been some sort of hiccup in time; one moment she was idly bantering with Endicott Gibbs at the museum then all of a sudden, without seeming to travel or think or want, she was sitting opposite him and a glass of pinot in a French restaurant. She literally had no idea how she'd gotten there or where exactly she was – this place could have been in Manhattan or Montmartre – but it wasn't creepy, like she'd blacked out or something; it was more like minutes and hours had ceased, leaving in their wake a series of disconnected moments that were already taking shape as sweet, distant memories even as she breathed them in.

"I shouldn't be doing this," she whispered.

"It's a difficult situation for both of us," he whispered back. The restaurant was oppressively quiet; murmuring waiters seemed to move on slippered feet, diners hunched toward one another in clenched groups, dark purple velvet wallpaper absorbed light and peripheral sound.

"You're not the one who's married," she reminded him.

"No, but I'm broke," he said. "I can't even afford the butter in a ritzy joint like this. And when the check arrives, well, I'm sure you can imagine how humiliated I'll be."

"Actually, I don't see feelings of humiliation as part of your psychological make-up at all." The truth was she'd never seen anyone so relaxed, so comfortable in his own skin. Who looked so good in a tuxedo.

"Oh really? How about feelings of emasculation when I have to let you pay for dinner?"

Just talking to this man was more laughs – more fun – than she'd had in months. "Who says I'm paying?" Adelaide teased. "And how is it someone like you is broke, anyway?"

"Someone like me?"

"Well you've obviously got money, Endicott. Or at least had it."

"That's true," he allowed. "But I grew up poor – or at least not worried about money. So it's no big deal not to have any. I'll get by."

She took a sip of pinot and asked him if he was being folksy again.

"No, I'm being sincere." He rubbed his lean jaw; in the cocoon of silence she could even hear the stubble scraping against his rough fingers. She had to stop herself from imagining those fingers on her skin. Too late. "You've always had money, haven't you?"

"Well, I haven't had to worry about it," she said. "Like you."

He laughed sardonically. "Not worrying about money in Manhattan and not worrying about it in Pennsylvania farm country aren't quite the same thing." He looked her in the eye, making sure he didn't accidentally come across as crazy or creepy, and said, "You can call me Endi, if you like." He was dying to hear how it sounded when she said it.

"All right," she said, then didn't say it because a waiter materialized and whisperingly requested their orders.

Their eyes locked across the table, each waiting for the other to speak.

"No, that's okay," Adelaide finally said. "We won't be staying."

"We won't?"

"You won't?" the waiter susurrated.

"We can't," Adelaide said. "We're late for the … thing. The very exciting thing we have to do. Right now." Time hiccupped again and she found herself out of her chair and running for the restaurant door – actually running – and not giving a damn how many people stared.

But he was just sitting there, staring at her like she was crazy. "Come on!" she shouted, jangling cutlery and craning necks up and down the room. "We have to hurry!"

When at last he grinned and stood up she could have screamed with joy. In fact, she may have – who could tell what did or did not happen in a swallowed breath of time?

Bethesda Terrace, Central Park

They were halfway around Bethesda Fountain when Charlie pointed over to their left. "See that kid over there, the one sitting on the bench, crying?"

The stone bench at the edge of the lake was unoccupied but Adelaide let that detail pass.

Charlie continued, "You know what's wrong with him? He dropped a record called "Little Shirley Beans" that he bought for his kid sister, broke it into a million pieces and now it's the end of the world. He's beyond consolation, the poor fella. Shall we go over and tell him everything's gonna work out fine?"

"*Is* everything going to work out fine?"

"Oh sure," Charlie said. "He's what – fifteen, sixteen? It'll be another five years at least before he finds out just how horrible life can really be."

Adelaide turned away from him as she smiled. "I think perhaps you're missing the point of 'The Catcher in the Rye'."

Charlie pulled his straightest face. "Of the what in the where?"

She turned back, unsure if he was joking. His face gave nothing away, and she didn't want to come across as either patronizing or naive. The pause in the conversation grew awkward.

When Charlie finally grinned there was audible relief in Adelaide's laughter. "Folksy *and* sly," she said. "That's quite a rare combination, Endicott."

"My folks made me take lessons." He was really getting used to this new name and wondered if maybe he'd like to keep it when all this was done. You stick a nice capital K in the middle and that was a fine name.

"In glibness as well?"

"No, that I learned by correspondence," he said. "It was a short course but very expensive." Charlie bent down and pretended to tie his shoelace, inserting a physical break in their conversation that allowed him to abruptly change the subject. "How old were you when you realized everything wasn't going to work out fine? Unless, of course, everything did."

"Everything didn't," Adelaide said firmly, clenching her jaw because that cheap little remark he dangled after the question actually made her mad. Of course, he had no idea just how wrong certain parts of her life had turned out so he couldn't actually have meant anything by it. So it was probably herself she was mad at, as usual. She added Herself to The List. "I was twelve," she said.

"What happened?"

She tilted her head. "Why am I telling you?"

"There's no-one else around," Charlie said. Then took a chance. "Besides, who else've you got?"

She wasn't sure if he meant what she thought he meant by that but decided what the hell, anyway. "Well, it wasn't anything explosive but it was profound," she said.

"It was simple disillusionment, the realization that everybody lies, no matter who they are or what their relationship to you is. This particular deception was trivial, banal even, but it was a lie nonetheless and when I discovered it, I was overwhelmed by it."

"What was it?"

"That's not important," she said.

"Well, it sort of is," he insisted.

"My mother had always said that she and my father had honeymooned in Hawaii, and I'd seen pictures of them there, pictures she claimed were of a trip in late November 'sixty-three. But when I was twelve I found out that they couldn't possibly have been there at that time."

November 1963. Charlie made sure that his next question came out calmly, as though he was merely interested rather than about to explode with curiosity. "Where were they?"

"Somewhere else," she said.

He knew not to push it, it would make her suspicious, but he had to know where. How else, he wondered, could he tease out such an intimate and seemingly irrelevant piece of information?

The way she was staring at him, it must have looked like he was thinking hard because all of a sudden she'd stopped in her tracks and said, "I know what you're doing. You're using the dates and trying to work certain things out." Charlie swallowed; it was like she was reading his mind. It was a little scary. "Let me save you the trouble – I'm thirty-four. I was born a long while after my parents were married."

Oh, right, Charlie thought. "Oh, right," he said. "Thanks. Numbers aren't exactly my strong suit. I'm more of a words man."

Adelaide looked up at the winged woman, the Angel of the Waters, standing atop the three-tiered fountain in the center of Bethesda Terrace. She carried a lily – the symbol of chastity and virtue – in her left hand, her right extending outward in blessing of the water below. Beneath her were four smaller bronze figures representing Temperance, Purity, Health and Peace. It occurred to Adelaide that she had very little in common with that statue. "What exactly do you do for a living?" she asked Charlie. "What kind of writing?"

I'm a reporter and I'm supposed to be working on a story that'll expose and ruin your company but I'm thinking about quitting because I'm falling for you except I'd really like to know where your folks were around midday on November 22, 1963 just in case one of them has anything to do with changing history, not that I'll hold it against you if they did. And my real name's Charlie Van Linden. Well, actually it's Charles Van Linden, but that's just nitpicking.

They'd completed another half-circle of the burbling fountain before Charlie spoke. "Did I answer yet?"

"No."

"Good," he said, relieved. "Well, I'm actually considering various aspects of my future, so right now I can't say for sure. What's your husband do that keeps him out this late?"

"I don't know what he actually *does*, but he's a magazine publisher," Adelaide said, her voice drained of color. "He puts out an insipid, anachronistic men's magazine called 'Primo'."

"A tits and abs number?"

"That's right," said Adelaide. "I think he thinks he's Hugh Hefner."

Charlie wondered if there was a connection here; Holly Hohenzollern's ex-boyfriend was a magazine art-director. But of course there were thousands of magazines in New York City. Or hundreds. Dozens, at least.

"And he wants me to be his Bunny."

"Then he's a damn fool," said Charlie. "If you don't mind my saying, you're no bunny."

"Well, I –"

"You're more of a goddess." He pulled his gaze from Adelaide and looked up at the lady carrying a lily on top of the fountain. A weighted silence told Charlie that the last few words had slipped from his tongue. Oops. But he wasn't particularly sorry.

Adelaide couldn't speak; no-one had ever said anything like that to her, and she was overwhelmed by it. She sat down on the low stone wall that encircled the fountain and let her fingertips dip into the cool water so that she would know that this moment was real. Then she looked across to the other side of the terrace hoping that she wouldn't see Holden Caulfield on a bench, sobbing inconsolably over a shattered record.

Kleinhooftersville Motel.
Room 4

"Well …" he said.

"Yes, well …" she said.

"Well, that was."

"Yes, it certainly was …"

A long pause followed. Given the situation – where they were, and what had recently occurred there, the fact that they were both hot, sweaty and naked – this was not the ideal place in a conversation for a pause. So the pause ached. It ached and it stretched and when Clayton couldn't stand it any longer he said, "You mean that in a good way, right?"

"Of course," Elodie said.

Clayton *phew*-ed then leaned over to the side table and shook a cigarette out of a pack.

"You don't smoke."

"I do after sex."

He lit up and immediately began coughing and spluttering.

"Been a while?"

The remark – quick and funny – reminded him of the

repartee they'd developed while they were taking improv classes. He laughed. And kept on puffing.

"I don't want to go to hell, Clay."

"That's quite understandable. It gets terrible reviews." *Okay, that's enough with the jokes,* he thought. *A smoker should try to be a little more serious.* "D'you actually believe in hell?"

"Of course not, but that's way beside the point. The point is that I'm having second thoughts – serious moral qualms – about this operation. I can't help thinking it's, well, wrong."

"Really? Have you had some sort of epiphany that I don't know about?"

"No. I don't know. I just …" As she sat up and leaned against the wooden bedhead, the sheet slipped and revealed her plump, pale breasts. "I don't think I can do this anymore. Any of it. I mean, what if I turn into Dwight?"

"Yeah, I know what you mean."

"You wouldn't be in bed with me if I was Dwight."

Clayton looked at Elodie's rack. "That's extremely true." He wondered if it was inappropriate to stare at breasts that he'd just had his face buried in. He looked away, wondering if that – the looking away – would make him appear as though he felt ashamed of looking at them – at her – in the first place. Which he wasn't, of course, either of those things, but you couldn't help –

Screw it. He looked at them – at her – again.

"You know you're not wearing sunglasses, don't you?" Elodie said. "I can see where your eyes are looking."

"What?" Clayton said. "When? I wasn't –"

"Stare all you want, Shifty," she said. "But only at these – no-one else's." She jabbed him in the shoulder with her finger. "As I was saying, if I was Dwight I'd be breaking us up. And I don't want us to be broken up. Again. That's not what should be happening. To anyone."

"What're you saying? There should be more love in the world?"

"Well I probably wouldn't put it like that, unless I wanted to throw up right here in bed. But yes, I suppose that's what I'm getting at." Elodie looked at the window near her side of the bed; the pane was black. She could see herself reflected in it as clearly as a mirror. "I mean, just think about what we're supposed to be doing tomorrow morning – separating a woman from her father, her community, her faith. It's disgraceful, Clayton. It's disgraceful and arrogant and sick and unconscionable and I'm not gonna do it anymore."

"Huh."

"And neither are you."

Clayton butted the cigarette. Blue and gray smoke wraithed around the lampshade.

Elodie took three deep breaths. "Okay, kill the lights," she said. "I'm ready to go again."

Strawberry Fields

He talked a lot, this Endicott Gibbs character. Really let his brain have its way with his mouth. Lucky most of what he had to say was pretty amusing and interesting. Insightful, in some ways, too, she had to concede. He was no dummy.

She and Gibbs were strolling past Strawberry Fields, the little garden on the western edge of Central Park planted in memory of John Lennon. She looked up at the crenellated silhouette of the Dakota Building, where Lennon had been living when he was shot. Rosemary of *Rosemary's Baby* had lived there, too. Nothing seemed to grow too well here in Strawberry Fields. They should try vegetables. Give peas a chance. Adelaide laughed to herself and for no reason the thought occurred to her that maybe she might actually want to have a baby. Not the devil's spawn, of course, not Rosemary's, but her own, a regular baby. Why not? A little girl. Or boy. It might make her life … better? More interesting? More worthwhile? Less self …

She realized that he'd been talking, had possibly even asked her a question. She slowed her thoughts down and waited to see if she could catch up with him.

"… wondering if ReStart is doing work that used to be the province of the clergy. Trying to save relationships, souls and so forth. Do you think that's true?"

Still grilling her. Jesus, ease up already. "I'm completely comfortable with what we do," she said firmly. "We do good."

Gibbs nodded. "But what if the various couples that come to you, what if these people were better off apart? Then what good are you doing?" Smiling.

Damn him. He turned her inside out and upside down and she didn't know what to make of him and she really wanted to kiss him. Damn him.

And *having a baby?* Where did *that* come from out of nowhere all of a sudden?

Kleinhooftersville Motel. Room 4

And then they did it again. And again. And once more after that. It was a record for both of them – one neither of them ever wanted to attempt to break. Because love could hurt, literally.

88 West 75th Street.
11.50pm

Charlie and Adelaide lingered outside her apartment building. She stood on the lowest of the wide stone steps that swept up to the entrance. Charlie was down on the sidewalk, allowing her to loom over him a little. Their night was drawing to a close but neither wanted it to end.

"You can't come up, you know."

"I know."

"I'm married."

"You mentioned."

She leaned down and kissed Charlie on the lips. It lasted just a moment too long. "You shouldn't have let me do that."

"I know," Charlie said quietly. "I apologize."

"Don't let it happen again." She thought about the next day, her birthday, the party at the weekend getaway in Sag Harbor. "Say, Endi, are you busy tomorrow night?"

Charlie thought about the most famous presidential assassination of all time, and whether the mother of the woman who had just kissed him was somehow involved.

He thought about what he wanted from life, and how things might turn out if he made one decision over another – not just for himself, of course, but for the accounting of history and for the good and decent people of America. He thought about putting his heart before his head and having it broken. "Well, that really kinda depends on what happens tomorrow."

To be completely honest, the whole thing actually made him a little queasy.

FRIDAY

Somewhere between Kleinhooftersville and Hartburg, PA. 9.40am

After getting up early and not having a "traditional Nord-Hollandse" breakfast of *hagelslag*, herring, sliced cheese, powdered coffee and *sinaasappelsap*, which was evidently what they called Tang in Holland, Clayton and Elodie cheerfully paid the motel bill and excitedly threw their stuff into the back seat of the Cadillac. It was a beautiful day, crisp and clear and cool. The sky was bluer, the clouds whiter, the grass greener. The air was pure and the birds sang more joyously! Here was Life that you could grab ahold of and make truly your own! It was hard not to think that Pennsylvania was the greatest state in the union, and tiny Kleinhooftersville, population 297, the greatest place in that state! Maybe they'd move there, settle down and raise a couple of kids and –

Or it could just have been that they were both terrifically horny. They checked into the motel again, tainted the sheets for a couple of hours then hit the road for real this time. The sky really *was* spectacularly cerulean, the grass almost edibly lush and green, and the birdsong heartwarmingly lovely; however, upon spent reflection, there would be no rural relocation, no fevered embrace of the heartland. Elodie and Clayton were back together and in love; they had not gone insane.

"Let's get the hell out of here," Elodie said, settling behind the wheel.

"So what happens now?" Clayton asked a few minutes later, as they passed a feed store on a piece of road called Lost Acres.

"In regard to what?"

"Not to put too fine a point on it, but everything," Clayton said. "There've been a few developments and revelations in the past twenty-four hours and I can't help wondering how they're going to affect us."

They passed the dilapidated wooden street-front of the Happy Horse Funeral Home and Crematory.

They passed House of Vacuums.

They passed a couple of all-you-can-eat-atoriums.

"Well, Clayton, if I've learned anything from bumper stickers, it's that today is the first day of the rest of our lives. We can do anything we want. What would you like to do?"

Clayton thought about what Dwight had done to him and Elodie, the many months of togetherness he'd cost them. He thought about how he might be able to make Dwight pay for that. "Let's swing by Dwight's dump," he said. "He has a pretty sweet pair of cufflinks I'd like to steal."

They passed a twelve-link chain of oldsters in ancient, rusted wheelchairs slowly filing into a VFW Hall for Friday morning bingo.

"Sounds good," she said.

The last thing they saw, as they left town on Locust Street, was a sign out front of a Baptist church praised God, Guns and Glory.

Boy, would they not be moving there.

Back in the city.
Around the same time

Charlie studied the messy diagram laid out on the floor of his living room. He'd begun working on it as soon as he got home from his night with Adelaide, and continued on it after rising at dawn. Laid out on large sheets of paper was everything he'd learned – and hypothesized – since meeting nutty, disgruntled, lawful-gun-carrying, possibly-Prussian Holly Hohenzollern on Wednesday morning. Names linked to dates, other names, locations, firm connections arrived at, tenuous connections guessed at. Lines, arrows, question marks all scrawled in the black marker Charlie held in his hand. The whole thing was a mind-spatter of hopeful conjecture, outlandish presumption and downright desperation. The key players were:

Adelaide Carter. ReStart boss?

Holly Hohenzollern. NYPD

Felix (magazine art-director/ex of Holly Hohenzollern) + an iguana + strawberry ice-cream. Dead parents = actors???

Rob Dolen (publisher/Adelaide's husband)

Clayton + the small woman he was with (her name?)

The priest/not-priest – who was he? ReStart?

Someone dressed as the Devil (or the Devil Himself? Unlikely)

Lainey Reardon & Thursty Brown aka Lulu & Fred

Adelaide's father – left his wife/Adelaide's mother in summer 1978

Adelaide's mother (deceased) – formed company when? '63? With Dwight K?

Dwight Kitchener (co-boss of ReStart?)

Arthur Munro (needs no introduction. Pal of Dwight K's)

Lyndon Johnson (died January 1973)/Lady Bird?

John F Kennedy (killed November 1963)/Jackie K?

But it was all forest and no trees. Or all trees and no forest – whichever way that thing was supposed to go. Even removing iguanas and ice-cream from the equation it was hard to see how it all added up. And if the company really *did* exist to break up relationships, how did the Kennedys fit into the picture?

He stared at Jack and Jackie … They hadn't been "broken up" – he'd been assassinated. How could the company have been involved in that? Wasn't it only supposed to act at the request of one of the parties *in* the relationship? So who in that relationship would have wanted …?

When it hit finally him Charlie's mouth fell open and the marker slipped from his fingers. He didn't hear it land.

Murray Hill. 10.50am

Dwight's cell phone lay on the table buzzing. Dwight sat nearby, staring at it angrily. It was Adelaide, no doubt calling to find out where the hell he was and if he was coming in to work. It buzzed a couple more times before he answered it. Pressing the tiny goddamn buttons and holding the goddamn thing up to his ear was a little difficult because of the goddamn handcuffs.

He told her he wouldn't be in today.

She asked why not.

"Because I damn well *won't*, Adelaide." His tone was even more sour than usual. Because of the *other* goddamn handcuffs – the ones biting into his ankles and shackling him to the chair in Holly Hohenzollern's tiny goddamn kitchenette. "I have my reasons."

She asked if he'd be coming to her party tonight.

"I dunno," Dwight said. "Just a second."

He muffled the phone against his chest; it felt cold against his naked flesh. "You want to go to a party tonight?"

Holly smiled and nodded. "Sure!" she said brightly. The dead-still barrel of her Beretta remained trained on his heart.

Dwight's gaze drifted down to her hips, just as it had last night when they were making their way down those stairs. And when the stair he'd forgotten to be wary of snapped underneath him, sending him careening forward, reaching out for her shoulders to break his fall but seeing her step neatly to the side, back flat against the wall and letting him take the tumble, ending up on his back at the bottom of the stairs, her standing over him with her Beretta pointed at him just as it was right now. Ah well … It'd gotten him into some trouble but if he was going to die anytime soon, Holly Hohenzollern's nice big can would be a fine last image.

He sighed and brought the phone back up to his ear. "Yeah, I'll be there," he told Adelaide. "Is it all right if I bring somebody?"

She asked if he meant a date.

"No, not a date" he said, looking into the nine milli-meter black hole of doom pointed at him. "More like an escort. See you tonight."

He hung up and said to Holly, "We'll take my car."

"If you say so."

Dwight watched her pick up her phone and dial. "Hey, Bobby," she said to some goddamn idiot named Bobby. "Sorry I didn't make it last night but something came up. Anyway, it's all set for tonight. I'll see you in a couple hours, honey. I miss you!"

Holly hung up.

"Boyfriend?" Dwight asked.

She shook her blonde curls. "Oh gosh, no," she said smiling. "Bobby D's a complete slimeweasel. I hate him and he's gonna pay for what he's done."

So maybe Holly's nice big can had led this Bobby into some trouble as well, Dwight thought, pleased that per-haps he wasn't the only chump around here.

57/57. Suite 5102

Charlie thumbed through the trades – *Variety* and *Hollywood Reporter* – as he waited in the hallway outside Lainey's suite. There was nothing in either magazine about her performance on Steve Lamont last night. He was surprised and a little miffed; no blowback might tank his deal with Clayton, and no deal with Clayton meant no file of Dwight's, which meant no proof of Charlie's JFK assassination hypothesis, which meant no Pulitzer.

The door to Elaine's suite opened and revealed Thurston.

Thurston slapped Charlie across the face.

"Hello, Thurston," Charlie said.

"If you say so." Evidently Thurston was expecting the line "good morning" and wasn't about to ad-lib his reply.

Charlie asked if Elaine was in.

"Sure," said Thurston, cracking his knuckles as though preparing to punch Charlie. "You know why I had to slap you, don't you, Van Linden?"

"For cutting out on Lulu last night at the ball?"

Thurston nodded solemnly and stood aside. "Enter, you," he said.

"You might want to stick with the French version of that particular phrase," Charlie advised.

He found Lainey, dressed in jeans and a white t-shirt and somehow making it look elegant, relaxed, chic and unpretentious all at once, doing nought but lolling on the chaise in the living room. She rolled off and marched up to him with her hand drawn back, ready to give him what-for right in the kisser.

Charlie held up a finger and stepped back. "Thurston already took care of the formalities," he said. "I'm sorry about last night, Lainey, I was following a lead."

Lainey's eyebrows shot up skeptically. "Oh yeah? Looked to me like *she* was following *you*."

Thurston sat down at the baby grand, lifted the cover and stared at the keys as though trying to figure out what they were.

"So, I see the manure hasn't been redistributed by the windmill yet," Charlie said.

"What?"

"Y'know – the fallout from last night's shenanigans."

Lainey glared at Charlie, putting a finger to her lips. She motioned toward Thurston, who remained seated at the piano, seemingly oblivious to anything else in the room.

"Attempts are being made to suppress it."

"Oh." Charlie's face crinkled up. "That's not good." Charlie chewed on his bottom lip. "But I thought it was live."

"On tape. Almost nothing's *live* live anymore, you know that." Lainey's hands found one of their preferred resting places – on her hips. "And pardon me for asking, Charles, but what's it to you, exactly?"

"Well, my Pulitzer kinda depends on it."

Thurston suddenly came to life. "What's what to him?" he turned around and asked Lainey. "Are you two back together? What about us, Lulu?"

"Elaine," she told him coldly. "Charlie and I are not back together, Thurston. As for us, there is no 'us'."

"America thinks so," Thurston pouted.

"America's kidding itself," she said. "Block your ears, Thurston."

Thurston dutifully stuck his hands over his ears. Lainey turned to Charlie. "So, what does the end of my career have to do with the continuation of yours?"

"I can still sort of hear," Thurston said. He began making loud noises to block out the sound. "Mwha-mwha-mwha-mwha-mwha-mwha …"

Lainey took Thurston's hands away from his ears. The mouth noises continued. "Boy, you really are an idiot," she said, clamping her hand over his mouth.

"Well, the whole end-of-career thing's kinda complic-ated," Charlie said. "But it'll all be worked out tonight. Do you and Thursty have plans?"

"Not together."

"Great. You're invited to a party." He wrote down the address. "Together."

Thurston pulled Lainey's hand away from his mouth. "I think we should check with the network before –"

Lainey put her hand back over his mouth and told him to be quiet. "Or Lulu won't marry Fred," she warned.

"She's gonna marry Fred?" Charlie said. "Since when?"

Thurston parted two of Lainey's fingers and spoke through the gap. "Yeah, since when?"

"Of course I'm not gonna marry him!"

Charlie *phew*-ed.

"What about the baby?" Thurston whined.

"What baby?" Charlie asked.

"There's no baby," Lainey told Charlie. She turned to Thurston. "Listen to me: there is no baby. There will *be* no baby. Block your ears again, please." Thurston stuck a finger in each ear.

Lainey's hands found her hips again, forming a little two-handled teapot. She thrust her chin up at her ex-boyfriend. "Anything else?"

Charlie nodded. "I need you to stay in touch with your feelings toward Fred tonight. The bad feelings."

"I have no others," said Lainey.

"Great. Anyone you meet, feel free to tell them it's over between Lulu and him."

"Uh huh. Only I can't help wondering, so tell me again – why am I doing this?"

"For love, Elaine," Charlie said, trying to soften the corn inherent in the sentiment. "You're doing it for love."

"Gosh, how sweet of me," she deadpanned, Lulu McGee-style. Charlie almost expected a burst of studio audience laughter.

"A couple more things," he said. The whole scheme was beginning to feel as though it might topple from the ponderousness of its complex complications and various variables. "From now on I need you to call me Endicott. Endicott Gibbs. And by midnight tonight I may not be working for the 'Sentinel' anymore."

"Right."

"But then again, I might, in which case I'll be known as Charlie again. It really depends."

"On what, *Endicott?*"

"On which is more important," he said. "Changing history or changing my life." The words sounded pleasingly weighty and dramatic.

Lainey folded her arms and tapped her foot. "So which is it?"

Charlie said that he hadn't decided, that he was waiting for a sign.

"From God?"

"If he's around," Charlie said doubtfully "But I'm not fussy. I'll take any kind from anyone."

Thurston removed his fingers from his ears, cracked his knuckles once again and took a deep breath. A moment later he brought his hands to the piano keys, releasing a busy but delicate Schumann toccata that rose and swelled and filled the room with beautiful sound.

"Is that thing a pianola?" Charlie asked.

"No," Lainey said. "That's actually Thurston."

Charlie looked profoundly impressed and profoundly confused; perhaps there were hidden depths and obscure sensitivities to Thursty Brown.

"He is an idiot," Lainey explained. "But he's an idiot savant."

Not far from Hartburg train station, Lancaster County, PA. Almost noon

It turned out Elodie was a pretty slow driver. Between all the detours she made and the sub-stately pace she was maintaining, it felt to Clayton like they'd never get out of Pennsylvania. She handled the Caddy like it was in the middle of a funeral cortège. And while it was all very scenic and unspoiled around here, he was kind of itching to get back to the greasy, noisy impurity of Manhattan. And twenty-five miles per hour just wasn't gonna cut it. He had to say something.

"Save your breath," Elodie said as Clayton unslung his jaw. "We'll get there when we get there. Until then relax and enjoy the pretty scenery."

When Elodie changed, she really changed: the cynical and sarcastic woman whose standard operating temperature was simmering had apparently been supplanted by some kind of a hate-hating, love-loving hippie crossed with a Stepford Wife. Who drove like an old lady behind the wheel of a hearse. Still, if that was the woman he'd slept with last night and woken up with this morning, then so be it. Whether he liked it or not, he was in love with her. She just drove a little too slowly; he could deal with that.

He saw a hitchhiker a hundred yards ahead, confidently negotiating the small path between tarmac and cornfield.

Elodie started to slow down even more.

Okay, this was getting just a little too much. "What're you doing?"

"Being neighborly."

"But we're not anybody's neighbors," Clayton said, his voice almost trembling with anxiety.

Elodie stopped the car beside the hitchhiker, a very pretty woman in her late-twenties. The long, straight blonde hair parted down the middle and collected into pigtails on either side gave her a kind of a Manson Family aspect, enhanced by the dowdy ankle-length skirt and red-and-white gingham shirt. Very 1972. Maybe that was the fashion around here, Clayton thought – the Linda Kasabian look.

"Where you headed?" Elodie shouted right across him, through his open window.

The hitchhiker bent down to the window, smiling right in Clayton's face. She had a very nice smile, he had to concede, and stunning pale blue eyes. "New York City," she said. Pretty good breath, as well.

"So're we," said Elodie. She leaned back over her seat and pushed aside the prop-filled suitcase on the backseat to make room for their new passenger. "Hop in."

"Thank you."

Okay, but letting in a possible psycho was probably pushing this "neighborliness" craze way too far.

After a few miles of small talk it became clear that despite her cult style get-up, the woman wasn't a maniac so Elodie decided to take her New & Improved Outlook up a notch, from Breezy to Sunny. "How'd you like to come to a party?" she asked the stranger.

Clearly Clayton wasn't as enthusiastic about the New Outlook as Elodie herself was. "But, honey," he said, "we have to do the ... *thing* before."

"What thing?" Elodie asked. "More sex? Can't that wait until tonight?"

"Not sex," Clayton said, turning red. "The thing. At Dwight's."

"Oh, right." She turned to the hitchhiker and told her, "we have to do a small robbery first."

12 East 67th Street.
3:41:45pm

Chester Polglase swallowed a nervous yawn and glanced at his watch; it was about fifteen seconds later than when he'd last checked the time. Not a lot had happened in that particular quarter of a minute. A pigeon had landed on the window ledge to his left; the car alarm that had been blaring for the past six and a half minutes had finally quit; and the breeze blowing across his face changed angles slightly. He'd been there for forty minutes, standing at the bottom of the stairs of the three-story brownstone he and Sara had called home, wearing his Brooks Brothers tuxedo and holding an enormous bunch of red and blue tulips. Clutching the flowers, and dressed the way he was, made him feel like a strange union of bride and groom in one. Which, considering the fact that he was here to resurrect his engagement – not to mention himself – was not inappropriate. He hoped Sara would see the coincidental logic in the gesture, if not its poetry. He promised himself that no matter what happened, he wouldn't cry.

He checked his watch again. Forty-five seconds had passed. Nothing much had changed. He didn't know what he was waiting for. He wasn't waiting for anything. He had to do this. He had to come back from the other side, present himself to his beloved and hope that things would work out okay.

He hoped that she wouldn't be too shocked. And then too angry.

He hoped that she would understand.

He took the stairs slowly, one at a time, breathing in deeply with each fall of his foot.

He lifted the heavy brass knocker and let it down heavily.

Nine seconds later the door opened and there was Sara. She was dressed entirely in black, from the tips of her toes to the top of her head, the face he missed so keenly shrouded by a black veil. It had been sixty-seven hours and forty-three minutes since Chester had seen her; it felt like sixty-seven *years* and forty-three minutes. She looked so lovely and sweet and beautiful Chester thought he was going to cry.

And when she squealed with delight and threw her arms around him, he did.

Rivington Street,
Lower East Side. 2pm

It never ceased to amaze Clayton that Dwight, worth however many millions he was, chose to live in a such a dive in such a divey part of the city. He knocked on the green door to the apartment. Waited. Knocked again. Looked down and saw green paint chips falling away from the flimsy wood and floating down onto the toes of his brown Tretorns. Man oh Manischewitz, what a dive.

But that was the thing about Dwight, Clayton supposed, as he removed the set of lock picks from his pocket. He was a man of striking contradictions; for one thing, he liked Elodie but hated Clayton and that just didn't make any sense. The lock bolt clicked, Clayton turned the handle and eased open the door. The windows were shuttered and it was dark inside. Clayton felt for a light switch on the inside of the doorway. The dim bulb hanging from a cord in the middle of the room did little to help.

The room was so small and there was so little to the depressingly ascetic place that unless Dwight hid things in the refrigerator the only place anything could possibly be secreted was under the Murphy bed.

But there was no refrigerator in the kitchenette. Clayton turned and saw a lockbox under the bed. He removed it and was about to take out his picks again when the lid simply opened. There was a file inside with some kind of serial number or code on the front: 221163.

"Are you freakin' kidding me?" Clayton said to himself. Here was perhaps the greatest contradiction of all – that a man so careful and secretive as Dwight Kitchener would leave something like this practically on display. It was almost as though he actually wanted it to be discovered. Or maybe it was hiding in plain sight. Except there was no actual hiding involved.

It's a trap! Clayton thought. And as he spun around to face the doorway Clayton knew that Dwight would be there, smiling, and ready to kill him.

But he wasn't.

And was *that* in itself some kind of a weird contradiction – that Dwight could be so vivid in Clayton's mind but absent in person?

Why am I even standing here having these thoughts when I should be –

Clayton closed the apartment door and ran back to the car.

Adelaide's office. Three hours before the party

She had no idea how long she'd been sitting there, doing that. Not that you could call what she was doing actually *doing* anything; just sitting at her desk staring at nothing, thinking about nothing. Not even The List.

Before her mind had whited out, Endicott Gibbs had been wandering her thoughts, along with the kiss that had concluded their night. Compelling as Mr Gibbs was, her mind had eventually let him go, and her ruminations drifted, ending up here, wherever, nowhere.

The office was quiet, practically deserted. Dwight hadn't been in all day. Clayton and Elodie hadn't called with any updates from Amish country. Rob had left the apartment that morning before Adelaide had gotten up. He hadn't left her a gift or even bent down to her dozing head and whispered anything along the lines of "Happy birthday, darling" much less "You don't look a day over thirty" or "Take a deep breath and hang on because I'm gonna screw you senseless right here and now." In fact, nobody had wished her a happy birthday all day. There'd be plenty of time for that at the party tonight, she supposed. Plenty of opportunities for her to plaster on a smile – hoping it wouldn't produce a sudden swarm of thirty-five year old wrinkles around her mouth – and say thanks.

Her gaze absently found the picture frame on her desk. For the millionth time in her life – and the thousandth time in the past few days – Adelaide wondered if her mother had known that Dwight had forced her husband to leave her. "Did you know, Mom?" she said aloud, picking up the photo frame and addressing the picture of Claudette. "And would it've made any difference if you had? Happiness is happiness, however you come by it, right?"

There was a knock at her door. Pete Valentine from Casting came in and handed her a large package wrapped in brown paper. "This was messengered to 101," he told her. "I'm outta here. See you tonight."

The package was from Rob, and she thought maybe he'd sent her a gift. But when she tore open the top and saw a furry black rabbit ear poking through she knew that he hadn't. And she wondered how she could have been so naive and hopeful, even for just that moment. And the three years that preceded it.

She sighed, switched off the lights and left the office, still holding on to the cumbersome package, wondering why she didn't simply let it all go.

Happiness is happiness, she thought to herself. *However you come by it.* Then added the Carter family clause: *whatever the cost.*

Arthur Munro's office.
5.45pm

As soon as he saw Mr Munro leave his office, Charlie dashed out from the partition he'd been hiding behind, ran in and scrawled a note on a page of *Sentinel* letterhead. He looked for something to hold the note down, to give it weight. He took one of the Pulitzers from Art's shelf and placed it on top of the paper.

He left the office and had almost made it to the photocopier when he decided the message lacked the proper hint of ambiguity, a nice finishing touch that would help to confuse his boss. Charlie bolted back to Art's office and added one word: *Probably*.

Finally, he photocopied the note, signed it and slipped it into an envelope with Adelaide Carter's name on the front.

Okay, so that was her birthday gift taken care of.

Probably.

Basement, 88 West 75th Street. 5.47pm

Adelaide was flicking through an old magazine while she waited for Tim to bring her car around when she came upon something that pretty much spelled the end of her and Rob. It was a simple image – a father and son holding hands and looking across the East River to the Brooklyn skyline. The father points across the river and tells the boy, "Brooklyn is the Manhattan of the other boroughs". The one halfway intelligent thing her husband had ever said in his life and he'd lifted it wholesale from a *New Yorker* cartoon.

That was going on The List – right to the number one spot, actually. Done.

But no, wait, this whole stupid List thing was so symptomatic of exactly what was wrong with her marriage and her life. Forcing herself to not think about whatever was wrong was morally weak, professionally hypocritical, lazy, self-defeating, self-destructive and childish. She was turning thirty-five in a few hours, for God's sake; she needed to grow the hell up.

Tim screeched up in the cobalt 1968 Shelby Mustang that Claudette had given Adelaide for her eighteenth birthday. He climbed out and held open the door. "Whatcha got there, Ms Carter?" Tim asked, pointing to the package by her side.

"Bunny suit," she muttered, snatching the keys.

Montauk Highway, between Watermill and Bridgehampton

The gun pointed at him wasn't even the thing that most irritated Dwight right at this goddamn moment; what really got under his skin was the same thing as every time he drove through the Hamptons – all those quaint, coy names for every damn thing in sight. The Little Shoppe on Sagg Road. Pond Meadow Lane. Contentment goddamn Cottage. As though these were quiet, unassuming little shacks instead of huge mansions and enormous yachts surrounded by stables and tennis courts and twelve-dollar coffees. Yes, he was personally worth more than $500 million, but at least he had the decency not to be so damn ostentatious about it.

"What happens when we get there?" Dwight asked, staring at the ugly brown monster on the road ahead of him. "You're not gonna shadow me with that gat the whole night, are you?"

"No," Holly said. She sat with her knees tucked up onto the seat, a quarter-turned so she and her gat – her Beretta – could more easily face him. "I'm meeting the guy who set this whole thing up."

"The reporter?"

"If you say so," she said cryptically. "And then I'm going to tell him it's over. To his face!"

"And why're you gonna do that?"

"Because he's a no-good, two-bit dirty rotten louse."

Dwight shook his head and sighed. "You don't know what you're getting yourself into, ma'am."

"Yes I do," Holly said firmly. "And it's *miss*."

Dwight tapped the brakes as that brown beast of a Cadillac suddenly veered into the oncoming lane and back again. Goddamn thing should've done everybody a favor and driven itself into Mecox Bay – the Cadillac Brougham d'Elegance was a disgrace to American automotive art.

Montauk Highway, between Watermill and Bridgehampton. Ten seconds earlier

Elodie swerved sharply to avoid a skunk loping across the highway. Everything inside the Cadillac jumped and slid. The suitcase full of props popped open, the contents near the top spilling across the backseat. Clayton watched as Sallie, the friendly, helpful, non-psycho lady hitchhiker leaned down to pick up the file that had slipped into the footwell.

Elodie asked her passengers if they were okay.

Sallie looked at the cover of the file; what she saw startled her. A lot.

"I'm fine, thank you," she said, a little tremulously. "But may I ask – why do you have a photograph of my brother back here?"

The Cadillac veered all over the road all over again.

Montauk Highway, between Watermill and Bridgehampton

Two cars back, Chester Polglase slowed down, opening up a little more space between his boxy Prius and the low-slung Porsche racecar-looking thing he'd been following since it left Rivington Street in the scary, decrepit, tenementy Lower East Side. He turned and smiled at Sara. She lifted the smoky layers of her veil and smiled back at him. Things had moved so fast since the afternoon – Sara had prised Dwight's home address from the printer who made the grief-counseling card Dwight had so kindly (although not really when you thought about it) given her, and right after she and Chester drove straight there just in time to see his car pulling away from the curb out front of a run-down building, giving them no choice but to follow him and the police lady with him to wherever they were headed, which so far was a pretty long way away! Naturally, there had been no time for either of them to change and so there they sat: the bride-and-groom driving, his widow by his side. Tulips were everywhere – clutches of them jammed in the cup holders, single bulbs poking out of air vents, one side pocket filled with blue ones, the other with red ones, a dozen strewn across the windscreen panel. Sara had arranged them all as they'd driven and she'd done a great job. She had a gift for this sort of thing – Chester could see that now – and she wanted to use that gift in creating the most perfect of all possible weddings where nothing went wrong and everybody had the greatest time of their lives. Where was the harm in that? There wasn't any – he understood that now – none at all.

"I rode in that Porsche the other night," Sara said. "It's the one James Dean was killed in."

"The same model?" Chester asked.

"No," Sara said. "The same *one*."

Montauk Highway, between Watermill and Bridgehampton

"So do you not want kids at all, or do you just not want them with me?" Thurston asked. He and Elaine were sitting as far apart as possible in the back of yet another black Escalade.

"Do you mean you?" Lainey said, clamping chapter thirty-two of *Washington Square* around her forefinger. "Or Fred?"

"Whichever answer'll get either of us into bed with you."

"With me?" Lainey said. "Or Lulu?"

"Does it matter?" Thurston said, helping himself to a Fiji Water from the mini-bar. "You've both got the same ..." He took a sip of the South Pacific.

"The same what?"

Thurston yawned extravagantly then said, "You know what I'm talking about." He stretched and spread his legs, making a wide open V of his crotch.

"I think I do and I really hope I don't," Lainey said. "So I need you to tell me: Lulu and I have the same what?"

He looked at her as though she was dumber than dirt. "Va-gi-na," he said, helpfully teasing out each syllable so she could keep up with him.

What depressed Elaine Reardon about this micromoment in her life – in time, in humanity's bleak history – was that there was nothing she could do or say that could ever penetrate the dense cloud of stupidity that permanently cloaked Thurston Brown.

On the other hand, she could kick him really hard in the balls – that would be something.

So she did.

Montauk Highway, between Little Long Pond and Bridgehampton

The Cadillac had been enveloped in stunned silence for quite some time.

Until somebody said, "Wow."

Then somebody else said, "Gosh."

"Remarkable," said a third person.

"What's the current Amish position on profanity, Sallie?" asked Clayton. "Because I'm leaning toward calling this whole thing 'fucking incredible'. Unless it'll tempt God to strike the car with lightning."

"Well, perhaps you'd better stick with 'completely amazing' or 'utterly astonishing'," she advised. "Do you really think God is quite that vengeful?"

"I do," said Clayton. "If only because we were created in his image and, as a race, humans are nothing if not vengeful."

Elodie said, "I just want to reiterate that we'd called the whole thing off last night. We have no business coming between you and your beliefs. Picking you up today was just a coincidence."

"A completely amazing, utterly astonishing fucking

incredible one," Clayton said, glancing nervously at the roof of the car.

Elodie leaned away from him in case there *was* a God and he was that vengeful.

Montauk Highway, between Watermill and Bridgehampton.

As he drove, Charlie looked for signs and spoke aloud to God (or whoever might be listening).

"Is that a sign?" he asked, passing the entrance to Bridgehampton Cemetery.

He passed a windmill. "Is that?"

"What about that?" A lighthouse.

A dog chased a cat across the highway. That could only mean one thing – dogs and cats were still at war.

A road sign: Sag Harbor 5 miles. "Well, I know that's a sign," he said. "But is it a *sign?*"

If there was a God, Charlie wondered, how long would it take for him to tell him to shut up?

Sagg Road, between Crooked Pond and Widow Gavits Road. Two miles to the party

Somehow, while she was driving, Adelaide had managed to change into the costume Rob had sent. Not for him, of course, for herself. Because if there was one thing worse than even *going* to a costume party it was showing up to a costume party not in costume. Traffic was pretty heavy and it was a miracle she didn't kill herself. Although what a corpse she'd have made: black fishnets, black gloves that went up past her elbows, the black bow-tie on a velvet choker around her neck, and a little white rabbit tail pinned to the back of a pair of black satin shorts. Pretty cute. But then, in the Mustang's rearview mirror, she caught a glimpse of the rabbit ears and it all came crashing down. She looked like a fucking idiot.

THE PARTY

Adelaide's house at Sag Harbor. 8.30pm

When Adelaide walked in she was so uncomfortable, so completely out of sorts, that she felt like she was crashing somebody else's party. The expansive living room was already crowded, noisy and star-studded: Marilyn Monroe stretched out languorously on one of the couches; Michael Caine in front of the floating slate fireplace doing card tricks for Spider-Man, Derek Jeter and Carmen Miranda; three bears with canapés in their paws surrounded Goldilocks; witches and warlocks threw back cocktail potions; Tracy and Hepburn stood lip-locked in front of the folding glass doors that led out onto the deck. Half a dozen waiters weaved in and out of the thickening crowd, keeping the party's gears well-oiled.

As she stood on the verge, scanning the room for Endicott or Rob, it occurred to Adelaide that, disguised or not, she didn't know who many of the people in there were. Maybe that was why nobody had seemed to notice her. She was tempted to turn around, take the stairs up to the bedroom and maybe crawl under the covers – no, under the bed itself – and wait for her party, her birthday, her night to pass.

But then Hugh Hefner saw her, winked and made his way over, sucking ostentatiously on his smokeless pipe. The closer he got, the more the light catching his red silk robe dazzled her, but not in a good way – in a flashy, blinding, annoying way. The *New Yorker* cartoon revelation probably had something to do with her irritation as well. He shook her hand and gave her a quick, dry peck on the cheek. "Nice outfit," Rob said, appreciatively. "I feel like I haven't seen you in days."

"You haven't," Adelaide pointed out.

"Right," he said. "But as busy Manhattanites, I sometimes don't know how we manage to balance our personal and professional lives."

He'd obviously read this somewhere and memorized it. Adelaide let it go.

"Happy birthday, by the way. I have something for you but it's upstairs in the bedroom." Rob winked again. "So ..." he said, nodding and looking around the room. Apparently he'd already run out of things to talk with his wife about. "*Qué pasa?*"

"What?"

"It's Spanish," Rob explained. "It means, like, 'what's happening?'"

"*Qué pasa ...*"

"That's right." He snapped his fingers. "What's happening?"

"I'm a little confused, Rob," she said. "Do you actually want to know or are you being sort of ... funky?"

Rob took a big sniff of his armpit. "I'm not funky. If you're smelling a smell, maybe it's my pipe." He looked over her shoulder and said, "Oh wow! I didn't know you knew those two." Seriously, he had the attention span of a toddler. His eyes widened in excitement. "What a surprise."

Adelaide turned as Elaine Reardon and Thurston Brown arrived. "Yeah, for both of us," she said. They weren't in special outfits, and Adelaide wondered whether it was okay for famous people to show up at a costume party dressed as themselves. If so, Charlie Chaplin must've had it sweet. She also couldn't help wondering what two people who were a major element of one of the strangest cases of her career were doing there.

Thurston held out his hand to no-one in particular. "Hi, I'm Fred. I mean, um –"

"He means Thurston," Lainey assisted. "I'm Lainey Reardon."

Hef turned on the charm. "Rob Dolen, pleased to meet you, guys. This is my wife Adelaide, uh …"

"Carter," Adelaide reminded him. "How are you?"

"I could use a drink," Thurston said. He flicked a finger at Lainey. "We just broke up."

Adelaide didn't bother hiding her surprise.

"*We* didn't break up," Lainey said. "Lulu and Fred broke up."

"The show's over?" Adelaide asked.

"I guess so," said Lainey. "Unless they find another me."

Rob directed the spit-glistening stem of his plastic pipe between the two actors. "But *you* two're still together, right?"

Lainey sighed; dealing with two idiots was exponentially more tiring than dealing with just one. She wondered exactly what it would take to be "broken up" with Fred and Thurston once and for all. His death, maybe. Or hers. "We were never together."

"Actually, we were supposed to have a baby," Thurston said. "But she wouldn't sign the contract."

Rob glowered at Adelaide, as though that very same situation was a part of their own relationship, their contract. He draped a sympathetic arm across Thurston's shoulders. "I feel your pain."

"My nuts are killing me."

"I hear you there, too, *compadre.*"

As Lainey rolled her eyes at the sight of the two men sharing their grief over phantom babies, Adelaide winced at Rob's last word; this Spanish thing of his was completely mystifying. Did he maybe think that Hugh Hefner was Mexican? Hugo Hefner?

Adelaide took Elaine by the arm and led her to a vacant space on the floating fireplace. "So what are your plans now, Elaine?"

"In the short term, drunkenness," she said, sitting down on the cool stone. "Long-term, probably alcoholism. You know how it is."

"I do, actually," Adelaide said, grabbing two glasses of whatever the nearest waiter was carrying and handing one to Elaine. "I'm curious about what exactly precipitated Lulu's decision to break up with Fred."

"Marital advice from an ex-boyfriend."

"Does he want to get back with you?"

Was this dame *serious?* Lainey wondered. Hadn't she been standing *right beside* Charlie as he literally *ran away* from Lainey last night? "Uh, no," Lainey said. "I'm just a regular girl. This guy's looking for something a little more elevated. He's looking for a ..." She looked Adelaide up and down, deciding whether or not to spill. But then she got distracted; a lady cop with curly blonde hair and a criminal in a black ski mask walked in, handcuffed to each other.

Dragging Dwight along with her, Officer Hohen-zollern marched straight up to Bobby Dolen, who was dressed for bed and standing with his arm around some stupid-looking actor she'd seen on TV way too much. She had a bone or three to pick with Bobby. "Hi, Bobby! How are you? Can we talk? Only it's kinda urgent. C'mon."

Holly pushed Bobby toward the nearest door that led out of the crowded living room. Thanks to the handcuffs, Dwight necessarily followed. The kitchen she found herself in was literally as big as Holly's stupid, titchy apartment, all gleaming silver and sparkling plasticky white, with a king-size marble-topped bench thing as a big as a bed plonked right in the middle. On top of the bench was a silver bowl filled with ice and bottles of Champagne. Holly got the impression that no matter what time of day a person walked in there, no matter the month or season or occasion, there would always be a silver bowl filled with ice and bottles of Champagne sitting on that bench. Just in case. There seemed to be two of everything, too – two microwaves, two refrigerators, two stoves (two!). As though this lady wasn't rich enough already she had to double up on everything to make sure everybody knew it! There was probably another kitchen somewhere else in the stupid mansion, just for emergencies. Holly noisily yanked open a few doors until she found a decent-sized cupboard. "This is between me and Bobby," she told Dwight. "So I'm going to have to ask you to step in here while we talk, all right? Great."

Dwight tried to resist.

Holly pulled her gun and poked it in his ribs.

Rob freaked.

She plucked off the ski mask so Dwight wouldn't suffocate, shoved him into the walk-in pantry then shut the door on the handcuff chain. It was hardly airtight but at least it gave her and Bobby a little privacy for what she was about to reveal. Bobby had no idea what was going on; as soon as the shiny white pantry door closed he leaned in for a kiss. She pushed him away. "It's going down tonight," she said in a hoarse conspiratorial whisper.

Smoochy Bobby was suddenly all business. "How will it play, Ho-ho?" he asked. "What's their, y'know, scam?"

"It's complicated, but one of them's pretending to be a 'New York Sentinel' reporter, doing a story on your wife's company," she explained. "He's acting like he's in love with her. I'm not sure what her feelings for him are but he's awful cute. If everything goes to plan you'll be wifeless before midnight."

"Great."

"Also, I'm breaking up with you."

"What!?" Bobby squawked. "*Qué pasa*, Ho-ho?"

"Oh come on, Bobby, I could never trust you after something like this. You're a complete slimeweasel." And that, as far as Holly was concerned, was about it between her and Bobby D. She pulled on her left wrist; Dwight necessarily followed. Naturally, being just three feet away, he'd overheard everything and there was a pale, shocked look on his face to prove it.

"You were together?" he said. "You two?"

"Not really," Holly said.

"Yes we were," Rob insisted. "I thought we were gonna have children."

"Children? We've been dating three weeks! And I only went out with you to annoy my ex-boyfriend." Holly turned to Dwight. "Bobby is my ex-boyfriend's boss."

"Felix," Dwight said, rubbing his wrist where the cuff had bitten.

Holly nodded.

"How do you know about that?" Rob asked Dwight. He turned to Holly. "Who is this guy?"

"Never mind who he is," Holly said. "You've got what you wanted, Bobby. You're getting out of your marriage the easy way. Be grateful."

"That wasn't what I wanted," he whined. "I want kids and Adelaide won't give them to me."

Dwight went paler. He tongued the scar lump inside his cheek. "Adelaide?" he said, his voice raw with disbelief. "Jesus Christ – you're Adelaide's husband?"

"Yes, I am," Rob said. "And who are you?"

Dwight was rattled; if there was some plan afoot that would separate this boob from Adelaide he didn't want to queer it by revealing who he was. He stalled, reaching toward the silver ice bowl for a bottle of Champagne. "My name is …"

*

Who will Endicott Gibbs come dressed up as? Charlie wondered. When he finally found his way to the living room the fact that he was not in some sort of costume was deeply accentuated by the fact that just about everyone else was. As a person who'd worn Amish clothes for a good part of his life, he found dressing up in costume a little embarrassing. But not as embarrassing as *not* dressing up when everyone else was extremely dressed up. In a way, of course, he had come as somebody else – Endicott Gibbs, who just happened to dress exactly the same as Charlie Van Linden. So who was Endicott Gibbs pretending to be?

Even though the room was packed with color and noise and action he spotted Adelaide immediately, sitting with Lainey and Thurston on the stone extension of a fireplace that seemed to float in mid-air. When he saw her, Charlie couldn't help glancing heavenward in disappointment. He'd finally received his sign, and it wasn't a good one: she was dressed as a Playboy Bunny. There was no God.

Lainey waved and Charlie held his breath, unsure of whether or not she'd play along with his deception. "Well, well, well – if it isn't Endicott Gibbs!"

He breathed a sigh of relief and squeezed through the crowd. "Evening, Lainey," he said. "Thursty."

"I prefer Thurston."

"Actually, he prefers Fred but it's best not to indulge him," Lainey said.

Charlie turned to Adelaide. "So, you're a Bunny after all. Seems kind of a shame. I really thought I was on the money pegging you for a goddess."

Lainey rolled her eyes; she'd forgotten just how much of a sap Charles could be when he let himself go. Turned out sappiness was way more attractive when you were the sappee.

Adelaide didn't reply but the finger self-consciously tugging at her long black ears said plenty.

"You know this is meant to be a costume party, right, Van ... Gibbs?" Thurston said.

"Yes, I do," Charlie said. "I've come as ... a reporter for the 'New York Sentinel'. An undercover reporter. That's why I look all normal and everything. Do I look normal?"

Lainey looked over Charlie's shoulder. "Compared to the Three Amishos you do."

Charlie turned and saw Clayton, Elodie and Sallie walk in, all dressed in Amish clothing; the outfits were a surprise in two cases, a disappointment in one. Elodie broke off from the group and began chatting with Eduardo/Che Guevara. Charlie noted a manila folder tucked under Clayton's arm, and saw that he was almost shaking with nerves, his eyes darting around the room, no doubt in search of the fearsome Dwight.

Things had suddenly gotten stratospherically complicated: Lainey and Sallie knew each other from when Charlie and Lainey used to date, but, of course, Sallie wasn't aware that Charlie was calling himself Endicott Gibbs, at least until midnight. And, oh yeah, what was his sister even *doing* here? Clayton began making his way over toward Charlie. "Would you excuse me?" Charlie said to anyone nearby. He then loped over to Sallie.

As Charlie put his arms around his sister and hugged her, Townsend wordlessly slipped Charlie the folder and kept walking.

Clayton was too nervous about what he'd just done to speak – not to Adelaide, or Elaine Reardon, or Elodie, or the actual, real live Derek Jeter, or anyone. And the living room was full of everyone. He pushed through the door to the kitchen.

Inside the kitchen – which was bigger than Clayton's entire living room – Dwight was standing in between a woman dressed as a police officer and Hugh Hefner. Dwight was drinking Champagne. Hefner was puffing on a smokeless pipe. A familiar-looking policewoman held a gun on Dwight. It was an interesting tableau.

Townsend had been in the kitchen for maybe a tenth of a second before Dwight told him to get the hell out. Even that blithering idiot probably hadn't had time to screw up whatever plan was in play to separate Adelaide and this clown Dolen. Meanwhile, Dwight was still stalling with his answer to Dolen's question: *Who is this guy?*

"I'm ..."

For whatever reason, Holly was trying to help. "He's ..."

At the other end of the kitchen, the back door opened. Holly, Dwight and Rob all turned. Dwight couldn't believe his eyes: "Buttons" Polglase and the Widow White walked in from goddamn nowhere. Polglase was dressed like he was about to get married and White was done up entirely in mourning black, even wearing a goddamn veil! They were holding hands tightly.

Polglase aimed a long, accusatory finger directly at Dwight, like Cotton Mather prosecuting a witch. "*This* is the man who saved our marriage!" he announced for all the world to hear. "*This* is the man who tore us apart so we could be reunited in even stronger betrothal! God *bless* you, sir! God bless you! I never knew how much I loved Sara until ..." He choked back a sob.

"Until he was *dead*!" panted Sara. "Thank you, Dwight!"

"Dead?" Rob said, the pipe falling from his jaw. "Are you some kind of a priest? Like a voodoo priest?"

Chester and Sara wedged themselves between Dwight and the policewoman, hugging their savior tightly. And all of a sudden it came to Sara: Lee Marvin! That's who Dwight reminded her of! Boy, was she ever glad to get that niggling thought out of her head. It had been there the entire last few days and had really taken her mind off her grieving!

Holly turned to Rob. "Shouldn't you..?" She waved her still unholstered gun toward the living room.

"What?" Rob said, sincerely wanting an answer. He glanced at the gun and took a guess. "Go kill my wife?"

From the look on Bobby's face it seemed to Holly that he'd actually go do it if she told him to. And she was giving it some serious thought when a waiter came through the door, his upturned-spider fingers balancing an empty drinks tray. "Wrong room, *pendejo*," Rob said to the hapless server. "This is the domestic kitchen. The catering kitchen is down the second hallway to the *right* of the entrance."

Holly *knew* it – they *did* have two kitchens!

The waiter spun around and went back through the domestic kitchen door into the crowded, roaring living room. On his way to the catering kitchen he passed a woman in Amish gear sitting on a couch talking with a guy dressed as … nothing.

"Charlie?" Sallie said.

"Sallie?" Charlie said.

"What are you doing here?"

"What am *I* doing here? You're the one in the cult in Pennsylvania." *Unless* … Maybe the company's plan had gone ahead. Couldn't hurt to ask. "Has something … happened?"

"Well, yes and no," Sallie said. "I've thought a lot about what you were saying the other night and I've decided to step out into the world. At least for a while."

"So nothing *unusual* has happened recently?"

"No, Charlie, it hasn't," his sister said. "Although I'm sure that *had* any strange events occurred, they'd have been well-intentioned."

She knew. She smiled. They hugged.

"So what's with the outfit?" Charlie asked.

"Well, it's a costume party and I'm dressed as an Amish woman," Sallie said. "What's with yours?"

"I'm pretending to be a regular citizen."

"That look'll never fit you, Charlie."

He stood up. "Listen, I have to talk with somebody. Go try some drugs or alcohol – there should be plenty around. It'll make a nice introduction to the world. A little mini-Rumspringa. But don't take anything stronger than marijuana though, okay?"

"I'll take the world as it comes, thank you," Sallie assured her brother. "That should be interesting enough for now."

*

Somebody turned up the music.

The bass from the stereo downstairs was really thumping up through the bedroom floor. Standing at the end of the bed, Rob and Adelaide could both feel it in the soles of their feet, and it was making an already difficult conversation grow steadily more tense and uncomfortable.

"He's not who he says he is, Adelaide, you have to believe me," Rob said, his voice edging perilously close to a marriage-ending wheedle. "This reporter, if he is a reporter, which he probably isn't, he's not really in love with you. His company made him do it."

"Which company?" Adelaide said. Her left Bunny ear flopped down in front of her left eye. She irritatedly flipped it back. "The 'New York Sentinel' Company?"

"No! This secret company which breaks couples up. He works for them." Rob sat down on the edge of the bed and put his face in his hands. "Oh God, what've I done?"

"Yes, what have you done, Rob?" Adelaide said. "Or do you prefer Bobby?"

It was all falling apart. And his palms smelled like corn chips. He licked them. They tasted kind of gross. He removed his wet face from his wet hands and looked up at his wife, standing in front of him with her arms crossed. She actually looked pretty hot in that outfit. He better explain what was happening before she got even more confused and he got even more of a boner.

"This is gonna sound crazy, Addy, but there's this evil company and they … I heard about it from one of our art-directors. And this company organized this thing for him involving some kinda lizard and some ice-cream. And I think that burglar downstairs in the kitchen is one of them. Anyway, to be completely honest, I was having a teensy little fling with Holly but I didn't know she was the one with the bicycle pump! How could I? Anyway, she organized the whole thing so now there's this guy pretending to be a reporter and in love with you. Oh God, it's all beginning to make sense. But it's over between me and her. I love you, babe."

"So you and this woman you're having an affair with – ?"

"*Was* having an affair with," he corrected. "I ended it."

"So you and her engaged this alleged company to somehow come between you and me?"

One of his wife's rabbit ears fell over her eyes. It looked pretty cute. "Actually, it was mostly her. But yes. Forgive me."

"Oh please."

"Is that a yes?"

"It's a no." She folded the cute ear back away from her eye; now both of them were giving him the evil eye.

"But I'm telling the truth, Adelaide," Rob pleaded. "Do you know anyone who says he's a 'Sentinel' reporter?"

"I know someone who says he's *pretending* to be a reporter for the 'Sentinel'."

"Well that's him!" Rob's fingers snapped in victory. "Even if he doesn't say he's not pretending to be ..." Boy, things got confusing fast in this situation. "No, wait ..."

Adelaide released the most despairing sigh of her entire life. "Oh God, how on earth did I spend so long with you?"

Rob couldn't believe his ears. "I can't believe my ears." Was she serious? "Are you serious?"

As his wife nodded sadly, Rob slipped out of his ruby robe and gave her Smoldering – that look was killer. "Your memory getting any better, babe?" He flexed his biceps then fluttered his fingers over his tanned six-pack. He was glad he'd decided to wear just a thong underneath the robe.

She'd had enough. Four years of enough. At the sight of her increasingly naked husband, Adelaide tore off her Bunny ears and her Bunny cuffs. She ripped off her black stockings and pulled down the black satin shorts with the white fluffy Bunny tail.

Rob smiled. "That's it, babe," he said, getting excited. He *knew* it – Smoldering always worked! "Come to Daddy."

Adelaide quickly scanned the bedroom. She grabbed some leather sandals from a shoe closet then, with all her strength, yanked the white Frette sheet from the bed, sending her husband spinning to the wooden floor which now seemed to be literally throbbing with the beat coming from below. Tearing the sheet in half, she let out a piercing, joyous scream.

Smoldering gave way to Frightened.

*

Chester and Sara smiled at each other as they heard a scream; someone upstairs was having fun! They moved through the living room, intoxicated with newly-revived love, hugging all the people they recognized from the incident that had "killed" Chet but reawakened their passion. There was Eduardo, and the soup waiter, the police and ambulance guys, and quite a few of their fellow "diners." But of course, Chester and Sara were completely unaware of the two people most responsible for their dissolution and subsequent resolution, the Emotional Architects who'd dreamed up the whole scheme, even though they were just a few feet away.

Clayton and Elodie occupied adjacent sofas in a relatively quiet corner of the huge living room, beneath an American flag signed and encausticated by Jasper Johns.

"We can't just let him get away with it," Elodie insisted.

Clayton agreed, with reservations. "No, we can't. But …"

"But you're scared of him."

"Well, he's very fierce."

"He broke us up, Clayton." Elodie poked her boyfriend's chest with her finger. "Using cereal and lipstick! He followed us to Rhode Island and crept around our hotel room! He's not getting away with it."

"It's already taken care of," Clayton said. He thought about lighting a cigarette, adding a little flourish to what really had been an excellently suave remark. But it was probably a non-smoking house and Adelaide would jump all over –

"How?"

He pointed at the kitchen door that Dwight, Holly and Charlie had just come through. Elodie recognized Charlie from the file photo. "That's –"

"My name is Charlie Van Linden," Charlie told Dwight as they walked through the living room and out onto the deck overlooking the bay. Thanks to the hand-cuffs, Officer Hohenzollern necessarily followed. Charlie sat on an Adirondack chair and breathed in the warm, salty air. "I'm a reporter for the 'Sentinel'."

"Good for you," said Dwight, peevishly.

"Your friend Arthur Munro's my boss."

"Then you know as well as I do he won't run anything you write about the company." Dwight sat down on another Adirondack; Holly remained standing. "So why am I even talking to you?"

Charlie removed the manila folder from inside his jacket and held it open before Dwight.

Dwight said nothing.

Charlie said nothing.

The sea and the sky said nothing.

Nobody was saying anything and it was beginning to annoy Holly. "What is it?" she said.

"Mr Kitchener here killed President Kennedy."

Holly's mouth fell open. "No shit? Really?"

"Yep. Only thing is, he was acting on orders from JFK himself."

Holly gasped. "The President committed suicide?"

"No." Charlie shook his head. "The order was to shoot Mrs K but a certain someone's aim was a little off, wasn't it?"

Dwight didn't even want to deny it. The most volatile, explosive piece of information in American history – in the hands of a goddamn reporter from the third-most authoritative newspaper in the city, for Chrissake – and all Dwight wanted to do was give it up, confess, get it all off his chest and spend whatever time he had left breathing easy, finally free not so much of the guilt over what he'd done – or failed to do – but of the crushing, malignant weight of the knowledge he'd carried around for so long. Van Linden knew everything, no doubt, the whole rotten, stinking mess. How JFK's sometime lover, Judy Exner, had approached her friend Claudette Carter with this insane plan the President himself wanted to put in play, one that'd get him out of his yoke of a marriage, free him up to chase trim with virtual impunity and practically guarantee him a second term. Claudette had given Dwight the job of finding a trigger and setting Oswald up as the patsy. And everything would've been fine if Dwight's man, a drunk named David Morales, hadn't been just a few inches off, accidentally taking out ... Well, everybody knew the rest.

"Doesn't matter how good a friend he is," Charlie said, without gloating. "Art will have to run this."

"So what do you want?"

Charlie considered the question. "That's a good question. What do I want?"

Holly told him what he wanted. "You want this stupid, evil company to quit its stupid, evil ways."

"Do I?" Charlie asked her. "Why?" He was sincerely curious.

"You know this dame's been playing you from the get-go, don't you, Van Linden?" Dwight offered contemptuously.

"She has?" he said. Charlie was truly surprised, not so much about being had as by the fact that everybody he met lately seemed to have some kind of a secret agenda.

327

Himself included, of course. Didn't anybody play it straight-up anymore? "How?"

"Her and Adelaide's half-wit husband cooked the whole thing up, getting you involved and threatening to do a story that would expose the company," Dwight said, half guessing.

Charlie said to Holly, "You made up all that stuff about the iguana and the zombie parents?"

Holly raised her eyebrows accusingly at Dwight.

"Well, that was all true," Dwight admitted, a touch sheepishly.

"So how many actual biscuits were on the baking tray?" Charlie asked Holly.

Her face scrunched up. "*What?*"

"How much of what you told me was the truth?"

"All of it," she said. "I just didn't mention that I was sleeping with Bobby Dolen."

"Adelaide's husband?" Charlie said, sort of maybe beginning to understand what was going on. A little. He hoped. "You and him were together?"

"That's right," Holly said. "But now that I've packed him off to Splitsville, I'd guess he probably doesn't want to bust up with his wife. Two break-ups in one night'd be tough on anybody."

"Gosh, what a mess." Charlie turned to Dwight. "What'll we do?"

"I'm handcuffed to a dame with a gun on me," Dwight pointed out. "There's not much I can do."

"You have a gun?" Charlie asked Holly.

"It's in my handbag."

"What if it goes off?"

"Well, I guess somebody gets shot," she said.

Charlie politely asked Holly to uncuff Dwight.

She wanted to know why.

"Because he's going to give his resignation to Adelaide," Charlie explained. "And I think he deserves a little dignity while he's doing it."

"Oh yeah?" Dwight said, with a pugnacious jut of his chin. "Who says I'm quitting?"

Charlie tapped the Kennedy file, reminding Dwight who had the upper hand. "Well, it's either that or jail."

Holly removed a key from her handbag and uncuffed her captive. "I can't believe you killed Mr Kennedy," she said, sounding disappointed as well as surprised. "There are plenty other of our presidents who deserved it way more than he did."

As it began to rain, Charlie got up off the wooden chair and took a few steps toward the bright, thudding living room.

Dwight asked him what he had planned.

"That depends," Charlie said, motioning to the party. "Shall we?"

"This oughta be interesting," Dwight muttered.

"Boy, I really hope not," said Charlie, sliding open the living room doors.

He almost fell back. The crowd was teetering right on the verge of mayhem – everything was louder, drunker, hotter and sweatier. Fate was in the air.

And Adelaide herself had taken things to an altogether higher plane. The Playboy Bunny's shift was over and she'd been replaced by a stunning Greek goddess who wore pale sandals on her feet, a frayed white sheet elegantly swathed around her hips and torso, a gold tasseled belt holding it in place, and a laurel wreath on her head. She seemed naked, utterly exposed, and yet veiled at the same time. As a sign from God – or whoever – Charlie was thrilled, aroused, moved, charmed and almost over-whelmed by it.

He found the stereo and turned the music down; this wasn't a scene he wanted to play out in shouts and repetitions. He patted his jacket to make sure the envelope was still in there then made his way over to the goddess. And her husband.

"Is this the guy?" Rob asked Adelaide.

Adelaide said nothing, just stared at Charlie.

Rob pointed his pipe. "Are you the guy?"

"Probably," Charlie said. "Which guy?"

"Are you pretending to be in love with my wife?"

"Who?" Charlie grinned at Adelaide. "Aphrodite here?"

Adelaide blushed. "You can tell?"

"I'm folksy, not ignorant." The Greek Goddess of Love and Beauty – it was a nice touch.

"Except you don't even know her *name*," Rob said. "Which is *not* Afrodiety. So are you in love with her or not?"

"No," Charlie said.

"Oh." Rob was flustered; Holly had promised him that the guy was in love with her, or at least pretending to be. "Oh ..." The word came out sounding disappointed. He tried again: "Oh ..." Now he sounded aroused. "Shit!" he said.

"'In love' is probably a little premature," Charlie clarified. "I like her, though. Very much."

Rob turned back to his wife. "Don't worry, babe, he's being paid to say that." He patted her bare shoulder.

"No I'm not," Charlie said with just a touch of indignation. "Who would pay me to say something like that?"

"The company you work for."

"The 'Sentinel'?"

Adelaide's eyes widened in surprise. "So you *are* a reporter?" she said.

Charlie glanced at his watch: five before midnight. "I am. And my name is Charlie, not Endicott. Van Linden, not Gibbs." Charlie attempted to lighten the load of his confession with a touch of levity: "Neither of us has a middle name."

Bad idea. He felt as though he'd just torn the sheet off her. Adelaide couldn't look at him.

She swallowed hard and began blinking rapidly. She didn't know where to look; it seemed like every person in the room was staring at her. Every person was. She'd been completely and utterly had by this guy, right from the gate. And now here she was, bared as a clueless dupe, as naive and oblivious as one of the countless casualties, known and unknown, direct and abstract, whom she herself had helped to wound. Her mind whirled as she wondered why; why he was doing this; why he'd gotten so close to her; why she'd let him. But there was no way she'd drop a single tear in front of all these people. Not a chance.

Dwight saw that Adelaide was right on the brink. He tried to pull her back by taking the heat off her and refocusing it on himself. "Not only is he a reporter, Adelaide," he said. "He has file twenty-two eleven sixty-three. It's over for me."

Bad idea. Adelaide's long legs wobbled; it looked like she was going to collapse. In an instant, Eduardo was behind her with a chair. She sat down gratefully as Dwight placed an avuncular hand on her shoulder and told her that everything would be okay, although he had no idea how.

"Oh man, what have I done?" Clayton said.

Elodie turned to him. "You?"

"It wasn't cufflinks I stole," he confessed. "It was history." Man, that sounded cool. What the hell – he lit a cigarette, sucked the smoke in deep and hardly coughed at all.

Rob was more bewildered than he'd ever been in his life, and even by his own estimation he'd spent a lot of it in a state of serious bewilderation: Was the reporter a reporter and was he in love with Adelaide or not? Why was she dressed in bedclothes and curtains? How come the old guy was touching her like that? "How do you know the burglar, babe?"

"Be quiet," she said sharply, shooting him a dark look. "I'm trying to think. And for God's sake stop calling me babe." She looked up at Dwight. "You're quitting?"

Dwight shrugged. "I don't see as I've got a choice."

"But the company's nothing without you," Adelaide said.

Rob thought he was going to vomit with confusion. Actually, literally hurl right there on the carpet. "You work together?" He pointed to Dwight. "He's in PR? *Him?*"

Dwight told Rob to shut the hell up.

"You're really a reporter?" Adelaide asked Charlie, finally able to look at him again.

He nodded and glanced at his watch. "But only for –"

"And you're doing a story on us?" Screw getting upset; now she was getting mad. And later she'd get even. "Why?"

Holly Hohenzollern threw her two cents into the pot. "Because I told him all about what you do," she said. "You and your dirty company with your schemes and your lies and your ruined lives!"

Adelaide looked up at the zaftig blonde dressed as a policewoman. "And you are?"

"*Maudite marde!*" Elodie said. "It's the strawberry iguana girl."

"I'm one of your victims," Holly told Adelaide.

Rob held up his hands, urgently crisscrossing them, as though he was trying to ward off insects and wave down traffic. "Don't say anything more, Ho-ho!"

Holly calmly continued telling Adelaide who she was. "You broke me and my boyfriend up."

"No, Ho-ho!" Rob cried. "No!"

"He's your boyfriend?" Adelaide said, pointing to her husband. "Hef?"

"Not *him*," Holly said. "Felix, my real boyfriend. Why'd you do it, huh?" She was beginning to get just a bit upset now, and reached inside her handbag for a Kleenex but came out instead with her gun. Oh well. "Why'd you break us up?"

Adelaide eyed the automatic, unsure if it was real or part of the woman's costume. Erring on the side of authenticity and mortality, she spoke to the woman quietly and carefully. "Well, he paid us."

"You think that's funny?" Holly said, waving her gun all over the place.

"No. But it's the truth," Adelaide told her as Charlie slowly began circling around the group, making his way behind the unbalanced policewoman. "Your boyfriend came to us, told us what he wanted – which was to let you down as easily as possible – and he paid us to help him do that. It's what we do. And we try to help both parties while we're doing it."

The gun stopped moving as Holly suddenly stood still, and a weird sort of calm descended on her, like she'd all of a sudden been wrapped up in cotton wool and put in a bath of warm cream. What this Adelaide woman said actually made sense. It was simple and stupid and sinister but it actually made sense.

For his part, Rob was pretty upset by what he'd heard from his very own wife; she'd been lying to him ever since they met! "You're not in PR at all!"

Holly pointed her Beretta at him. "Okay, you better not speak anymore, Bobby."

This had gone on long enough. Charlie leaped at Holly from behind, reaching around her ribs for the gun.

There was a gasp.

There was a bang.

And there was a scream from the other side of the room as Chester Polglase fell to the floor, bleeding.

Eduardo immediately rushed over.

Sara was instantly – and understandably (you'd have to agree) – wary about the situation. "Are you trying to break up with me, Buttons?" she said. *"Again?"*

"No, ma'am," Eduardo said, pulling off his green revolutionary shirt and making a tourniquet from one of the sleeves. "He's really been shot."

Well that was different. Sara bent down, close to her superbeloved's face, cradling his head in her hands. "You *better* have been hit, mister!"

"The bullet passed right through," Eduardo told her. "He'll be okay."

Sara pushed Eduardo to one side. "Let me see the hole."

"I can't help thinking it should have been you," Adelaide told her husband.

"I agree," said Holly, her arms now firmly but gently pinned behind her back by Dwight. And this was maybe the worst thing about the whole entire night – realizing that she enjoyed just a little bit having this silver fox man-handling her like that. She wondered if maybe she'd been on the wrong side of law enforcement all this time.

Adelaide turned to Charlie. "Or perhaps you."

"I understand," said Charlie, with yet another look at his watch. It was 11.59. "But before you take out a con-tract on me, happy birthday." He handed her the envelope from inside his jacket.

Adelaide read the card inside. The words he'd written inside were astounding. "Is this for real?" she asked. "You're giving up a Pulitzer?"

"Well, potentially," he said. "Probably."

Adelaide smiled. "You'll actually quit your job – for me?"

"Absolutely," Charlie said, smiling back. "Effective midnight tonight."

"God, that's the most romantic thing I've ever seen," Elodie told Clayton.

Clayton felt kind of nauseous but knew better than to say so. Besides, it might have been his nerves making him feel that way. Or maybe the cigarette smoke; he really needed to think about giving up.

Thurston turned to Lainey. "So what's the message here – if you love somebody, quit your job? Is that why you're leaving the show?"

Lainey sniffled and fought back tears. "It's not about quit-ting a job, you pinhead. It's about following your heart."

"How about you, Adelaide?" Charlie said. "Are you prepared to give up yours?"

It was ten seconds to midnight. She had all the time in the world to make up her mind. And when she was ready, she took a deep breath and gave Charlie Van Linden her answer.

TODAY

An off-Broadway theatre

On a small theatre stage a show is in progress. The set is very simple; a series of Warhol-style prints of Woody Allen and Mia Farrow, Liz Taylor and Richard Burton, and relatively recent additions Ashton Kutcher and Demi Moore hang at the rear. In front of these artworks, in the middle of the otherwise bare stage, are Clayton Townsend and Elodie Frontenac, sitting side by side on tall stools. They are nearing the end of a performance piece about their true life experiences in their former job. The sold-out show is called "The Splitsville Duologues." They talk to one another as though oblivious of the audience.

"God, that's absolutely the most romantic thing I've ever seen in my life!" Elodie says.

"Really?" replies Clayton. "I thought it looked kind of nauseous."

There is laughter from the room.

"It wasn't nauseous, Clay, it was absolutely beautiful." She whacks him on the arm. "You *have* to quit your job for me!"

Clayton slowly shifts his attention from Elodie. "And that's exactly what I did," he tells the audience.

Elodie puts a hand to the side of her mouth and offers an inevitably theatrical aside. "After *I* did it first."

More laughter from the three-hundred strong crowd.

"When we tell people about what we used to do, they often ask –"

"– if they even *believe* us."

"They ask us how the hell we could live with ourselves. It's a good question, one with some serious moral weight. And we've thought about it a lot, the people we helped, the others we … didn't. And our answer is this – if you're in a good relationship, thank your lucky stars. But if you're out of a bad relationship –"

"Thank us."

The stage falls black. The applause is long and loud.

Primo Magazine
editorial office

Rob Dolen is hunched over his desk staring intently at a pleasingly generous selection of 8 x 10 portraits of his favorite subject – himself. Finally he chooses one and adds it to the mock-up he's working on for the cover of this month's issue. It's a full-bleed black and white shot with the headline: "Manhattan's Most Illegible Bachelor?"

After considering it a while he calls in a colleague.

Felix the art-director enters and Rob presents the mock-up. "Something's not right, is it?" Rob says.

Felix looks at the headline, the appalling misspelling, and nods.

Rob smiles in recognition. "Gotcha," he says. "Lose the question mark, right?"

The Old Town Bar

Dwight Kitchener's standing at his favorite bar downing a whisky. He is dressed in a suit and tie, and he looks nervous. He places his empty glass on the long wooden bar and walks out into the bright sunshine. He knows he has to hurry, so there's a quickness in his step as he walks around the corner to St George's Episcopal, where the organ player inside is just beginning the Wedding March. Waiting out front, at the top of the stairs, is Sara White, who smiles with bright delight as she sees him. Dwight can't help himself from grinning back at the bride, all dressed in white, as he briskly climbs the stairs, takes her arm and walks her down the aisle.

When he reaches the altar and hands Sara over to Chester, the groom whispers: "When this is done, can I call you Dad?"

"Take a guess," Dwight mutters quietly. "Buttons."

A living room in Beverly Hills

The large television screen shows Lulu and Fred at home in their huge Manhattan apartment. Thanks to Elaine Reardon's network-mandated departure, the once-beloved series exists now only in re-runs and on disc.

"Aw, Fred," Lulu says lovingly, holding her screen husband's rubber cheeks in her hands, puckerizing his lips.

"Oh, Lulu," he responds, holding her face the same way.

"Aw, Fred," she repeats.

"Oh, Lulu," he replies.

"Aw, F–"

Suddenly the screen explodes in a shower of glass and smoke. Sitting opposite the pulverized television is Thurston Brown, a smoking gun in his right hand, a thickening dick in his stroking left.

"Oh, Lulu ..." he says tearfully.

A living room in
Kenilworth, Illinois

Morton Havisham's latest fifty-eight inch plasma television screen is covered in a fine scrim of cobwebs and
dust. It's been months since it's been switched on; literally and theatrically, it is dark.

Dolores Havisham is pleased; there is no longer any
at-screen shouting and gunfire and shattering glass and
TV innards. There is peace and quiet and crossword
puzzles and vodka and Xanax.

But there is no Morton.

The Millionaire Meat King of Chicago has decamped
to Los Angeles, where he has been engaged in a one-man
picket protest outside the entrance to the CBC broadcasting network, his placard demanding the immediate
return to air of "Lulu & Fred." Briefly gratified as he had
been by the dissolution of Lulu's relationship with Fred,
it quickly became apparent that Morton Havisham loved
hating "Fred & Lulu" more than he hated hating "Fred
& Lulu." It was a rich, gratifying, and deeply-sustaining
hatred which, even above his protein-based millions and
the love of his shapely and forbearing wife, kept him in-

terested in life, and without it he felt bereft. It was an irony almost sitcomical in its architecture.

"Yeah," Morton says as the thought occurs to him. "Futzing hilarious."

Lancaster County, Pennsylvania

Lainey Reardon is in the front yard of a farmhouse. She is dressed in Amish clothing that is almost extravagantly unflattering: a black one-piece dress, a black apron over the black dress, a black triangular shawl over the shoulders, and a black prayer cap, all of them homemade in extremely authentic Amish style. The whole ensemble brings modesty – not to mention discomfort – to a new low. The minimal amount of make-up on her face is designed to appear as though she is wearing none at all. It sort of works – she looks like a very beautiful woman made to look extremely plain. Seated at the rough-hewn oak table opposite her is a man in his sixties. He, too, wears typical Amish clothing and facial hair – a beard but no mustache. They speak to one another with painful gravity and ponderousness.

"I love him," Lainey says.

The old man holds up the gnarled finger of wisdom. "But he is –"

"I know what he is, Father. It's *who* he is that I love."

The man takes her hand. "Pray with me, child."

Lainey swallows. "For ... for ... deliverance from the deviled blemishments of my clouded heart?"

She puts her head in her hands, sighs deeply and yanks off her bonnet. Then she looks up to somewhere beyond the man opposite her.

"I cannot say that," she says to the director. "It's the stupidest line in the history of cinema."

The director calls "Cut!" as Lainey gets up from the table and walks toward the vast green field beyond the set. Then she throws her arms wide, beginning to run, quickly and greenly swallowed by the endless rows of cornstalks.

Bleecker Street, Manhattan

Charlie Van Linden is walking along the busy street, with his face to the sky, trying to remember if this is a Tuesday or a Thursday and whether or not it matters either way. He's so preoccupied that he doesn't notice that Holly Hohenzollern, who is not in police uniform, is less than twenty feet behind him. Or does he? Sometimes it's hard to tell with him, that dopey yokel routine he's got down so well.

There's a leash in his hand, and he's being pulled along the street by a wire-haired terrier he calls Smitty.

Charlie and Smitty arrive at the florist shop at 172 Bleecker: S and A Flowers. A sign in the window says they specialize in weddings. Good for them. As Charlie enters, a bell hung over the door tinkles.

Sallie and Adelaide – S and A – look up from behind the counter and smile. Charlie gives his sister a peck on the cheek, a little something extra for Adelaide.

Adelaide bends down and tickles the terrier's auburn muttonchops. "How are you, Asta?" she says in a special voice she reserves for canine conversation. "How are you, baby?"

"How's the book coming along, Charlie?" Sallie asks.

"He's still gunning for that Pulitzer," Adelaide says with a smile. "No matter what he might've said back in Sag Harbor." She has to hold her breath for a moment and fight back the nausea rising in her. How would she explain it if she barfed right here on the shop floor? And how would Charlie take it if she told him the truth?

"I won't deny it, but now I'm chasing the prize for fiction," he says, plucking a pale pink peony from a bucket and placing a couple of dollars on the counter. (Sure, he's dating the boss of the store but he doesn't like to take anything for granted. You never know what small thing might lead a relationship toward doom.) "What I promised to give up was a prize for reporting. Along with yet another solid writing career. Both of which did actually happen." Charlie tongues his lateral incisor, even now still wobbly from where Art Munro belted him when he turned in his story about the Armenian Hot Dog Syndicate. "In extremis," he adds, then asks Adelaide if she's ready to leave for lunch.

She has a final bit of housekeeping with her business partner. "Everything set for the, um, Bloomfield reception?" Adelaide asks Sallie. "She's due in at two."

"It's under control," Sallie answers, taking Smitty/Asta's leash from Charlie. "You guys go enjoy yourselves."

Adelaide and Charlie leave, hand in hand. Back outside beneath the purple awning of the cantina next door, he asks if she misses her old life of suspicion and intrigue.

"And marital misery?" she replies. "No, Charlie, I don't. My work in that area is done and done."

"What about all the unhappy, bitter and emotionally paralyzed people of America?" he says. "There's millions of them."

"They'll just have to learn to get along." Adelaide pauses pointedly. "Without my help."

"Well that's a nice sentiment, giving the people back their free will and all," Charlie says, looking upward, his face darkening in the shadow of the canvas awning. He lets out a sigh. "But don't think I'm unaware of what really goes on back there. I know your secrets, Adelaide. I'm not a complete dimwit."

Adelaide grabs his shoulders, turning him around so she can look right at him, right into him.

Oops. Did he actually say that out loud?

He probably did, but what the heck.

"And I really wouldn't care if your company was still going, really and honestly and truly, I wouldn't. It's your life and you're entitled to live it any way you choose. I'm just happy to be a part of it, Adelaide, I really am, because ..." Choking a little he unstrangles the knot of his tie, still not sure if his stray thoughts are being given voice. "Because ..." He gulps for air and for courage and gives her the peony hoping it'll maybe distract her. "I love you."

Judging by the tears on her face all that definitely got out.

"You said 'secrets'," she says... "What else do you imagine is going on?"

Charlie gently places his hand on Adelaide's ever-so-slightly swelling belly, looks into her eyes and doesn't say a word.

*

A little further back down the street, Holly H approaches S and A Flowers, looks around, then slips inside the store. Sallie nods hello as Holly goes past the counter through to the storeroom in back. There, she enters a series of numbers on a digital security pad and a small section of brick wall disappears. On the other side is the vast headquarters of the new company, Splitsville Inc. Holly heads straight for her desk to see who the next target is.

And now we must leave Miss Hohenzollern. We must do so because she's a private person, because she has a lot of work to do, and because the next name on her list could very well be yours.

Acknowledgements

The book you have (hopefully) just finished took many years and a lot of work to become what it is. Along the way all of these people[*] all helped it get there and I'm very grateful to every one.

Chris Burns. Kitty Flanagan. Clare Forster. Dan Kirschen. Tendo Nagenda. Michael Williams. Barrington Williams. Michael Weldon. Yasmine Wick-Kopita. Anthony Jones. The late Pat Kavanagh. Jo Jarrah. Jo Butler. Joe Dator. Joel Naoum. Alasdair Kay. Anne Treasure. Tara Goedjen. Igal Hodirker. Vincent Casey. Alex Gott-Cumbers. Anna Bowen. Marcos Valle. Tahiti-80. And Sally Van Es.

---

[*]   Or musical acts.